FROM THE RUIN

OF EXTINCTION

Also by Bradford Combs

Romantic Suspense (Anderson novels):
Cicada Song
Not Quite Home

Juvenile Fiction (3rd grade reading level):
The Adventures of Flitter & Plank
Flitter & Plank 2: A Pixie Problem

FROM THE RUIN OF EXTINCTION

Refuge: Book One

Bradford Combs

This book is a work of fiction. Names, characters, places, and incidents are the product of the author's imagination or are used fictitiously. Any resemblance to actual events, locales, or persons, living or dead, is coincidental.

All rights reserved. No part of this publication may be reproduced, distributed, or transmitted in any form or by any means without prior written permission from the publisher.

From the Ruin of Extinction
Refuge: Book One
By Bradford Combs
Copyright © 2013 by Bradford Combs
Cover and interior art by Ryan Campbell

bradfordcombs.tk

Printed in the United States of America
ISBN-13: 978-1484965627
ISBN-10: 1484965620

This book is dedicated to my friend Kyle Deckard, whose encouragement during the initial writing of this novel kept me from giving up on my dream.

Part I: Refuge

...and in the shadow of your wings I will make my *refuge* until these calamities have passed by.

Psalms 57:1

2 | Refuge

"How did we die?" the boy asked inquisitively.

"What do you mean, Randall?"

This was said with a playful smirk. The question was quite possibly the oddest Silus Rook had ever been asked.

"I mean us, our people. How did we die?"

It took a moment, but Randall's meaning eventually sank into Silus' aging mind.

"You mean the human race? Yes, well, it is my belief that man's descent began when we stopped believing in fairy tales."

"Fairy tales?"

"Impossible stories of things seemingly uncanny. The thing is, fairy tales were often steeped in truth in one form or another. The last truth to become fairy tale was God Himself. When the last of our kind deserted God, roundabouts five hundred years ago, He kindly removed his Spirit from the Earth so that we could experience the fullness of our freewill. Without God's guidance, mankind's moral code deteriorated until nothing mattered save power and greed, and family to some small extent. War became the proper course of debate. Many died."

Randall Whitaker listened eagerly; he had always been an attentive child. Silus watched as his words fell into place within the young boy's mind. Then Randall's brow furrowed.

"So, if God is a fairy tale, then why do you still read that old book?"

Silus lowered his eyes to the book resting in his lap. Its pages were torn and dirty but for the most part complete. Its leather cover, however, was so scuffed that the title was hardly legible, and the back cover was missing entirely. In fact, if one were to simply glance at the book, they might miss the title altogether, but a flip through the first several pages would reveal the name of its story.

"We read this Holy Bible to remember the fairy tales. Remember, the decline of man began after they deserted their gods. Recovered texts show this to be a rapidly growing theory in the final days of man... before the elves came. And so we read to never forget."

"But *you* believe in God."

The man smiled as he ran his withered fingers over the worn leather.

"I do. It's amazing what works of the old world can do by simply reading them. This book, there aren't many like it left, but it gives me hope."

"Like we give others hope?"

Silus laughed and pat Randall on his head. "Very good, my boy. This world may hate mankind for our part in its near-destruction, but there is forgiveness to be found in the remnant of men. It was for this reason—and for the words in this ancient text—that I formed Refuge. My hope is that, in time, this community will become a home for all races, no longer separated by fear or pride."

"Even the elves?"

"Especially the elves." Silus sighed and put an arm around his youngest student. "They will stop hunting us in time, and they will listen. I have faith."

Refuge was razed exactly one year following this conversation. The Elven Nation leveled the small community and slaughtered its residents so that their ancient views would never again be taught. Silus Rook came to a painful end. The books were burned. Few survived.

Forty-seven years later

Smoke rose from the Roclä Mountains, cascading in great billows as it darkened the distant sky. Watching this frightening display, Orlan Rook wondered if his friends were burning. Four days had passed since Randall Whitaker led a party of five men to the caves of Uuron Plauf and two more since all communications had ceased. Call him a pessimist, but Orlan feared the worst.

Something caught his eye, not from the mountains beyond Uuron Plauf, but from the tree line near the base of the hill where Orlan sat. A man whose face was concealed by a black hood weaved in and out of the trees as if searching for something. The man suddenly buckled over and grabbed his side. Then, after a moment, he stood upright again, twisted in the waist a bit, and continued on his way.

This man was not a member of Orlan's tribe, but it *was* he who had warned of the attack on Uuron Plauf, prompting Randall to act. He had wandered out of the forest seven days ago, hurt and bleeding, and collapsed at the foot of the hill where Orlan now sat. After two days of being nursed back to health, the man shared a rumor that he had heard. The elves feared the birdmen's unification. An extermination order had been given. Uuron Plauf—the birdman kingdom within and atop the Roclä Mountains—was to fall. None were to survive.

"You can't save everybody, Randall," Orlan whispered to himself.

"What?" a young boy asked from nearby.

Orlan looked up and found his adopted brother Joshua sitting in the branches of a nearby tree.

"How long have you been up there?"

"Since the sun came up. I'm waiting for Father to get back."

Two hours? Joshua had been sitting above his head for two hours without making a sound?

"You're spying on me?"

The boy laughed. It was the humor of youth. Being twelve years old, Joshua maintained the ideology that nothing bad could ever happen, that everything would turn out alright in the end. Orlan lost that mentality six years ago when his parents had died. He was only ten years old at the time.

"I didn't want to interrupt your intense focus," Joshua said with a smile. "I miss Father. I can't wait to hear his stories. Do you think they'll fight some elves?"

Orlan groaned. "I'd say there's a good chance of it. We'll have to move again if they're seen."

Joshua shrugged. "What else is new?"

It was true. Their tribe had been on the move for as long as Orlan could remember. They were nearly destroyed once already, forty-seven years ago. If Kïer was to learn of their continued existence, his elves wouldn't stop hunting them until everyone in Refuge was dead.

Now, here in the Greysong Forest, Randall was tempting fate. They'd been here just shy of a month, their second longest stay since leaving Hamil Hill, and Orlan was beginning to like it. The smoke, however, made him wonder where they'd be a week from now.

"You do realize the danger they're in, right?" Orlan asked.

"You do realize they have Father with them, right?"

"Gabe's strong but he's no match for what hit Uuron Plauf two days ago. They could all be dead right now, your father included"

Joshua laughed again to Orlan's utter annoyance.

"Sorry," Joshua said, "but if anyone thinks they can stop not only Father, but Randall, Kris, and Tramin as well, they've got another thing coming."

"No love for Payson?" Orlan asked, referring to the head of their medical staff.

Joshua just shrugged. He slipped from the branch and landed cat-like in the grass. "Have you tried calling them?"

"Trent won't let anyone else touch the radio."

"Alright. I guess I'll go see Trent then."

"Let me know if he's heard anything."

Joshua gave a thumbs-up and headed down the hillside toward camp. Trent hadn't heard anything, Orlan knew, because Trent promised to find him if anything came through the radio. The radio, unfortunately, had been silent for two days now.

There weren't any other two-way radios nearby, or quite possibly in existence. They substituted quality for quantity and low-cost in mankind's later years. "Objects with no sense of longevity," Orlan remembered his father saying. Most technology fell into disarray after the Fall of Man, though simple radios continued to be made during mankind's war with the elves, but even those fell into obscurity over time. These radios, found in a bunker in their original casing, seemed to be an exception. It took Trent and his brother Tramin a few weeks of tinkering, but the radios were eventually salvaged. They were likely the first to be used in decades, possibly a century or more.

Orlan didn't like how his voice sounded through the radios but that didn't matter. He wasn't allowed to use them anyway. They were Trent's babies and he'd become stingy with them in Randall's absence—something to do with battery power.

He looked over his shoulder. Joshua was a good kid; it was the age that Orlan found annoying. Trent's son, Benjamin, was the same way. They would outgrow this naive stage soon enough and be better off for it; but then, was it so bad being oblivious to how the world worked? Maybe not, Orlan conceded. The world could probably use a bit more innocence.

While smaller living tents were strategically positioned throughout the camp, a large tent with multiple rooms stood at its center and served as the base for the tribe's medical staff. Payson Harlow was in charge of that staff, but with him off assisting Randall, the leadership duties fell to Payson's wife Debra.

"Hello," Joshua said as he entered the medical tent.

"Hello, Joshua," Debra replied. Her curly red hair was pulled back into a ponytail. "Benjamin's off playing with Jillian."

"Oh, I know," Joshua said. "I was looking for Trent."

Debra's smile faded a bit as she directed Joshua toward a side room. There he saw Trent, the tribe's second-in-command, sitting on a tree stump with his head bowed and his fingers intertwined. He was praying. The radio sat on a makeshift cot, silent. Pillar, a dog belonging to Tramin, Trent's brother, lay at his feet.

"No word?" Joshua asked Debra quietly.

She led Joshua away from the room and spoke softly. "Not since the smoke started rising two days ago. I think it might be best if Trent was left alone until we hear something."

"When will that be?"

"Soon I hope. Now go find Benjamin and Jillian. I think they're playing tag in that field near your family's tent."

"Yes, ma'am."

Seeing Trent so focused on his prayers unsettled Joshua, and he wasn't sure why. He wasn't so naive that he didn't know there'd be fighting, but his father and the others were the best warriors in all the Earth. Joshua was excited. So why wasn't Trent, or Debra, or Orlan? He was eager to see his father again, to hear his stories. More than that, he was curious how many birdmen they were going to bring back.

No one ever walked the same path home; it left trails that could be followed. So Joshua playfully jumped on the supply cart that sat behind the medical tent—often used to haul tents and supplies whenever they moved to a new location—and propelled himself further into the woods, burying his feet in some swirling mud. Then he leapt over a fallen tree trunk and splashed through a shallow creek in the right general direction. It wasn't long before he heard the squeal of a young girl.

He arrived at the open field and saw Benjamin dodging Jillian's frantically waving hands. She was ten years old, younger than Joshua and Benjamin by two years, but they played with her anyway.

"Jillian, look!" Benjamin shouted, pointing at Joshua.

The girl bolted for him. Joshua laughed and dodged the tag, and the game continued for nearly an hour. Then a loud and recognizable whistle carried through the wind.

"Kids! Dinner!"

The three children entered the woods and headed toward the Shepherd family's tent. Joshua's adopted mother stirred something in a pot set over a nicely kindled fire. Her gray hair frizzed with the heat.

"Smells good, Phyllis," Benjamin said politely as he sat on a stump. Jillian sat beside him, Joshua opposite her.

"Squirrel in broth, kiddos," Phyllis said as she dipped a bowl for Jillian to test. "How is it?"

Jillian made a sour face.

"Always the picky one, aren't you?"

They were soon eating, and Jillian's eyes were beginning to droop. It was getting late.

One benefit of being adopted into the Shepherd family was that your mother was the finest, and typically only, cook in the tribe. She took it upon herself to prepare meals and to care for the children whose parents were dead or distracted. She was a mother through and through despite having never had children of her own. Benjamin's father, Trent, and Jillian's mother, Debra, had both been preoccupied of late which resulted in Benjamin and Jillian spending more time with the Shepherds. That was perfectly fine with Joshua as that meant more playing time with his friends.

Phyllis and Gabe had taken Orlan in after his parents' accident and Kris before him. Joshua considered them brothers, though neither shared his blood. As for Joshua, he had been a Shepherd since Gabe found him as an infant, deserted in an old silo. They loved him very much and he them. The Shepherds were an irregular sort of family but a family none the less.

"Have the others eaten yet?" Joshua asked.

"Angela sent for them, but everyone's so busy. I'm not expecting them all at once."

"I don't know why everyone's so worried," Joshua said. "Father's there—and so is Kris."

"And Dad," Jillian offered with her cheeks full of squirrel meat.

"Add Tramin and Randall to the mix and those elves don't stand a chance," Phyllis said with a silly chuckle.

Joshua noticed that her smile didn't seem quite right, almost forced, but maybe it was just a trick of the firelight. They ate in mostly silence for the next few minutes until something caught their ear. They turned and saw someone rushing through the distant trees.

"Orlan?" Phyllis called out, but her second adopted son passed by their camp without acknowledging her beckon.

"Why's he running?" Jillian asked, sitting up straight and suddenly awake.

"Because he saw something," Phyllis replied quietly.

Joshua noted that she was no longer smiling.

Angela Whitaker, Randall's daughter, set her bowl on the ground so that Pillar could lick clean what was left of the broth. She patted the dog's head and ruffled his short gray hair. It was good seeing him eat.

They found Pillar three years ago while hiding in a cave further south, not long before they found the radios. They almost killed him, food being scarce in that area, but Tramin petitioned that the mutt could be useful, so they adopted him into their family.

She had been twelve years old at the time and remembered being cautious because Pillar was a bit savage, but he mellowed in time and Angela grew to love him. True to Tramin's word, the dog became a valued member of the hunting party, often tracking deer and squirrels, and he was typically all too eager to devour dropped food, which prevented unwanted four-legged creatures from visiting their camp. Sadly, Pillar hadn't been eating well since Tramin set out for Uuron Plauf.

"That's a good boy."

"He always is," Debra said, coming out of the tent. "Shëlin left to gather some fruit, but she'll be back soon. We'll head up to the Shepherd's tent after that."

"Will Trent be coming?"

"I doubt it. I'll have Jillian bring him some food."

Angela always liked Debra. She wasn't old enough to be her mother, but when Angela's own mother had died it was Debra who picked up the slack. Most of the orphaned children turned to Phyllis and Gabe Shepherd, but there was just something about Debra Harlow. Perhaps it was her thin frame and long red hair—so similar to Angela's mother—but from the day Bethany Whitaker died, Debra became that womanly figure lacking in Angela's life. That is, until Angela found interest in other things.

"Do you think Kris will be alright?" she asked.

"That's the big question isn't it? Will any of them come back?"

There was no answer. Angela knew that. She was worried, just like everyone else above the age of twelve, and it was exhausting. How Phyllis could keep up with those children while fearing for Gabe and the others was beyond Angela.

"What do you think of Ivan Shaymolin?" Angela asked, changing the topic.

"I think he needed our help."

"He knew about the extermination order on Uuron Plauf and talked my father into going. What if he set them up?"

"Your father taught you better than that, Angela," Debra said sternly. "Silus Rook formed Refuge as a place of grace. Ivan Shaymolin gets the benefit of the doubt like everyone else. We shouldn't judge him."

Oh, yes. Silus Rook. Orlan's ever-so-wise grandfather and founder of the tribe.

"Yeah," Angela said quietly, "and that mentality's cost a lot of lives, or don't you remember that Refuge was on the receiving end of its own extermination order fifty years ago?"

Debra glared, and Angela knew she had misspoken. She didn't really think negatively of Orlan's grandfather or the purpose of the tribe. She was just frustrated and afraid for her father and Kris.

Static.

The sound caught their ear and they froze. The static came again. They raced inside and found Trent with his mouth to the radio.

"I couldn't understand you. Please repeat."

There was more static but nothing decipherable. Angela's heart leapt when a recognizable voice came through. It was Tramin, Trent's brother. What he said was broken, but it was clearly his voice. She heard "coming" and "hurt," something about "birdmen" and "blood," then a long run of static and the term, "dying."

"You're breaking up," Trent said into the radio. "We can't understand you. If you can hear me, the medical tent is prepared. We'll be waiting for you."

Orlan burst through the entrance a moment later.

"They're coming. I saw torches."

"How many?" Trent asked breathlessly.

"Four."

"Only four?" Angela asked, her hand covering her mouth.

Four was not good. When they were close, Randall's men were supposed to light torches signifying that they were okay. Each member was to light a torch. Five set out; four were lit. Angela thought of Tramin's broken message. Dying. Somebody was dying. Was it her father Randall? Was it Kris whom she…?

"Who didn't light their torch?" Orlan asked rhetorically, but Trent brushed by him without an answer.

"Angela, find Shëlin," he commanded. "Make sure she's ready for however many wounded we bring back. Let Phyllis know that they've returned, but make sure she stays with the kids until we can gauge the damage. After that, meet us at the hill. They'll need a hand carrying the wounded."

Or the dead.

"Go!" Trent said, and Angela went.

"We should go to them," Joshua said, but Phyllis shook her head.

"No, we'll wait until we're called for."

"But why?"

"Because they've been through a lot and will likely need a few bandages and some rest. Not to mention they might have birdmen with them. We don't want to overwhelm our guests, now do we?"

Phyllis smiled, but her eyes betrayed her jovial words. They were tired, and the mug in her hands shook as she spoke.

"I want to see my father," Benjamin said softly. "I miss him."

"As do I, love. We'll see them soon enough."

Phyllis forced a smile again, but her hands shook the mug loose and it clattered against the stones surrounding the fire pit.

"Blast!" she said, and Joshua noted her tone.

"You're scared, Mother."

Phyllis forced another smile, but it faded quickly.

"Phyllis?" Benjamin spoke up. "Phyllis, what's wrong?"

"Nothing," Phyllis said forcefully. "Nothing is wrong. Let's just sit here quietly, shall we?"

Joshua and Benjamin exchanged glances, and suddenly Joshua wasn't as excited as he had been. They weren't sitting in the silence long when another sound caught their ear. Jillian was the first to hear it. She stood and the others did likewise.

"Phyllis?" Angela called out as she stepped through a pair of trees.

"Has there been news?" Phyllis asked desperately. "Gabe and Kris, are they…?"

"We don't know," Angela interrupted. "Tramin radioed in, but the reception was bad. We couldn't make out much."

"And Orlan? What did he see?"

Angela stole a glance at Joshua and the others.

"He saw four torches."

Phyllis gasped and covered her mouth. A whimper escaped through her fingers.

"What?" Benjamin asked, his nerves showing. "What's wrong, Phyllis?"

The nervousness in Joshua's stomach intensified. He didn't know what the four torches meant, but something had obviously gone wrong. Was someone hurt? Missing?

"Trent's asked that you stay here with the children until he sends for you," Angela said.

Phyllis laughed nervously.

"Stay here?" she said, as if Trent's order was the most ridiculous thing she'd ever heard.

Never in his life had Joshua heard Phyllis sound so afraid. He began to shake.

"My husband and son are out there," she continued. "One of them might be hurt or worse. How could I possibly... Joshua!"

Joshua darted into the forest. His father was invincible, and Kris would lead the tribe someday. The possibility of one of them getting hurt was ridiculous, but the fear in Phyllis' voice terrified him.

Something *had* gone wrong. He recalled the billowing smoke. How high must the flames have been to send smoke that far into the sky? How hot would they have been? He felt an uncontrollable urge to be held by his father again, to wrestle with his brother. He wanted his family back... now.

His stomach lurched as he ran through the trees, and he stumbled a bit. It took him a moment to realize that someone else was running behind him. A quick glance revealed Benjamin. Someone else was there as well.

"Joshua, stop!"

Angela.

He didn't stop. He pushed harder, splashing through the creek and dodging low branches. He could hear voices nearby, and as he burst through the trees, he saw Orlan and Trent on top of the hill.

"There they are!" Orlan shouted, and they vanished over the hill beyond Joshua's view.

Benjamin and Angela were at his side now. They passed over the crest of the hill and saw a small gathering of silhouettes pushing through the tree line where Ivan Shaymolin had been earlier that day. It was too dark to determine who each silhouette was, but it didn't matter. They were back, and the fear Joshua had been feeling faded.

He could hear indecipherable voices as Orlan and Trent merged with the silhouettes. Then they broke free again and raced up the hill, carrying someone by the shoulders and legs. Was it a birdman? Despite the creature's less than desirable condition, Joshua felt a sliver of excitement. He'd never seen a real birdman before. He had a pre-conceived image of what one might look like, but he never expected to actually meet one. He laughed as he raced down the hill to get his first look, but then, when Orlan and Trent passed him by, Joshua saw that it wasn't a birdman at all. The blood on his face was too thick to see through, but the victim was obviously human. Joshua was confused at first, and then he began to panic.

"Father?" he whispered as Angela and Benjamin joined the others. "Father!"

"Joshua!"

He turned and his heart leapt. Gabe Shepherd, his adopted father, wrapped two overly muscular arms around Joshua.

"Help us, Joshua. We have injured birdmen, and we've carried them a long way."

Joshua saw Benjamin taking a the arm of a wounded birdman from his uncle Tramin. Dried blood covered half of Tramin's face, but he looked alright otherwise. The birdman, however, did not.

He couldn't determine the creature's coloring due to the blood covering the majority of its body, but its eagle-like head hung low, and its wings dragged the ground behind it. Its thin and bare, three-toed legs stumbled under its own weight, supported only by Tramin and Benjamin. It wheezed and coughed.

Joshua ran to them and relieved Tramin of the birdman's other arm—surprisingly human-like. Tramin raced ahead as the boys bore the birdman's weight—what little of it there was. Then Joshua gasped. The warmth of the creature's blood-soaked feathers startled him. He began to cry.

"No... tears... little one," the creature whispered. "It is... only blood." Then it coughed and stumbled.

Joshua tightened his grip.

"It'll be okay," he said. Whether he was speaking to the birdman or himself he wasn't certain, but it felt like the right thing to say. "Everything's going to be alright."

He peered behind him and saw Randall with a second birdman. That one seemed to be in better shape than the one he and Benjamin were carrying, as it partially carried its own weight. Beyond them were Angela and someone else he couldn't make out. They were carrying a third birdman. It could have been Kris or Payson, either one, but that made his stomach lurch again. He prayed that the person helping Angela was Kris, because if it was Payson, then that meant the bloodied human that Trent and Orlan had been carrying was Joshua's own brother.

"Oh, God," he blurted out while Benjamin sobbed.

"Every...thing," the birdman said again, "will be alright...children... as you said. Just keep... just keep moving."

The birdman winced at some unseen pain and coughed. Joshua swallowed his tears and quickened his pace. Benjamin did the same.

"Mom!"

Debra Harlow turned to find her daughter and Phyllis rushing into the medical tent.

"Jillian can't be here!" Debra shouted.

"They're not back yet?" Phyllis asked. "We heard they were coming and thought maybe..."

"They're on their way but..."

"Is Dad coming back?" Jillian asked. Her face lit up.

"You have to leave. Phyllis, you have to take Jillian away from here before they get back. We don't know what to expect, and I don't want Jillian here if..."

"Debra... Shëlin," a static voice interrupted from a side room.

"This is Shëlin," answered a soft, yet beautiful voice.

Phyllis pulled back the curtain and found the only non-human member of their tribe with the radio in hand. She was dressed the same as everyone else, but her perfect, porcelain skin, pitch black hair, and pointed ears set her apart from the rest of the tribe. Shëlin-Vin was an elf. She had been scrubbing the dirt from her fingernails and stood alert now with water running down her elbows. A basket of fruit sat on the floor beside her. Debra pushed past Phyllis and stood at Shëlin's side.

"Thirty seconds," came Trent's voice through the radio. "We've got Payson. He's bad."

Debra froze. Payson. Her Payson was the unlit light. She felt the lump in her throat growing and barely noticed Phyllis's arms wrapping around her. Shëlin's gaze bore into her, but she couldn't register the meaning.

"Debra," Shëlin began, her voice heavy with concern, "do you need me to..."

"Dad!" Jillian said in a panic. "Daddy!"

Debra stooped and hugged her daughter.

"It's going to be alright, Jillian. Daddy's going to be alright. Oh, God, please let him be alright."

Jillian sobbed into Debra's shoulder. She didn't hear the rest of Trent's message giving the count of injured birdmen, but she didn't care about that. The man she loved was hurt, too hurt to light his own torch. Then she remembered what Trent had said. Thirty seconds.

"You have to leave, Phyllis. Take Jillian. Hurry before…"

Jillian cried as Phyllis pulled her toward the entrance, but then they skidded to a stop. Phyllis quickly diverted Jillian to the nearest room, pulling the curtain shut behind them.

"Debra!" Trent called from just outside the tent. They carried Payson through the flap a moment later.

Debra attempted to bark orders, but the words wouldn't come. She could do nothing but stare at her husband's bruised and swollen body.

"In the back," Shëlin ordered, usurping control. "What are his injuries?"

Orlan ran off a terrifyingly long list of broken bones and lacerations, but all Debra saw was her husband's face. It was unrecognizable. Blood clogged his nose, and his mouth hung agape; his eyes were swollen shut; an ear was missing; his throat was purple and stitched, and his light brown hair was now matted black. The rest of him, she quickly noted, was no better. He was barely breathing.

Her whole body convulsed as she fell on him, despair overcoming her shock. Orlan and Trent nearly dropped Payson under her weight until Shëlin pulled her away.

"Stay out here, Debra," she said. Her elven eyes were cold and demanding. "Let us work."

Debra attempted to push past Shëlin but fell instead. Her legs had betrayed her.

She watched as Shëlin, Trent, and Orlan disappeared into the back room with her dying husband and she sobbed. Phyllis was with her then, comforting her, but there was no comforting Debra.

She glanced back and saw Jillian peeking from behind a curtain. Tears were streaming as she quietly called for her daddy again and again. Debra ran to her, and they cried and prayed together as a family.

Others poured into the tent, three bloodied birdmen in their arms.

The tribe worked long into the night under the medical leadership of Shëlin-Vin, saving the lives of each and every birdman.

Debra prayed for God to heal Payson, her faithful husband who had selflessly offered his services so that the birdmen of Uuron Plauf might live. He was the most loving husband and father a family could ask for, but God chose not to heed those prayers.

Payson Harlow died in the early hours of the morning with Debra by his side. Alone with her dead husband, Debra cursed the God who refused to heal him. She cursed the elves and the birdmen of Uuron Plauf. Then she cursed the mysterious Ivan Shaymolin, the hooded man who had sent her husband to his death. And when her anger passed, she cursed herself for having lost control when the tribe needed her to be strong—when *he* needed her to be strong.

She cried in such a way that all the tribe could hear, and they mourned with her.

Part II: Repercussions

Randall Whitaker grunted as he swung his legs over the side of the cot. They popped and cracked, and a pain shot through them starting somewhere in his lower back. He touched the stitches on his chest. They were tender. How close had that birdman's sword come from ending his life? If not for Kris...

"Daddy?"

"I'm up, Angela."

Angela pulled aside the curtain that separated her cot from Randall's and sat beside him.

"How are you?" she asked while eyeing the stitches.

"I hurt," he answered somberly, "but I'll take it. How's Debra and Jillian? Have you spoken with them?"

"I've not left our tent, but I heard Debra last night. She was cursing everybody."

He understood how she felt. He had felt the same after losing his wife.

"I'll check on her."

"No, you won't," Angela said sternly. "You were nearly stabbed through heart. You're staying in this cot on Shëlin's orders."

"I'm sorry, but Shëlin-Vin does not lead this tribe. One of our own is mourning, and I will be with her. Besides, Kris deflected the blade. It only scratched me."

"Only scratched you?"

"This conversation is over."

He stood and grimaced against the pain that ran through his joints and conceded that Shëlin's orders were probably for the best. Despite his condition, Randall was still the tribe's leader, and there were responsibilities to uphold. He grunted with his first few steps, stabled himself, and wobbled out of the tent. The sun was just rising, and the crickets and birds sang together. That was good. It meant that the tribe had evaded pursuit—for the moment. He grimaced again. The pain was worsening.

"Maybe it *was* more than a scratch. I won't be gone long."

Angela wrapped her arms around his neck. It startled him at first, but then he returned the embrace. He ran his fingers through her hair, so much like her mother's, and kissed her forehead.

"I love you, Angela."

"I love you too. I was so scared."

"I know, but it was necessary. Those people needed us."

Angela stared inquisitively at her father, tears in her eyes.

"Was it worth Payson?"

This was a question that Randall had been asking himself since leaving Uuron Plauf. Were the lives of three birdmen worth what it cost the tribe? The creatures were known to look down their beaks at all races save their own. Would they appreciate the sacrifice that was made for them? He wasn't sure.

"I suppose we'll find out."

"Good morning, Randall," Shëlin offered as he approached the medical tent. "How are you feeling?"

"Could be worse," he replied. The ache in his chest was the worst of it, but the rest was tolerable. "Is Debra inside?"

"She and Jillian are with Payson."

"How is she?"

"She's not spoken all morning."

"And Jillian?"

Shëlin sighed sorrowfully. "About as well as you'd expect."

Randall remembered the feeling. He lost his parents in the fall of Refuge, skewered while he hid in a chest. He mostly remembered his mother lying in a pool of blood, slowly shaking her head, warning him to stay hidden. Then they beheaded her.

"Might I see them?"

"Of course."

She stepped aside, and he made his way through the tent. Passing by a room with the curtain left open, Randall peered inside and saw a birdman on a cot. It eyed him wearily. The blood had been washed from its fur and feathers, and Randall was struck by the creature's golden color. The birdman did not speak. Randall merely nodded.

"May I come in?" he asked upon reaching a room at the back of the tent.

Jillian sat on a stump beside Payson's cot. She looked up at him with red, broken eyes, and his heart sank. He would take Jillian's place in a heartbeat if he could. Sadly, she was just the next in a long line of shattered children. Debra sat in the far corner and refused to look at him, his question regarding admittance going unanswered. He entered anyway.

A third stump had been brought in, so Randall sat down and took Jillian's hand.

"Dad's dead," she said in a numb tone.

"I know," he answered.

"I don't want him to be dead," she said as she leaned against Randall's shoulder.

Randall pulled her close.

"I know," he said. "We're all mourning him, and there's no shame in that. I tried to be strong after losing my parents, but pretending to be strong only made things worse. We need that release so that we might recover. So you just mourn for as long as you need."

Randall held her as she sobbed into his shirt.

"Here," he said, reaching into his pocket. He pulled out a stone and placed it into Jillian's hand. "Your father made me promise to give you this."

The stone was white, plucked from the base of Uuron Plauf. Jillian had always found rocks fascinating, and Payson picked this one because of its shape: a nearly perfect heart. He had scratched Jillian's name onto one side of the stone and his own name on the other. He had later pressed it into Randall's palm and made him promise to give it to her. It was Payson's last request.

"He took it from Uuron Plauf because its beauty reminded him of you. He loved you very much." He let that sink in a moment. "He can still hear you, you know? Or at least, I believe he can."

"He can?" Jillian asked, suddenly hopeful.

Randall nodded.

"Do you remember my telling you about a man named Silus Rook?" he asked. Jillian nodded. "Silus taught us that God, never intending for us to be apart, arranged for our souls to be accepted into Heaven once we've died. There would be no more pain or death, and we could all live there together forever. I believe that with all my heart, and your dad did as well."

"He can hear us in Heaven?" Jillian asked. "Is he there now? Can we see him?"

"I'm sorry, but we cannot see him. Not yet, at least," Randall confessed. "I'm not sure if he's already there or if that comes later, but if he *is* in Heaven, then I think it's very possible for him to hear you. I don't understand how it all works, but there's a thing called prayer, which is when we speak with God. If your daddy is in Heaven with God, then perhaps he could hear your prayers as well?"

"So, when we die…" Jillian began but seemed to falter at the thought of dying.

"When the time comes that you leave this place, and God willing it won't be anytime soon, I believe that you and Payson will be reunited in Heaven. I believe that we will all be together again in time."

Randall watched as the lessons that were taught to him as a child ran through Jillian's mind. It was a lot to grasp, he knew, but Jillian was a smart girl and deserved a little hope. Her eyes moistened again, and she began to cry.

"I miss you, Dad," Jillian said through broken sobs, "and I want to hear you talk again."

She wrapped her arms around her father and cried until Debra, who had been sitting silently until now, came and held her.

"It is good to cry," Randall reminded them, "but remember, Payson would probably like to hear positive things as well."

He watched as Jillian considered this. Then she held out the heart-shaped rock and turned it over in her fingers.

"Thank you for the heart," she said. "I like it very much." Then she gripped the rock in a fist and held it to her lips, tears running over her hands.

Randall stood to leave.

"Remember, Jillian," he said as he reached the curtain, "you are not alone. Everyone in this tribe loves you very much. Even as he did."

"Thank you," Debra said softly through her own tears, and Randall nodded in return. Then he left them to their mourning.

Once clear of Jillian's ears, he allowed himself a moment to mourn as well. Shëlin held him as he cried. There was a pain deep in his chest, deeper than the stitched wound or the ailments that came with his age. It was the pain of a man who had lost a friend.

This was not the first death that Randall had had to bear. Payson was just the next in a long line of loved ones lost under his watch. Each death simply built upon the last and upon the one before that until the pain was so great that he could barely breathe.

"It's alright, Randall," Shëlin said as he sobbed into her arms. "We do not blame you. This was not your fault."

Orlan groaned as he sat up. He could have slept on through noon if he'd been allowed, but the smell of food cooking over a campfire woke him. His grumbling belly refused to let him sleep a second longer.

"What's for breakfast?" he asked as he approached the campfire.

Phyllis and Joshua were preparing the wooden plates while Kris rested in a hammock hanging from two nearby trees.

"Eggs," Joshua replied as he left for the stream with a basket of canteens.

"Is Kris still asleep?"

"No," Kris answered for himself. He sat up and stepped off the hammock, rubbing his eyes. "I couldn't sleep."

Orlan and Kris found a seat around the fire pit as Phyllis handed them their plates. Joshua returned shortly and distributed the filled canteens. They ate silently, but Orlan's mind wasn't on the food. He studied Kris as subtly as he could and saw the bags under his eyes. He hadn't slept all night, maybe not for days. He had several deep bruises and some shallow cuts, but of everyone who had come back, Kris was in the best shape.

"So what happened?" Joshua asked once Kris put his plate down. "In Uuron Plauf, I mean."

"Joshua," Phyllis said sternly. "Breakfast is not the time for..."

"No, it's fine," Kris said, rubbing his eyes. "We got there just after the raid began. We never intended to fight and did our best not to be seen. We were there to rescue as many birdmen as we could, that was all. Engaging the elves in a swordfight wouldn't have solved anything.

"Anyway, we managed to make it all the way up the mountain and into their throne room without being seen, but the birdmen were all dead by the time we got there. We searched for survivors and found two. Payson did what he could for them, but one died shortly after, so we hid the one that still lived and continued our search. We found another survivor in a hall several levels down. His throat had been slit. We didn't think he'd make it, but he did. Payson and Tramin carried him to where the other birdman was hidden while Gabe, Randall, and I went on."

"You separated?" Phyllis asked, surprised.

"The birdmen needed care, and Tramin refused to leave Payson alone with them. Randall wanted to help more survivors, so we agreed to separate provided Tramin and Payson remained hidden."

"Then what happened?" Joshua asked.

"Then Randall decided to head toward the sound of battle. We entered a cavern that was littered with dead elves and birdmen. We found a wildman among them, decapitated."

"A wildman?" Phyllis asked. "Why would a wildman be in Uuron Plauf? A prisoner?"

"A soldier," Kris corrected. "They were fighting alongside the elves."

"But the elves hate all mankind," Phyllis protested. "They've never distinguished us from those cannibalistic Neanderthals."

Kris nodded and rubbed his eyes again.

"It confused us too," he said, "but there they were. Anyway, we left the room and found several birdmen trapped in a hall, cornered by some elves and wildmen. We shouldn't have intervened, but we couldn't help it. The birdmen were getting slaughtered."

"So you attacked the elves?" Joshua asked, suddenly excited.

"That's not a good thing, Joshua!" Phyllis shouted.

Orlan couldn't believe it. The idea of them actually attacking the elves, making themselves known, it was suicide!

"We caught them off guard, and I think that's what gave us the edge. They had us outnumbered, but between us and the birdmen, we were able to kill them all—or so we thought."

"You killed them?" Phyllis asked. "We don't kill!"

"We had no choice."

"You always have a choice!"

"Trust me, we agonized over it the whole way back. If we didn't kill them, they were going to kill us. We did what we had to do."

Phyllis nodded, but she didn't look comfortable with the idea of her eldest adopted son killing anyone.

Kris continued.

"The birdmen were confused by our presence, and they scoffed at us when Randall offered to help." Kris laughed humorlessly. "In fact, one of them promised to kill us if we didn't leave their home immediately. Anyway, they flew off. That's when Gabe realized that one of the elves had escaped. We chased him, but he found help, so we fled. I'm guessing the wildmen had our scent because they caught up to us as we reached Payson and Tramin."

"And then what?" Joshua asked.

The boy's excitement was sickening. It wasn't real to him, Orlan knew, and that made it exciting. He wanted to yell at his younger brother, wake him up, but it wouldn't do any good. He was too naive.

Then Gabe stepped from his tent quite suddenly and punched the air. "Then we had ourselves a fight!"

Orlan rolled his eyes. This was a serious matter, and everyone knew it. Why Gabe insisted on portraying such things as sport was beyond him, but Joshua always ate it up. Gabe acted out the battle, telling of how the elves wavered beneath their might and how that same group of birdmen flew in and returned the favor. He was in the middle of describing the neck of a wrung wildman when

Kris slammed his plate against the rocks surrounding the campfire.

"Stop it!" he shouted, and the camp went silent. He pointed a finger at Gabe and shook his head. "You play these games with Joshua to keep him innocent, but that's not at all how it happened. We were terrified. We were nearly killed before those birdmen showed up. We were trying to escape with their injured kin on our shoulders and they didn't like that, so their leader attacked. Randall would have been stabbed through the heart if I hadn't deflected the blade.

"The elves attacked again, and most of the birdmen went down in a flurry of arrows. Payson was hit and then trampled by a wildman before Gabe gutted it with his ax. A hunter showed up and nearly cut Tramin's face off and would have likely killed him if not for a birdman intervening. We escaped in all the confusion and hid until the battle was over. We found that the birdman who had attacked Randall was the only one left alive, though he was in a lot of pain, so we took him and the other two and ran for our lives."

No one spoke. Orlan digested this and watched as Joshua's face faded from excitement to dread. Gabe sat and began eating his eggs.

"The truth is," Kris continued after a moment, "if those wildmen have our scent, then they might be able to follow us here. That's why I haven't slept. Everyone else needed their rest, but I've been up on the hill keeping watch."

"Did you spot any?" Orlan asked.

"No, but that doesn't mean anything. Wildmen are incredibly stealthy. We wouldn't even know they were here until they were throttling our throats."

"And they're coming here? To our camp?" Joshua asked, terrified.

"Not necessarily," Orlan replied, feeling a sudden need to reassure him.

"But they could be," Kris reiterated.

"That's enough," Phyllis broke in. "I hate what you went through out there, Kris, but frightening Joshua is no way to…"

"No, he's right." Gabe set down his plate and ran a hand along his thick, red beard. "Those wildmen have our scent, and if given the order, there's a real chance they could follow us here. We have to leave."

"Should we pack our things?" Phyllis asked.

"Get a start on it," Gabe said while standing. "I'll talk to Randall. We need to decide what we're doing now that we're rested and in our right minds."

He attempted to hug Joshua, but Joshua pushed away. The boy seemed shaken but suddenly stern.

"I'm alright," he said, and then he began kicking dirt on the fire. "I'll help pack."

Orlan and Kris exchanged glances.

It bothered Orlan that Joshua was pretending not to be afraid. Kris had informed him of a world very different from the one that Gabe often portrayed in his silly stories. That, in addition to Payson's death, would likely begin Joshua's long, difficult path to adulthood. Orlan felt sorry for him. Suddenly, he realized why Gabe always downplayed the world to preserve the boy's precious innocence.

"We can handle the packing," he said reassuringly. "Why don't you go find Benjamin and play?"

Joshua seemed to wince at the word *play* but didn't argue. With a forced calm, he walked into the woods. Then, judging by the sound, Joshua took off in a sprint toward the Bishops' camp.

"Get some sleep, Kris," Gabe said, interrupting the silence, "Phyllis can handle the packing. Orlan, get over to that hill and keep an eye out. I'll send relief after I've spoken with Randall."

"Yes, sir," Orlan said. He was suddenly very nervous.

Joshua was throwing every rock he could find into the creek, trying to make the biggest splash possible. He was not having fun.

He felt invincible two days ago. His father was the strongest man alive, and nothing could ever hurt the people he loved. There wasn't anything they couldn't handle. But then he saw the condition that they returned in, and his faith was shaken. They lost Jillian's father, but he wasn't strong like Gabe and Kris and Randall. He waited all night for his father to wake up and tell him how strong they were, to remind him that they were invincible, that Payson was a fluke, but then Kris had to open his stupid mouth.

He wondered if perhaps Kris had over exaggerated but knew better. He saw the fear in his father's eyes after Kris corrected him. They were both afraid—afraid of elves and wildmen—and suddenly Joshua was afraid too. He picked up the largest rock he could find and chucked it into the water with an angry scream.

"Joshua?" He turned to find Benjamin coming through a gathering of bushes.

"What's wrong?"

Joshua didn't know what to say. He didn't know what to think. He just shook his head as Benjamin picked up a rock and tossed it in. Neither of them spoke. They eventually made their way to a fallen tree trunk and sat in silence for a while.

"I'm scared," Joshua finally admitted.

"Of what?" Benjamin asked.

"I don't know," Joshua said with a shrug. "That maybe we're not as strong as I thought we were, that maybe we're not as safe, that we could die."

"Like Payson?" Benjamin said. "I've been thinking about that too. Seeing my father pray so much, I realized that maybe they weren't going to make it back. I pretended not to worry, but I could barely sleep. Phyllis noticed, I think, but she didn't say anything. I don't think she's been sleeping either."

Joshua remembered how his mother had been forcing her smiles. Why hadn't he understood then? He could vaguely remember Benjamin having quiet moments, and now he realized why that was.

Neither Joshua nor Benjamin spoke for a while. He was relieved to know that he wasn't going through this alone. Benjamin had realized their frailty first, but they were in the same boat now.

"So what do we do?" Benjamin asked. "Should we talk to someone?"

"We need to learn how to fight," Joshua said abruptly, sounding a little bit like Gabe.

"We're too young. They won't send us out there to…"

"We're going to be attacked."

Benjamin's eyes grew wide. He tried to form words but his mouth simply hung agape.

"There were wildmen at Uuron Plauf, and both Kris and Father think they could track us here. Father went to talk to Randall about it. Mother's packing our tents right now."

"Oh, no!" Benjamin exclaimed. His eyes glossed over, and Joshua could see the panic beginning to form.

"Calm down," Joshua said, trying to sound reassuring. "They don't know for sure, and it might not happen at all. Let's just wait and see what Randall has to say."

"We have to tell my father or Uncle Tramin!"

"Shouldn't we wait for Randall?"

Benjamin took off running. Joshua followed him and easily caught up.

"Where are you going?"

"The medical tent. Uncle Tramin should be awake by now."

Joshua followed his friend. They were approaching the tent when something caught his eye and he startled. He grabbed Benjamin by the shoulder and pulled him down behind a tree.

"What are you doing?"

Joshua pointed ahead of them to the left. There, sitting on the low branch of a forked tree, was a man with a black hood draped over his head. His arms and feet were crossed, and he was smoking a pipe. He didn't move or say anything. He simply stared at the medical tent up ahead. It was this man, Ivan Shaymolin, who had sent Randall and the others to Uuron Plauf on a suicide mission.

"What's he looking at?" Benjamin whispered.

Joshua was about to answer when the man turned his head, ever so slightly, in their direction. The hood cast shadows over his face, but a bright, sunburnt-looking chin gleamed beneath the shadows.

"Move along children," the man demanded.

His voice had some rasp in it but was, for the most part, smooth. The boys stumbled out from behind their tree and moved quickly toward the medical tent. Joshua kept his eyes to the ground as they passed the man, but he heard Benjamin gasp.

"Children," Ivan said as they neared the tree line. Joshua couldn't meet the man's eyes. "Which way to your leader's tent?"

Joshua saw Benjamin point and listened as Ivan Shaymolin stood and began walking in that direction. They were frozen in place until the footsteps faded moments later. Benjamin covered his face and sat on a rock.

"What is it, Benjamin?"

"His face," Benjamin said. His hands were shaking. "I mean, I didn't get a good look at it, but what I saw... it was like he didn't have any skin; like it was all burned off."

Joshua glanced in the direction that Ivan had wandered. Phyllis had kept him away from the stranger while Gabe was away, and Joshua often wondered why. Was it because something evil had wandered into their camp?

"Let's go see your uncle," he finally said.

He didn't much like thinking about Ivan Shaymolin. Something inside him trembled at the thought of the man, a dormant part of himself that had suddenly come to life—that part which feared death.

Debra watched as Jillian slept. She had fallen asleep in Debra's arms not long after Randall left, still clutching the stone heart that Payson had engraved for her. The thought of her husband left Debra hollow. He was gone, and the empty shell that rested before her was all that remained of the man she loved. It was torture sitting here, staring at his body, but she couldn't leave him.

"Take care of her," she remembered him saying. He had been referring to Jillian of course. "If I don't come back, and we must both acknowledge that as a possibility, I want you to make sure she's taken care of. Mourn, but not so much that she finds herself alone. Do not give in to the grief."

Those words had been running through her mind since he left, especially these last few hours. The worst that could happen did happen, and now she had to face raising Jillian alone. No, not alone. Randall said it himself. The whole tribe was mourning with her. They were her family, but were they enough? Why did this have to happen?

"This is a suicide mission!" she remembered shouting at Payson before he left. He had attempted to soothe her.

"This is something that we must do," he answered softly, and she cried into his chest. "It is our responsibility to help people in need and to offer them a chance at life free from elven tyranny. If what this stranger says is true, then those birdmen are going to need all the help they can get. Don't worry, we won't be caught. They won't even know we're there."

"But what if you *are* caught?"

"We won't be."

They weren't caught, but they were seen. Payson was murdered. Fire erupted in her chest at the conceived image of it all.

That deformed man had sent them. Ivan Shaymolin. He just wandered into their camp, his side half ripped out, and sent them on their way. Why did Randall have to listen to him? He should have said no. She was being selfish, she knew, but she didn't care. She just wanted her husband back—the kind, selfless, handsome man who rescued her from life as a forest vagabond. She missed Payson terribly, despite him lying only a foot from where she was sitting. If only Randall hadn't listened to Ivan Shaymolin. The name was quickly becoming a curse.

"Ivan?"

She startled as if her thoughts had been spoken aloud, but no, it wasn't her voice. Shëlin was quoting someone. She gently laid Jillian on the floor and stepped out of the room for the first time in hours.

"He was just staring at the medical tent," Benjamin was saying. "Then he asked where Randall's tent was and headed that way."

"Then I'm sure Randall will greet him when he arrives," Shëlin said as she patted Benjamin's head. "We're a little busy at the moment, so you boys will have to come back later."

"There might not be a later!" Joshua shouted. "Wildmen are coming! Father and Kris both think so."

"Wildmen?" Debra asked. She joined the others at a cautious pace.

"They're right," another voice said from a room near the entrance. The curtain flipped open and out stepped a tall man with blonde hair and a blonde beard. A bandage covered the left side of his face. He slid a shirt over his muscular frame, and it was obvious from Shëlin's expression that she did not approve of his moving about. This was Trent's brother, Tramin—Benjamin's uncle. Pillar stood at his heels.

"What do you mean they're right?" Shëlin asked.

"There were a lot of wildmen there," Tramin answered. "I don't know why they were helping the elves, but our scent could lead them here. We were in too much of a hurry to cover our trail adequately. We need to leave."

"We should probably wait for Randall to..." Shëlin began but Tramin waved her off.

"Randall will make the call. I was just beginning to consider the wildmen myself when these two ran in. We were all too tired to think last night, but Randall will have put it together by now."

"Father went up to talk to him," Joshua said.

"Good, then he'll be there when I arrive. I'll wake Trent up along the way. You should start packing this place up."

"What about Payson?" Debra asked nervously.

"We'll bury him before we go," Shëlin chimed in, "but what about the birdmen?"

"What about them?" a harsh voice asked.

A large, white birdman entered the tent, its talons spreading in the dirt. From its inverted knees up through its neck, it could almost pass as human save for a coating of white fur that covered every inch of its body. Its head and the wings extending from its back, however, were entirely birdlike. With the blood washed away, its brilliant coloring glared in the morning sunlight.

"What do you mean, Nikiatis?" Shëlin asked.

The white birdman growled in its throat. "We are not your people, and we did not ask for your help. My kin and I will be leaving this rotting encampment soon enough."

"Your people are injured..." Shëlin began, but Nikiatis crouched as if preparing to pounce.

"No!" Debra shouted. "My husband died saving you people! You cannot talk to us as if..."

"I will talk to you however I wish!" Nikiatis replied. His hand went for the sword strapped to his hip.

Debra felt anger and fear boiling up inside her. She wished she had her bow; she'd shot more than one bird out of the sky in her day.

"We do not deserve your taunts, birdman," Tramin said calmly, stepping between Nikiatis and the others. He pointed at his bandaged face. "I've taken my own wounds at your defense. Whether you stay here or not is of no matter, but you at least owe us some courtesy."

"I owe you nothing."

Shëlin grabbed Debra, suddenly pulling her back as curses filled the tent. She could feel herself pulling away from Shëlin, demanding a bow to kill the beast, but it was as if she were looking through someone else's eyes. She couldn't hear what Shëlin was saying due to the drums beating in her ears, but she didn't care. She saw only Nikiatis, sword in hand, preparing to attack the whole lot of them. Tramin stayed between her and the birdman with Pillar growling at his side.

"You owe us!" he shouted again.

Nikiatis hesitantly stepped back, though not out of fear or concern. His sword remained tightly gripped in his hand as if anticipating an excuse to use it.

"When can my people leave?" he asked. Hate saturated every word.

"When they are fit to leave, likely in a week or two," Shëlin answered.

Debra was no longer fighting her friend; she fought the tears that were intruding upon her cheeks instead. She spied Joshua and Benjamin nearby, pointing their daggers at the birdman, and she suddenly regretted having lost control. Not only did she put *them* in danger, but Jillian might have gotten hurt as well.

The danger never came, however, as the white birdman turned and stormed from the tent. Then he lifted into the air with a flap of his mighty wings and was gone.

"He wasn't worth..." Debra began, but the clearing of a throat quieted her.

"Do not fault Nikiatis," came a broken voice from a nearby room. Debra and the others followed the voice and found the birdman with golden feathers sitting up in his cot. "How must it feel to witness the fall of a race that you were bred to rule?"

The birdman's words stilled the tent. He coughed and returned their glare.

"Nikiatis was our king" he continued, "and he is undoubtedly blaming himself for the extermination of an entire race. Such a thing is bound to drive even the most noble of birdmen to grief-given madness. He failed his people. I know how he feels." He coughed again. "Could you shut the curtain please? I wish to rest."

Shëlin did as the golden birdman asked, and Debra was struck by how differently the two creatures behaved. The golden one seemed kind enough. She was decided on one thing, however; Payson's life in exchange for Nikiatis' was a detestable trade.

"It is our duty to show this world compassion," she remembered Payson saying, "and pray that it will one day remember how to pass it along."

"I'll collect my brother," Tramin finally said. "I'll see if he wouldn't mind preparing a grave once we've finished discussing things at Randall's. I advise that you begin packing immediately."

"We will," Shëlin said, suddenly sure of Tramin's order. "Why don't you boys go play? There will be little time for fun in the coming days."

Debra noticed Joshua and Benjamin again. Benjamin was obviously shaken, but Joshua hid his nerves better.

Their daggers were still clenched in white fists. Since when did they become little warriors?

"Take Jillian with you," she said, surprised to hear herself suggesting it. "She shouldn't be here when we prepare Payson's…"

Her voice broke.

Shëlin hugged her as Tramin retrieved Jillian and sent her out with the boys. Then he left the medical tent with Pillar at his heels. Shëlin agreed to prepare Payson's body for burial while Debra distracted herself with packing supplies. She wasn't ready for this. She wanted to curl up in a ball next to Payson and fall asleep. She wanted to give in to the depression and join him in the heavens, but she refused.

"Do not give in to the grief," he had demanded of her, and she would obey no matter how badly it hurt.

Randall rubbed his neck and coughed a great deal. In addition to the throbbing in his chest, it seemed he was coming down with something. He blamed it on stress and lack of sleep, neither of which would be getting better any time soon.

Gabe had come to him with Kris' concerns, and Randall agreed, as did Trent and Tramin once they arrived. There might not be anything to worry about, but then, there could be. Randall wasn't going to take any chances. He'd sent the others out to help prepare for Payson's funeral, and after their friend was laid to rest they would leave.

He had been questioning whether it was wise or not to intervene in Uuron Plauf, but debating hypotheticals was useless. He had to move forward; he just didn't know what to do about their guests, the three birdmen and...

"Are we alone?"

Randall stood as the black-hooded man walked into his camp.

"We are," he said. "To what do I owe this honor, Ivan?"

"Please, sit." Ivan motioned a hand toward the stool that Randall had been sitting on. "I just wanted to talk for a bit. I hope you don't mind that I waited for your friends to leave?"

"You were eavesdropping?"

"I was. My apologies."

The man knelt a small distance from the fire pit. It was unlit, but Ivan glanced wearily at it anyhow. His burnt face was unsettling.

"You fight well for a group of pacifists," he said.

"We learned to defend ourselves long ago. Is that what you've come to talk about? Our swordplay?"

"No," Ivan answered. "Your tribe, it is strange."

"In what way?"

"You have an elf."

"Shëlin-Vin is not like those under Kïer's rule. She's proven herself trustworthy time and again. I like to think of her as the epitome of what the elves could become if they were to let go of their hatred."

Ivan seemed to consider this then glanced in the direction of the medical tent. He snickered. "You've brought birdmen back with you. Three, I believe."

"We have."

"They hate you."

"The hate is theirs alone."

"You do not fear them?"

"I would be a fool not to fear them, but what is important is that I do not give in to those fears."

Ivan shook his head and released a frustrated sigh.

"Why?" he finally asked.

"Because we believe in something bigger. The hatred and turmoil that the elves breed is secondary."

"Mankind bred it first, remember."

"And it nearly destroyed us."

"If not for the elves."

Randall sighed. What was the point in all this? He studied Ivan, but the man gave nothing away. "We owe the elves a great debt for nurturing the world back to health, but they have fallen. The world darkens with every dawn. The races grow further apart. Wars will be fought again, and those few who thrive now will be cast down into the shadows of what we've all created. The elves are blinded by their hatred and cannot see that they are repeating the same mistakes that mankind had once made."

Ivan's eyes narrowed. "And why do you tell me this?"

"Because I refuse to let this world fall again. We are a tribe of hope, accepting everyone and loving them regardless of their race or past. We are a safe haven as the cathedrals once were in the old world."

"Cathedrals?"

"Places where people of faith gathered. It was where people could be forgiven of their sins and start life anew.

A man named Silus Rook formed our tribe based on that principal so that every person who finds us might receive a new start."

"And where is this Silus Rook?"

Randall hesitated.

"I'll tell you where he is," Ivan said. "He is dead, killed forty-seven years ago on the banks of the Sïren River. Silus founded not only your tribe but Refuge as well, a faith-based community that challenged elven law with ideals. His religion frightened Kïer, so he placed an extermination order to have the believers eradicated. Silus Rook died in a tent full of old books, and Refuge came to its untimely end—or so it was believed."

Randall crossed his arms and studied his guest.

"You know our history," he said. "Did you recognize us by our ideals?"

"You have an elf. That intrigued me, and your march to Uuron Plauf only strengthened my suspicions. Your mentioning Silus Rook confirmed them."

"So you mentioned the extermination order on Uuron Plauf to test us?" Randall asked. He was becoming angry. "You wanted to see if we'd risk death for another race?"

"Yes, in part. It was a test."

"And the other part?"

Ivan did not answer. He stood again and studied Randall, and then he smiled.

"You have nothing to fear from me, Randall Whitaker. I think your ideals are foolish, but I have no qualms with you. You treated my wounds, and for that I owe you a dept. I will accept your offer to stay… for a while at least."

"I have not yet extended that offer," Randall sternly corrected.

"But you will. Am I below that of an elf or birdman?"

"That is yet to be determined. We lost a good man in that test of yours, and you…"

"And you," Ivan interrupted, "acted in a way that would have made Silus Rook proud. You followed your ideals. Do not fault me if all did not go as planned. It was you who decided to take your men into Uuron Plauf, after all. Not I."

Randall turned away as a dull pain hit him in the gut. Ivan was right. The man had been lying in the medical tent when he whispered the extermination order into Randall's ear. It was Randall's idea to seek for survivors.

"Besides," Ivan said with a smile, "it would be quite hypocritical of you to turn me away, sins be forgiven and all that."

"I don't trust you."

"I do not ask that you do. It would probably be best if you didn't to be honest. You trust far too much already. Do you need any help preparing for our upcoming journey?"

"No. We move frequently enough. We know what to do."

"Very well."

He turned to leave but then paused, discomforted. Randall remembered the wound—four deep gashes along his right side.

"How are your injuries?" he asked.

"Healing," Ivan replied without turning around. "And yours?"

"Healing." He coughed, as if the question had reminded him of his health. Ivan took another step.

"You still haven't told us how you were wounded," Randall said.

Ivan did not move. He simply stood, his head tilted slightly toward Randall. He was perfectly still as if paralyzed by a terrible memory.

"I escaped from a prison."

He vanished in the shadows of the Greysong Forest, and Randall was left with too many questions. How did Ivan get so hideously scarred? Had he really escaped from a prison? How did he learn of the extermination order on Uuron Plauf? And most importantly, what were his true motivations for staying with the tribe? Only one thing was certain, Randall did not trust Ivan Shaymolin. Not one bit.

"Your name is Debra?"

The voice startled her. She wasn't expecting to hear it again so soon, yet here it was. She put down the bag of ointments that she had been packing and slowly made her way to the golden birdman's room.

"It is," she answered while tying back the curtain, "Debra Harlow. And what would your name be?"

"Fagunol," the birdman answered. It was hard to tell with his beak, but he appeared to be smiling.

"It's nice to meet you, Fagunol. Is there anything I can get for you? Would you like some water?"

"I have plenty of water, thank you. Your elf is very accommodating."

Debra nodded. She didn't know what else to say and was about to turn away when the birdman spoke again.

"Payson was your husband's name, was it not?"

Her throat constricted, but she showed no outward sign of her emotional state. She nodded.

"I am sorry to have learned of his passing. I want you to know that I am grateful for his sacrifice, but his efforts were in vain."

"In vain?" she said angrily.

"Do not misunderstand me," Fagunol said. "I recognize the selflessness of his actions and relate to your tribe's grief, but the trade was not fair. Your people, they saved only three of us, all males. We cannot breed. We cannot multiply. Nikiatis, Vetcalf, and myself—we are the last of our kind."

"And what do you want me to say?"

"Nothing. You say nothing. I simply wished to relay my condolences. But if it is of any consolation, I've never liked humans much. Seeing the actions of... Payson... and the others, I am inclined to admit my mistake, and that is a difficult thing for a scholar such as me to do."

Debra didn't know how to respond. She didn't know anything about birdmen, but this one seemed friendly enough. She was reminded of the other.

"So the white birdman..."

"Nikiatis," Fagunol corrected.

"Nikiatis. He was your king, and you are a scholar. What of the blue birdman?"

"Vetcalf was merely a low-ranking soldier. So low, in fact, that he didn't even warrant my attention. Nikiatis had to inform me of his name."

"I thought birdmen were supposed to be wise."

"Regal would be a better word, I think. We thought ourselves above other races. Perhaps it was our high perch that created that illusion. I do not know. Anyhow, Vetcalf had not yet reached the level of importance that I would have considered respectable."

"That's a horrible thing to say. Were you all so vain?"

"Perhaps, yet I now find myself longing for Vetcalf's company. I would like to learn more about him and about what life was like in the lower levels. It is strange how, in the face of extinction, we realize how unimportant we really are. I mourn for what the Aerie put our people through, those of Vetcalf's rank. We were not kind."

"The Aerie?"

"The high council of Uuron Plauf of which I was a member."

"And your king? Was he a member?"

"We advised Nikiatis, but he was nothing like us. He was a far better birdman than I've ever been. He loved and was therefore loved by all."

"I saw no love when last he came to visit."

"I fear his love has been overcome by bitterness and guilt. He was a young king with much to prove, less than a year on the throne. Now he must live, knowing that he failed his people."

This saddened Debra. She was a caring woman, as mothers often were, and she could perhaps understand a portion of what Nikiatis was going through. How heavy must the burden weigh, having led an entire species to its death? What would that do to a person's mind?

"I will pray for him," she replied after a slight pause.

"Pray?" the birdman asked. "To a god?"

"Yes. We believe in God here."

Fagunol appeared astonished.

"Interesting," he said excitedly. "I was not aware that there were any belief systems still in play in this day and age. I believed religion to be rather antiquated."

"Then I suppose the scholar has much to learn."

The birdman studied Debra and smiled. "Perhaps I do."

Angela had grown up with Kris and Orlan, being only a year younger than Orlan and two years younger than Kris, yet something had changed over the past couple of years. When she looked at Orlan he was still the same boy she used to play tag with, but Kris was different.

She wasn't sure when it happened, but it was like Kris suddenly grew up. He began hunting and going on missions with the men of the tribe—scavenging for clothing and weapons. He sprouted and built muscle. He matured. It wasn't that Orlan hadn't matured; Kris just seemed better at it.

There was more to it, of course. She knew of Kris' heritage and what that meant. After Refuge was razed, it was Kris' grandfather, Rand Medair'yin, who led the survivors to safety. Rand, and then his son Damian, led the tribe until Damian, Kris' father, passed away. Kris was too young to lead, so Angela's father took over with

Trent serving as his second-in-command. Everyone knew that Kris was being groomed to replace Randall, and the idea of leading the tribe beside him made Angela smile. A lot of things made her smile.

"Hey, Angela," Kris said as he strapped his sword to his waist. It looked elven. He must have picked it up in Uuron Plauf.

Angela caught her breath and felt silly for having lost it. Since when did Kris start having *that* effect on her? She had asked to accompany Gabe Harlow to his family's camp so that she might check in on Kris. She was glad to find him awake and seemingly healthy.

"I was about to relieve Orlan," he said.

"You're not relieving him," Gabe said pointedly. "We need someone out there with rested eyes. You need more sleep."

"I slept an hour. I'm fine."

"Maybe we can watch together?" Angela offered. The idea of being alone with Kris on the outskirts of camp was alluring.

Gabe offered a sly grin, and Angela nudged him. The bearded man was apparently more observant than his eldest adopted son. Kris, fortunately, hadn't noticed the exchange.

"Fine," Gabe said, "but keep your eyes on the trees."

"Yes, sir," Kris consented.

They headed out, talking very little, and this bothered Angela. They could typically talk about nothing at all without pause, but it was like Kris didn't even know she was there.

"Are you alright?" she finally asked.

"No, I'm not."

"What's wrong?"

Kris sighed. "I'll explain when we get to the hill."

It took a few minutes, but they eventually got there. Orlan was sitting on the bottom branch of the hill's lonely tree with his eyes fixed on the forest, his sword ready. He didn't look like he needed a rest.

"We're here to relieve you, Orlan," Angela said as they approached.

Orlan looked back at them and smiled, but there was no humor in it. There used to always be humor in Orlan's smile.

"I'm fine," he said.

"Then do you mind if we join you?" Kris asked, and Angela was struck by the fact that she and Kris wouldn't be alone. They were never alone in this godforsaken camp.

Orlan dropped from the branch and leaned against the base of the tree. Kris scanned the forest briefly, adjusted his sword, and sat beside Orlan. Angela sat beside Kris.

"Anything?" Kris asked.

"If there were, do you think I'd still be here?"

Kris didn't answer.

They sat in silence for a while until Kris stood again. He scanned the trees, and Angela watched as his eyes focused on the smoke that still rose over Uuron Plauf.

"I've never seen anything like it," he finally said. "I've only seen a handful of elves in my life, Shëlin aside, but never like that. Their numbers were overwhelming, and their eyes—the hate that filled them—it was like they were possessed."

Angela took his hand and pulled him back down beside her. She put her arm around him, but he shrugged it off and continued.

"When they saw us, it was like they wanted to rip us apart, drag our intestines out for the crows to eat. I've never realized how much they despise us. I've never seen hatred like that. They know we escaped, and they'll do whatever it takes to make us pay for intervening. They have wildmen with them. They'll find us eventually."

"Can we cover our scent?" Orlan asked.

"Maybe. Trent and Tramin would know more about that than I do."

"So then it might not be so bad?" Angela asked.

Kris didn't answer, and that was answer enough. She didn't know what their future held, but the men of the tribe all seemed to share Kris' mentality. It frightened her. It made her want to leave immediately to get a bigger head start, but they couldn't. They couldn't take Payson with them, and two of the birdmen needed more time to recover.

"We'll be ready," Orlan said.

Kris nodded in agreement, and they both focused on the line of trees below. Angela studied Kris and Orlan. The three of them had been friends for as long as she could remember—inseparable—but somewhere along the way her friends grew up. They were young men now; worrisome, burdened, and fearful. She missed how playful they used to be, how they used to chase one another around trees. If only they could get back to that. But then, why couldn't they?

"Tag," she said, pushing Kris over in the grass.

She stood up and walked backwards for a few steps.

"What are you doing?" Kris asked, righting himself.

"That was my attempt at making you ease up. You're too tense."

He looked at her in a way that made her stomach drop, and not in a good way. It was as if she had said the dumbest thing ever spoken. She chose to ignore it, moved forward a few steps, and pushed him again.

"This is when you chase me."

"Knock it off, Angela!" Kris shouted.

Angela's smile faded. Never once in all their years together had he shouted her name like that. Not with that much venom behind it. It hurt, and she felt tears forming in her eyes, so she blinked them away and plopped herself down a few feet from where she had been standing.

Maybe wanting to be children again *was* foolish. But was it so wrong of her to want to see Kris' beautiful smile again before they died, if it came to that? Maybe it *was* too much to ask. Maybe she was just being childish.

Orlan tried his hardest to focus on the tree line, but his mind wouldn't cooperate. He kept thinking about Joshua's expression after hearing Kris' account of what had happened in Uuron Plauf. He wondered if the fear had faded yet, if Joshua was playing tag with Benjamin and Jillian, but he doubted it. He recalled the days when he used to play tag with Angela and Kris, and suddenly he missed it.

He felt guilty for having been annoyed by Joshua's youthful enthusiasm. It wasn't until he saw it stripped away that he recognized how beautiful it was. But then, when was the last time he felt that enthusiasm himself? Not since before his parents died when he was ten. Now here he sat, sixteen and somber. Well, that wasn't always true.

He felt butterflies in his stomach—that playful nervousness that fluttered—whenever Angela came to visit. He'd always felt that way when she was around, even when they were children, and for a time he wondered if perhaps she felt the same, but he knew better now. She was in love with Kris. Everyone could see it. Well, almost everyone.

For all his importance and high promises, Kris was one of the least observant people in the tribe. Orlan didn't condemn his best friend and adopted brother for that—Kris had a lot to take on—but it sometimes frustrated him how Kris ignored Angela's advances. She was fifteen, Randall's daughter, and beautiful. Kris was strong, seventeen, and being primed to take over Randall's position as leader of Refuge. As much as Orlan wished it wasn't so, Kris and Angela seemed destined to be together. If only Kris would notice her. She deserved that much.

Like right then, just a moment ago. Angela was trying to ease Kris' mind and he scoffed at her for it. It pained Orlan to see him do that, to see the hurt in her eyes. He wished more than anything that she would play with him like that, like when they were children. He considered coming to Angela's defense but then remembered all that Kris had been through, and he understood. This watchful task was important, but Angela didn't understand. She appeared to be close to tears, and it reminded him of how Joshua had looked that morning. It broke his heart all over again.

Orlan took a breath and studied the tree line. There was nothing there—nothing he could see anyway—but he had a feeling. They were coming. Sometime soon they would burst through those trees and likely kill every member of this tribe. He looked at Angela as he thought this.

Something shifted inside Orlan.

He would never allow it. He would gladly feel the jaws of a wildman or the arrow of an elf before letting her or Kris come to harm. These could very well be their final hours together, and he refused to spend them like this—afraid. He would rather fill the hours as children would: saturated in youthful innocence.

He took a deep breath, stood, and stretched. Then he walked over and kicked Kris down the hill.

Angela couldn't stop laughing. Despite Kris' frustrated expression, she still found Orlan's unexpected assault funny. There was no smile on Kris' face, no sign of the boy from their childhood, but there was in Orlan. He wasn't laughing like she was, but he had a grin on his face.

Coming to the conclusion that Orlan needed to lighten up even more, she ran and collided with him, knocking him over the crest of the hill so that he rolled a part of the way down before stopping beside Kris. Orlan laughed heartily and immediately charged back up after her.

Angela screamed, and the rest of the afternoon was spent playing, chasing, wrestling, and attempting to prod Kris into joining them. He refused, however, and remained perched on the side of the hill, his eyes glued to the trees.

Angela and Orlan rejoined Kris as the sun set, but he didn't comment on the fun they were having. He simply moved his sword so that Angela could sit down and continued studying the trees.

"Anything?" she asked, but Kris just shook his head.

It took a few minutes, but Kris eventually glanced at them. His expression was sad.

"I wish it could be like that again," he said sorrowfully, "like when we were kids. You have no idea how badly I wanted to jump in."

"Nothing was stopping you," Orlan offered.

"Responsibility stopped me. What if something happened while we were goofing around? What if the elves or wildmen had gotten by us? We can't afford that chance. Refuge deserves better than that."

"Always so serious," Angela said beneath her breath. She understood Kris' concern but still felt the sting of his words.

"I have to be," Kris replied softly.

They sat quietly for a while. It was Orlan who broke the silence.

"You're not obligated to take over, you know."

"Yes, I am. My grandfather led us out of Refuge as it burned, and my father took over from him. Randall only took the reins because I wasn't old enough to lead, but I am now. I'm the last of the Medair'yins. I have to be ready for when Randall steps down."

"You don't have to do anything," Orlan said. "My grandfather *formed* Refuge. You don't see me jumping to take Randall's place."

Kris didn't reply, and Angela knew why. She and Kris had often discussed Orlan's decision to stay out of all leadership roles. Yes, Silus Rook may have been Orlan's grandfather, but Orlan had never met the man and felt no obligation to step into his footsteps. That mentality had always frustrated Kris.

"Randall's tired," Kris finally said. "He pretends not to be, but he hasn't been the same since Bethany died. It's like he just wants to mourn but won't let himself."

Angela studied the grass at her feet. She felt the familiar pang in her gut, the pain that always came with mentions of her mother. It hadn't been that long since she died, only three years. She was the tribe's most recent loss before Payson.

"So you think he's pushing you to be ready so he can just give up?" Orlan asked, obviously not agreeing with what Kris was insinuating.

"Maybe. You're not in the meetings with us, Orlan. You weren't there when we raced back from Uuron Plauf. He talked to Bethany's ghost more than he talked to us. He's still broken over losing her."

"He talks to her when he thinks I'm asleep," Angela said quietly. She hugged her knees and hid her face behind them. "He still cries when others aren't around. I do too. We both miss her a lot."

Orlan put an arm around her, but something kept her from leaning into him. This wasn't about her, and it certainly wasn't about her father.

"You can't take away his burdens, Kris," she said. "My father is a strong man, and he'll bear whatever he needs to until you're ready. The last thing he'd want, what any of us would want, is for you to be rushed into his position. You're not ready."

"And Trent is Randall's second-in-command," Orlan added. "He can take over anytime Randall needs him to. You have time."

Kris was about to reply when a flock of birds flew from just beyond the tree line, and then another flock to their immediate left. Something had spooked them. Kris and Orlan stood, drawing their blades.

"I'll keep watch. Go, tell Randall," Kris said, and Orlan obeyed.

Angela stood with Kris, slowly drawing the dagger that she kept with her. She reached for Kris' hand but he pulled away.

"Go with him," he said. "Spread the word. We must leave now."

"But..."

"Now!"

***

"Focus on me, Joshua."

He tried focusing on Gabe, but his legs shook and he felt as if he could throw up. He had been training with his adopted father for years, but today was different. He'd never needed to use the techniques that Gabe taught him. Now he might. If the elves or wildmen came, then he would have to fight, and the idea of having to defend himself terrified him. What if he wasn't strong enough? What if he failed? What if…?

He screamed and thrust the dagger at his father's chest, but Gabe deflected it, grasping Joshua's arm and pulling him close. If Gabe were a real threat, Joshua would likely have had a sword thrust through his abdomen. Gabe stepped back and looked Joshua in the eye.

"You need to calm down, Joshua," he said. "I've protected you all these years, and I will continue to do so. This training, it's precautionary. Just in case."

"But what if they show up tonight while we sleep?"

"Then I'll cut them in half before you even know they're here. Try it again."

Joshua stepped back and prepared to thrust. He did so, and Gabe sidestepped him again.

"You're announcing yourself. A scream, a grunt, clenched teeth; they all tell your enemy that you're about to attack. You need to keep that held in until the attack is over."

Joshua slumped and looked at his dagger. He had fought Benjamin with it during imaginary games of war—he even cut his friend once on accident—but now the weapon felt heavier. It had always been a toy before, a sharp toy that he helped Phyllis cut meat with, but a plaything nonetheless. Now he looked at it differently. The dagger was deadly, and the hand that held it shook continuously.

Gabe studied Joshua for a moment and then sat on a fallen tree trunk.

"Come, boy," he said, patting the bark beside him. Joshua did as he was told. "You were a baby when I found you in that old silo, when we took you in. You know that. But the truth is, your mother and me were more frightened in that moment than ever before. Kris and Orlan, they were older when we took them in, but you we named from infancy. We'd always dreamed of having a baby but couldn't conceive. Despite our love of children, we didn't know how to raise one so little. Taking you in was more frightening for us than fighting every wildman in the world." Gabe laughed to himself. "I could at least shut those beasts up."

He seemed to be looking into some distant memory, but then he smiled and put an arm around Joshua.

"I knew a day would come when you'd progress from a child to a man. A boy's childhood is precious, and I wanted to prolong those years for as long as I could, but Kris was right. I've kept you sheltered for far too long, and now you're being bombarded with fears that you've never known. But know this: if danger comes, I will be fighting beside you the entire time. Under no circumstance will I leave you. I will keep you safe, your mother will keep you safe, and your brothers will keep you safe. We're your family."

A knot tightened in Joshua's chest. He tried to fight it but the emotions surging through him were too much to bear. Tears began to fall, so he leaned into his father's chest and sobbed. He confessed his every fear and insecurity while Gabe simply listened.

"There is everything to be afraid of, Son," Gabe said once Joshua had regained control of himself, "but through it all, I will be here. I love you, Joshua. Let me carry these burdens for you."

"But if the wildmen come," Joshua said through tears, "and I have to fight...?"

"Then we will fight together, and I will keep you safe. You'll remember how to use that dagger when the time comes."

"I'm scared, Father."

Gabe hugged his son.

"I'm going to tell you a secret, Joshua. How you feel right now, that's how I feel every time I go into battle. I fear that I'll never see you again, that if something were to happen to me, I wouldn't be able to protect you and your mother. And that fear, if you embrace it, can be a weapon. The day you stop fearing, Joshua, is the day you have nothing left worth fighting for."

They sat together for a few more minutes while Joshua composed himself. Then they headed for the medical tent. Payson's funeral would begin soon, and they didn't want to be late.

"Did I ever tell you about the story of when I rerouted a whole river so that Kïer himself had to thirst while we drank aplenty?"

Joshua offered his father a wary glance, but Gabe grinned through his bushy, red beard and grew suddenly animated. He acted out the story, culminating with him digging a looping path through the dirt with his ax, and Joshua laughed at the absurdity of it all.

But then Gabe stopped.

Joshua laughed for only a moment but was then struck by his father's sudden grim expression. Gabe surveyed the ground and then knelt, fear etched on his face. He traced something in the dirt with his finger while looking up and down a trail that they had just crossed. Joshua joined him and stared at the footprint. Muddy water was still settling in the deeper indentations.

"Why weren't they wearing boots?" Joshua asked.

Gabe stood, gripped his ax, and studied the trees around them. Then, without warning, the forest burst to life as a wildman leapt from an overgrown bush with a savage, lion-like scream. Gabe swung his ax, wedged it into the creature's side, and imbedded the body into the mud. Then a second and third wildman fell from the trees above and tackled Gabe to the ground. He was pinned. One of the attackers bit into his neck, but Gabe pulled an arm free and broke the cannibal's neck.

Joshua screamed for help, but none came. Not knowing what else to do, he charged the wildman with his dagger, screaming despite Gabe's lessons. The attackers didn't seem to notice him before, but as his dagger dug deep into the last wildman's back, it screamed and leapt at him. Its blood splattered Joshua's arms, but then it fell, thrashed, and died.

Joshua stared at the creature he had just killed. Its skin was deeply tanned and leathery, and hair grew from its head and back in long, black strands. The wildman's hands were almost twice the size of Joshua's and inconceivably muscular. They were stained with blood and dirt. Then he saw the wound that emptied the wildman's contents onto the dirt. The blood on Joshua's own hands felt warm and sticky, and he could taste it in his mouth. He felt as if he were going to be sick.

"Come on, Joshua!" Gabe said, grabbing him by the arm. "These were scouts. There will be more."

He ran alongside his father, but his mind was still with the dead wildman. The immediate shock subsided, and he recalled the creature's face as he had stabbed it. It was terrified. Its eyes were fully black and emotionless, but its every feature screamed with pain. Horror was frozen upon its face as it lay still.

Was every battle like this, every death just as horrifying? Was Payson's face just as…?

"Stay with me, Joshua," Gabe said, still pulling him by the arm. "You did what you had to do, and I'm proud of you. Just stay with me."

Kris was seemingly alone atop the hill when a massive, horrifying call suddenly rang out. A long series of howls filled the forest, echoing from every direction like the call of a million dead souls, and it was getting louder. The sound dragged on as Kris slowly moved away from the hill's crest.

Then, all at once, the forest came alive as shadow after shadow, silhouette after silhouette—seemingly hundreds of them—burst through the trees, running on all fours like dogs. The wave of wildmen was like an ocean pouring through the forest. It broke upon the field and was now preparing to crash upon the foot of the hill. Their howls were disorienting.

Kris had been right. The raid on their camp had come, but it came sooner than expected. They were going to die. Kris held out his sword in a quivering hand. He intended to stall them, knowing that it would be his death, but then someone grabbed him by the arm and pulled him back.

"Don't be stupid, Kris!" Orlan shouted, knowing his friend's thoughts.

He had arrived just in time to hear the howls and was frozen by it. He was sobered, however, by the sight of the wildmen's rapid approach. He steadied Kris as the wildmen reached the bottom of the hill, and together they tore through the Greysong Forest, swords in hand.

The raid had begun.

Part III: The Wildman Raid

Randall froze as howls filled the air. He and Tramin had been discussing Uuron Plauf when the call went out, and their hearts fell. They had waited too long. They exchanged a single worried glance, and each knew what the other was thinking. The howls frightened Randall, but a deeper fear came in knowing that his daughter was now in danger.

With his sword in hand, he ran faster than his aging knees should allow. Tramin, the younger of the two by several decades, ran ahead with Pillar at his side. The large man disappeared through the trees, and a frightened scream immediately followed. Breaking through the foliage, Randall found that Tramin had plowed over Angela.

"Kris is still back there," she said breathlessly as Tramin helped her up, "Orlan went back for him."

"We'll get them," Randall said. "Get to the medical tent and tell them to leave immediately. We'll follow you if we can."

Judging from her expression, the thought of leaving camp without her father and friends horrified Angela, but they could reconvene later.

"Angela, go!" Randall shouted, so she ran.

"Go with her, Pillar," Tramin commanded. The dog obeyed.

Randall and Tramin wasted not another second. Kris and Orlan, the future of their tribe, were in danger. There was no time for words.

***

Debra tied Vetcalf to the cart with shaking fingers. This birdman, blue in coloring, had yet to awaken and would have to be pulled.

"How dare you!"

Debra jumped as Nikiatis, the white birdman, shoved her aside. He cut the bonds with his sword and lifted Vetcalf into his arms.

"A birdman should never be tied down! I will carry him to safety."

"Will you return for us?" she asked.

"He will," Fagunol answered, walking up behind Debra, "because we birdmen are in your dept. You aided us in our time of turmoil. Now we will aid you."

Debra noted the stern, challenging glare that Fagunol offered his king. They stared at each other, each measuring the other, until Nikiatis offered a frustrated hiss.

"I will return soon enough," he relented. Then he took to the air and flew east.

"Thank you," Debra said.

"You are welcome."

Fagunol glided over to where Shëlin and Phyllis were lighting rows of torches. They had been in the process of tearing the medical tent down when the howls echoed. Now they focused on creating a barrier of fire to keep the wildmen at bay. The torches were a precaution conjured by Shëlin-Vin, based on the wildmen's known fear of fire.

To what extent they feared fire, however, none of them knew.

With Vetcalf taken care of, Debra ran to the small, wooden table on which Payson slept. Trent stood over him, his eyes closed, prayers proceeding from his lips. Sweat glistened on his brow. Jillian stood nearby as well, refusing to leave her father's side.

"We can't bury him," Trent said after whispering a final prayer, "and we can't take him with us."

Debra's belly ached.

"We can't leave him here," she said worriedly. "They're cannibals."

"Then we'll have to burn him."

"What?" Jillian shouted. "You can't burn my dad!"

Trent replied calmly, despite the impending chaos. "It is said that in the old world some would burn their loved ones to ashes as a way of sending their bodies to Heaven. I believe it was called a…" he hesitated a moment, "a funeral pyre, or something of that nature. It was considered an honorable send off, and your father deserves the best, right?"

"But fire really hurts."

Debra knew where Jillian's fear was coming from. She had gotten too close to a fire pit when she was seven years old and burned her fingers. It took Payson a long time to convince her that fire wasn't bad, only dangerous. She had obviously not taken the lesson to heart.

"Payson's spirit is in Heaven, remember. His body no longer feels pain. He won't feel the fire. I promise."

Jillian was still in denial, but they didn't have time to comfort her. Debra took the nearest torch that Shëlin had lit and handed it to Trent.

"Mom, no!"

"I'm sorry, baby. It has to be this way."

Trent said a prayer and set fire to Payson's body. Debra and Trent pulled Jillian away as Payson and the table he rested upon burned. Smoke and flames licked the sky. Jillian cried into Debra's arms, and she wished she could comfort her daughter forever.

Then she saw the eyes.

They were black, but the flames of Payson's pyre reflected orange in them. Three wildmen inched out of the woods but faltered, fearing the flames.

Debra pushed Jillian behind her.

"Wildmen!" she shouted.

Trent drew his sword.

She grabbed her bow and strung an arrow. The wildmen were soon joined by others, all hooting and shouting, some beating the ground with their fists, but none dared approach the circle of fire.

"Phyllis?" Debra called over her shoulder.

Phyllis took Jillian and tucked her beneath the cart that Vetcalf had been strapped to. Then she knelt beside it while making hollow promises of safety. Jillian's tears flowed nonetheless.

Trent took up a bow and moved away from Debra so that, between the two of them, they covered more ground. Debra glanced back and saw that Shëlin and Fagunol were doing the same. Of them all, the wildmen seemed to fear the birdman most. His golden feathers reflected the firelight as if he himself were a pillar of flames. Shëlin's pale skin had a similar effect.

Trent released an arrow.

A wildman had tempted fate by creeping close and kicking at a torch. It lay dead with an arrow in its throat.

"God forgive me," Trent whispered.

Debra found his prayer silly.

A wildman attempted to clear the torches, so she sent it fleeing back into the woods with an arrow in its ribs. Wildmen surrounded them now, each testing the barrier of flames. Some succumbed to fear and retreated before getting too close. Others were stopped by arrows.

"Where are the rest of your people?" Fagunol shouted over the hoots and screams.

"Let's focus on keeping ourselves alive at the moment," Shëlin stated.

"Stay with me, Joshua," Gabe said.

Two more wildmen crossed their path and were dead in seconds. Joshua hid himself behind a tree as Gabe had previously instructed him to do, but as he stepped back out, a pair of large, powerful hands grabbed his arm and cupped his mouth. He tried to scream, but his voice couldn't escape the wildman's massive palm. But he still had his dagger. He sliced the wildman's forearm, and when the creature howled and released him, Joshua turned and buried the dagger deep into the wildman's stomach. The creature fled but fell against a nearby tree, screaming. Gabe finished it off.

"Hurry, Joshua. We have to…"

A wildman leapt onto Gabe's back, and then another, and another, and another. Wildmen carried no weapons; they didn't need to. Instead, they used their massive hands to choke the life out of their prey. They were now strangling Gabe with those massive hands while simultaneously yanking his beard and beating every inch of his body. They wanted him dead.

Joshua had been told to run if Gabe was ever outnumbered, but Joshua couldn't just leave his father to die. He ran toward the wildmen with intent to kill, but then another tackled him and he dropped his dagger. He screamed and fought, but the beast wouldn't let go. Unlike those who fought Gabe, this one did not try to kill him. It dragged him further into the woods, but then it screamed and fell, writhing in pain. Joshua scrambled away and turned just in time to see the enigmatic Ivan Shaymolin pulling his sword from the creature's back. Joshua pointed to where his father was being strangled, and Ivan ran in that direction without speaking.

"Joshua!"

"Benjamin?"

Joshua's best friend ran and fell beside him. His clothes were torn, and he had blood and dirt caked on his face; otherwise he seemed fine. He helped Joshua up.

"He saved me too," Benjamin said.

They found Ivan a moment later, kneeling above Gabe and surrounded by dead wildmen. Ivan's hood was down and his scarred, hairless head stood revealed, shining in the dim moonlight.

"He's alright," Ivan said. "Give him a moment."

"Thank you," Gabe struggled to say as he sat up. His face was covered in blood. His beard was matted with it. "We have to move."

He stood with Ivan's help and reassuringly patted Joshua on the back.

"Where should we go?" Benjamin asked.

"The medical tent," Gabe answered hoarsely. He cleared his throat, picked up his ax, and led the way.

�֎

Angela pressed her back against a tree and waited. Each heartbeat felt like a clap of thunder alerting the wildmen of her presence. They were following her. There were others up ahead. Where else could she go?

She could hear a battle taking place near the medical tent and wanted to help, but she was exhausted. Her legs felt weightless, and her whole body shook. She needed a moment to catch her breath.

A howl.

She didn't have to look to know that at least one of them had caught her scent again. She'd dodged most of them, but one wildman seemed determined to find out where she'd gone. It was ignoring the sounds of battle and heading her way.

She waited.

It was getting closer. So close now that she could hear it breathing. It approached the other side of the tree and began to growl. It knew she was there. The wildman screamed as it reached around the tree, hoping to grab her, but she was ready. Her dagger dug into its ribs and it screamed again, this time a wounded, painful scream. She withdrew the dagger and struck again, this time in the heart. No creature should have to suffer, even if the wildman *was* trying to kill her.

She ran again. The wildman's screams would have alerted others of her presence. She headed for the sounds of battle, but three wildmen came at her from the west and she had to cut east to dodge them. She could take on one wildman, but she wasn't Gabe or Tramin. She couldn't handle three simultaneously.

She ducked beneath fallen tree trunks and weaved through living ones. Then she saw the creek and splashed into its stream up to her thighs. She ran, stumbling over loose stones, until she saw the spot she had been looking for. A tree had long ago fallen from the bank, and its roots hung deep into the water. She hid behind them, stooping in the creek water.

The wildmen stopped at the water and sniffed. The creek water was covering her scent, but it wouldn't hide her completely. She tried holding her breath but instead gasped. Her lungs were straining after all the running, and she couldn't appease them. She prayed that the water and tree's roots were adequate enough protection.

The wildmen drew nearer. The first two passed by her. They would have seen her if they'd have simply turned their heads, but they didn't. The third one did.

The wildman screamed as her dagger dug deep into its eye socket. She scrambled from behind the roots and started wading through the water when the bleeding, screaming wildman grabbed her leg. She turned to kick the creature, but then the wildman collapsed under an unexpected weight. Pillar had leapt onto the creature from the bank. The dog bit and tore into the wildman as

Angela dug her dagger into its neck, silencing it. Then she and Pillar ran back up the other bank, shouting so that someone might hear her.

Someone had.

She saw the shadow overhead and cowered, not knowing what to expect. Then she heard the screech, and when she looked back, there was the golden birdman splashing down into the creek, slashing away with a sword. She could see the pain in Fagunol's face, likely caused by wounds yet unhealed, but he did not relent. He killed the nearest wildman and then leapt at the last one, decapitating it with a single swipe. More creatures poured from the surrounding forest, so Fagunol leapt for Angela, scooped her up, and carried her high above the trees.

"Pillar!" she shouted, but the birdman did not descend.

Wildmen chased Pillar away from the creek, and Angela looked away sorrowfully. She knew that this was likely the last time she'd ever see the dog.

Her stomach lurched, and she clung tighter to the birdman's neck. She never dreamed of flying. She didn't even like climbing trees.

"I will not drop you," Fagunol promised, but she could hear the strain in his voice. He was struggling.

Wildmen filled the forest below them for as far as the eye could see. Their number was uncertain, but they were everywhere like frenzied ants over a disturbed anthill. Then Angela saw the fire surrounding what was left of the medical tent. Her people were firing flaming arrows into the northern most group of wildmen, and she saw why a moment later. That was where Gabe, Joshua, Benjamin, and Ivan Shaymolin were attempting to fight their way through the crowd.

Trent and Shëlin were killing wildmen that stood between them and their tribe members, trying to thin the herd, while Debra protected their border. Her red hair glowed in the firelight. Phyllis was kneeling by an empty cart.

They were all so distracted that no one saw the wildman slowly creeping between two torches, opposite from where Debra focused her arrows. Angela watched in horror as the wildman sprinted and crushed Phyllis' skull with two mighty fists. She collapsed awkwardly as if her body was made of jelly. Then the creature pulled Jillian from beneath the cart and dragged her into the forest, screaming.

Debra pursued the wildman a moment later, desperately shouting her daughter's name. Fagunol followed. They dipped low, passing over Debra's head, and caught up with the wildman. Then as they hovered above the creature, Fagunol dropped Angela right on top of it, and she wrestled the beast to the ground. She stabbed it in the back and then ran to where Jillian had been dropped. Fagunol landed beside them as more wildmen arrived. He attempted to frighten the cannibals away with an ear-piercing screech, but the creatures challenged the birdman with a deep and horrifying howl of their own. Fagunol attempted to screech again, but his voice gave way to a croak, his injuries getting the best of him. He stumbled to one knee.

The wildmen howled even louder. Then they attacked.

Joshua fought at his father's side, their backs against Benjamin and Ivan. The creatures were not warriors; they were animals with no plan of attack. They simply threw themselves at the nearest target. Due to this, Gabe led the four of them in a calculated defense that pressed forward while protecting their every side. Despite the fear that Joshua saw in his father's eyes, Gabe really was the warrior that he portrayed in his stories. This encouraged Joshua to fight on.

They had been struggling, and Joshua thought they were going to have to flee, but then he saw the first flaming arrow. The fire thinned the herd, but there were still enough wildmen to keep them away from the medical tent.

Fagunol had joined them for a brief time but then flew away, something in the woods having caught his ear. A small part of Joshua felt panicked when the birdman left. He heard Fagunol's screech a moment later, and a large chunk of wildmen followed after it, leaving too few to stop Gabe's men. It took some time, but Ivan eventually slew the last of the wildmen that stood between them and the medical tent. They darted between the torches and collapsed.

"Keep your bows nocked," Trent ordered as Benjamin rushed into his arms. "They'll fill in again. It's not over."

"Phyllis?" Gabe said quietly.

Joshua and the others turned to find his mother lying on the ground, a black pool forming around her bloodied head.

"Phyllis!" Gabe shouted. He ran to her, and Joshua followed.

"Where's Jillian?" Trent asked. "Where's Debra?"

They heard the nearby battle, and Gabe cursed. He darted through the torches and into the trees.

"Benjamin!" Trent shouted.

Joshua watched, horrified as his best friend raced after Gabe. Benjamin was already covered in wildman blood, mixed with some of his own, but that didn't stop him. He ran toward the sound of battle, and Joshua was dumbstruck. Trent pursued his son. Then Joshua turned and saw that only Shëlin and Ivan remained.

"Take up a bow," Ivan demanded of him. "Shoot as many as you can. Protect their backs."

Joshua did as he was instructed and soon fired an arrow into the back of a wildman that had taken off after Trent. He was still frightened, but he no longer hesitated. He couldn't stop, couldn't hide. All he could do was fight, die, or watch someone else die, and so he fought. And suddenly, a small piece of him wished he had followed

Benjamin, Trent, and his father into those trees. A piece of him still considered it.

"I'm out of arrows!" Ivan shouted.

Joshua realized that he was down to his last two. He fired them off, killing a wildman that was kicking at a torch, and tossed the bow aside.

Taking Ivan's lead, he drew his dagger and charged after his friend, his father, and what could be the last surviving members of his tribe. Only Shëlin stayed behind, racing to treat Phyllis' wound. Joshua worried for his mother but needed to defend those he loved. This, he assumed, was what it meant to be a man.

※

Jillian was screaming. Debra could hear her child through the chaos of howls and grunts, but she couldn't reach her. She was half-running and half-fighting off wildmen, and it was for this reason that she fell, her foot having gotten snagged in a root. The wildmen pounced. She skewered the first one with her sword, but the second wildman overpowered her. She struggled as it forced its hands around her throat—the pressure of its grip was immense—but then the wildman was pulled off of her and lifted straight up into the air. She caught her breath as the wildman crashed into a nearby bush, having fallen from a great height.

She bolted up as a flash of white collided with an oncoming group of wildmen. Nikiatis, the white birdman, had returned. Then he screeched. Unlike Fagunol's tired, wounded screech, Nikiatis' voice was strong and terrifying. Many wildmen fled while others simply cowered. The white birdman flew ahead, and Debra freed herself and followed after him.

She spotted Fagunol, who could barely stand, blood covering his wing and left side. Nikiatis reached him just as his kin's legs gave out.

"Where is Jillian?" Debra shouted.

"I... do not... know," Fagunol replied. "She was taken... and the other girl... Angela... followed. I held... as many here... as I could."

"You fought well, my friend," Nikiatis said.

"Not... enough..."

"Fly," Debra demanded of Nikiatis. "You could spot them from the air. If you..."

"I will see to my kin first."

"No... Nikiatis," Fagunol said, wheezing between words, but Nikiatis did not listen.

The white birdman lifted his golden kin into the air, turned east, and was gone. Debra shouted after him, but Nikiatis did not heed her plea. The frightened wildmen returned now that Nikiatis had gone, and Debra ripped her sword through the neck of the nearest one. She attempted to push through the cannibals, desperate to find her daughter, but then a strong hand yanked her back by the arm. She turned with the intent of attacking the creature but found Gabe Shepherd instead.

"I'm sorry Debra, but she's gone."

Debra broke his grip and attempted to run deeper into the forest. Gabe stopped her once again.

"It's suicide. We have to go back."

But Jillian needed her. And Angela, who was also like a daughter, needed her. She had to be strong for them. She had to...

She cut Gabe's forearm and attempted to run, but he was quick for his size. He grabbed her shirt and pulled her back.

"I'm sorry, Debra. I really am."

Then he hit her... hard. The world flashed white and spun for a second, and then it went black. She could barely hear Gabe's muffled voice apologizing as he lifted her from the ground, but then that faded as well and all was silent.

Joshua heard Trent's voice but couldn't see him. He was screaming for his son.

Joshua fought beside Ivan and was amazed by the man's athleticism and skill. The tribe's guest killed every wildman that approached with a single stroke and fluidly moved on to the next as if he were the composer of some horrific dance.

Then Joshua was relieved to spot Trent rushing toward them.

"Where's Benjamin?" Trent shouted.

"We haven't seen him," Ivan replied. "We were coming for you both."

The panic in Trent's eyes told Joshua that something had happened. Benjamin was missing.

"They took him," Trent said, panicked. A sob escaped his throat. "I tried to stop them, but there were too many."

Ivan tilted his head, and Joshua looked up just as Nikiatis flew by with Fagunol in his arms. More wildmen came, and Gabe showed up a moment later with Debra in his arms. They warded off the attack quickly enough.

"Father!" Joshua shouted and ran to him.

"Back to the torches," Gabe ordered, dismissing his son. "More are coming."

"But they took Benjamin!" Trent said.

"And they took Jillian and maybe Angela too. They're taking our children. We can find them if we survive, but we have to get back to the torches. I have a plan."

Gabe led them through the woods, having to stop twice to ward off attacks. The wildmen were fewer now, Joshua noticed, but he didn't care. He thought only of his friends. Wildmen were cannibals. What if they had stolen his friends for food? He tried to push the thought out of his mind, but it lingered.

He fought on.

"Randall, stop!"

Randall turned and saw that, in his haste, he had run right by a pair of booted footprints. Then Tramin pointed out prints that were bare.

"They were being chased by four wildmen," he surveyed the dirt around them, "no, more like seven, maybe eight."

Randall followed as Tramin ran in the direction that Kris and Orlan had gone. They were headed west, not south toward the medical tent, and that made him nervous. The boys would have known to reconvene at the medical tent. If they were headed west, then it was because they had no other choice.

Tramin slowed his pace. Randall could see the dead body nearby. It was naked with black hair down its back. The wildman had been stabbed through the neck. A second wildman was nearby and then more after that.

"They took a stand here. The tracks are muddled but I'm estimating nine wildmen. There are only seven bodies."

Randall and Tramin split up, searching their surroundings. Then Randall found something he wasn't expecting: a three-toed print.

"A birdman!" he shouted as Tramin joined him.

"And there's a booted print," Tramin said, pointing beyond a mess of vines. "Orlan's I think. This is where they stop. The birdman must have carried him away."

"Fagunol would have been too weak to come out this far," Randall stated. "Maybe there's hope for Nikiatis yet? What do you make of Kris?"

"I don't see his prints here. He might have fought the wildmen off while Nikiatis flew Orlan to safety."

"That sounds like him."

The two men continued their search and found more booted prints, but they did not belong to Kris.

"Whose are these?" Randall asked.

Tramin studied them and finally shook his head.

"I don't know. Ivan's maybe, but I don't think so. No one in our tribe have prints like this. The tread is wrong."

"An elf?" Randall suggested.

"A hunter," Tramin said with a scowl.

Elves and wildmen weren't the only threats in Uuron Plauf. There were hunters as well. Hunters were traitorous beings, often humans, who hunted their own kind for immunity and profit. Tramin's hand went to the bandage hanging from his face, long since dirtied and torn. A hunter with a long coat had given Tramin his wound.

They followed the booted prints until they heard voices. They knelt behind a pair of trees and watched as two hunters stood in a circle of wildmen, barking orders. They were both human.

"What did it say?" asked one who wore a metal breastplate.

Randall grabbed Tramin's shoulder as the second hunter began to speak. He wore a long coat and motioned with a knife.

The hunter clicked his tongue and grunted. The wildman nearest him replied. This continued for a moment before the first hunter stepped forward and kicked the wildman in the jaw. The creature fell over and the others growled but none attacked. The man in the long coat simply stared, ill amused.

"When I ask a question, Maximus," the hunter with the breastplate said, "I expect to be answered."

"And when I have answers to give, Lobos, I will give them." Maximus adjusted his hat and pointed the knife at his ally. "Do that again and I'll run this across your throat."

"I look forward to it," Lobos said sarcastically. Then he reiterated, pausing between each word, "But what did the ugly thing say?"

Maximus shook his head and sheathed the blade.

"It said that there were a total of three children and two teenagers, possibly three, who could be made into slaves."

"I don't care about that!" Lobos shouted. "How many kills? We're getting paid by the head; that's all I care about!"

"I wouldn't know. You kicked him just before he could tell me."

Lobos stomped toward the wincing wildman and dragged it up by its black mane. "Then ask it again."

Maximus spoke the wildman tongue, and the creature answered weakly.

"None, apparently."

"None?" Lobos screamed. He cursed and held a blade to the creature's neck.

"Don't be foolish."

Lobos was about to mock Maximus, but then growls echoed from the surrounding wildmen. He laughed and slowly released the wildman's mane. He held out his hands in surrender.

"At ease, monsters."

Then Randall heard a sound that made his stomach lurch. Someone was screaming. Tramin cursed as two wildmen burst through the trees, dragging a boy by the foot. His arms and legs were bleeding, and mud caked his face. Randall's voice was caught in his throat.

"Benjamin!" Tramin shouted upon spotting his nephew. Then he leapt from behind the tree.

"Put the boy with the others," Maximus ordered while drawing his sword.

Randall followed Tramin, his chest burning, but that pain was nothing. To see one of their youngest treated so barbarically, it lit a fire in Randall that he hadn't felt in years. The wildmen attacked, but Tramin plowed through them. His nephew was in danger, and he would rather die than let them take the boy. Randall would do no less.

"Finally!" Lobos said as he swung his sword at Tramin's head. Tramin deflected it and tossed the hunter aside easily enough.

Lobos cursed, and not wanting to let two pass him by, kicked Randall's legs out from under him. The hunter tightened his grip on a knife and leapt at Randall, pinning him to the ground. He did everything in his power to bury the blade into Randall's throat, but Randall clutched Lobos' hand and fought for control of the knife. Despite an urge to end this quickly, Randall had not yet healed from his time in Uuron Plauf. His chest burned, and his body ached. He could feel the tip of the blade cutting into his neck, but then Lobos screamed.

Blood and dog breath hit Randall in the face as Pillar sank his teeth into Lobos' neck. Lobos rolled, fighting to get the dog off his back, and this gave Randall a chance to recoup. Then, without a word, he pushed Pillar aside and drove his blade through Lobos' neck. The hunter gasped and gurgled, attempted to stand, but then fell over and died.

There was a pang of guilt for having killed the man, but Randall disregarded it. He had killed in self-defense. There was no other choice.

"Good boy," he said with a quick pat on Pillar's head.

He could hear metal clashing nearby and raced to where Tramin and Maximus were battling. Tramin was pushing their battle in the direction that Benjamin had been taken, the boy's screams dimming by the second. The wildmen were howling, and Randall feared that they were calling for others. He had to reach Benjamin and quickly.

He raced past Tramin and Maximus but then felt a sudden sting in his shoulder. The pain caught him off guard and he stumbled, hitting the ground.

"Can't have that now," Maximus said while deflecting Tramin's blade.

Randall reached around and felt the hilt of a knife sticking out of his shoulder, slippery with his own blood. If Maximus hadn't been engaged with Tramin, he would have likely put the blade in some vital organ. Randall struggled to his feet but paused as the sound of wildmen approached. The wildman's call had been heard.

He wanted to push forward, to ward them off and rescue Benjamin, but it would have been suicide. He was already tired and hurting. The knife in his back, he now noticed, hindered his swordsmanship, and he wondered if perhaps Maximus' aim was true after all. He held his sword with his left hand and raced to help Tramin.

Maximus had just thrown Tramin to the ground and was likely to slay him if not for Randall's intervention. He wasn't a match for the hunter in his condition, but he couldn't do nothing.

"Run, Tramin!" he shouted as Maximus deflected his blade.

Despite being a skilled swordsman, Maximus was obviously winded. Defeating Tramin was no easy feat, and the hunter was paying a toll for having achieved it. Every blow was deflected. No wounds were placed. They seemed evenly matched in their fatigue, but Randall—the elder of the two by twenty years easily—was tiring fast.

It was then that the wildmen arrived. They burst through the trees, dozens of them, their black eyes looking for blood. Randall clung with Maximus and turned him so that a lurching wildman struck the hunter and tripped up the other cannibals that followed.

Randall scrambled to regain his footing but fell as a pair of strong hands reached for his throat. First one, then two, then three wildmen piled on top of him, beating his head and chest. He could not move, could not defend himself. Through the flurry of fists he saw Tramin on his feet again, fighting, but then Tramin was tackled as well.

This was how Refuge would end, at the hands of cannibals.

Then an ear-piercing screech filled the air and the wildmen cowered. The creatures abandoned Randall, his body constricting with pain, and they pursued a great white birdman that hewed them in half as they approached. In one hand he held a great sword, and in the other a torch.

"Come, Randall," Tramin said, helping him to his feet. "The birdman's bought us time."

Tramin dragged Randall from the battle, but Randall steadied himself and refused to go any further.

"Benjamin…" he said, but Tramin forced him to move.

"Nothing can help Benjamin now," Tramin said heavily.

Randall could see the battle as Tramin dragged him away. The birdman was fierce, and a bloodlust glinted in his eyes, but Nikiatis was not yet fully healed. Could he outlast the wildmen? Then Randall saw Pillar gnawing on a wildman's throat.

"Pillar," Randall said.

"Be quiet, Randall!" Tramin said through tears. "I know what we've lost."

They hid as several wildmen passed by, then Randall and Tramin moved on until they neared the medical tent.

A mass of dead wildmen lay before them, but a crowd of hungry cannibals still gathered near the border of torches. The creatures howled and screamed. Some beat their chests like animals while others simply ran from left to right, as if expecting some hole to form in the wall of fire. Randall and Tramin knew better than to push through the wildmen—they would never have made it—but they were glad to spy survivors within the torches.

"Can we reach them?" Tramin asked.

"No," Randall said as he sat against a tree, catching his breath, "not through here, anyway."

"Can you go further? If we find a weak spot in their ranks..."

Randall stood again. His body throbbed, and the pain in his chest and shoulder threatened to shut his body down, but he pushed through it.

"Let's keep moving."

Joshua tried to stay strong for his mother, but it was difficult. He knelt beside Phyllis and held her hand, but she couldn't return the pressure. She couldn't move at all.

"Does it hurt?" he asked.

"No, dear," Phyllis answered, but he didn't believe her.

She lay limply where the attacking wildman had left her. Shëlin had mentioned something about broken bones in her neck and back. How could a broken neck not hurt? How could this have happened?

Joshua glanced at his father, who stood nearby. He was holding a bundle of rags, and Shëlin was not happy about it. She was yelling at him. Their argument seemed silly with all that was going on around them, but they were taking it seriously.

Shëlin had lit more torches while they were away, and it seemed to be working. The wildmen kept their distance, though they seemed to be getting louder. Joshua wondered if that was out of frustration or anticipation. He didn't like thinking about either.

"How long have you had these?" Shëlin was asking. "Does Randall know?"

"No one knew, Shëlin," Gabe replied. "I kept them hidden in case we'd ever need them, and it's a good thing I did. What was created for evil, God might allow us to use for good—if you can call massacring these cannibals good. They might help some of us survive at the very least."

"We're not even sure how they work exactly! Orlan's parents died trying to understand them!"

"They set fire to the wire," Gabe said. "The fire made the sticks explode. It was unfortunate, but Fredrick and Danielle's accident could save us all."

"They could kill us as well," she replied while pointing at the rags, "or do you not remember how large that explosion was?"

"Then we send them out there. We're out of arrows, so it'll have to be by hand. Someone will have to run them into the crowd. I'm more than willing…"

"Father, no!" Joshua cried out.

"That's suicide!" Shëlin shouted. "Why can't we just throw them into the crowd?"

"Frederick said they were unstable, that they might ignite if jostled too much. They could explode before leaving our hand."

"So you're going to kill yourself?"

"If the rest of you live, then…"

"That's enough!" Phyllis shouted. "Come here, all of you."

Gabe and Shëlin rushed to Phyllis' side. Gabe took her hand, and she stared at him with a furrowed brow.

"You will be doing no such thing, Gabriel," she said. "Joshua needs his father, and so will Kris and Orlan when they get back."

"They'll have you," he said, but she stopped him.

"No, they won't," she said. Her voice was as broken as her body, and her eyes betrayed the pain that she was feeling. "I will deliver the devilish things."

"No," Gabe said sternly. "I won't allow it. You can't even…"

"You have no say in the matter. My body is broken; I cannot move. How will I flee the explosion?"

"I will carry you," Gabe said, his eyes running now.

"You'll be dead, remember?"

"Then Trent…"

"That would only further my injuries, possibly killing me anyway."

"We can put you on the cart…"

"I would slow everyone down and threaten their survival."

Joshua sobbed. Gabe fumbled for more answers but found none.

"You can't," he finally whimpered. "You just can't."

"I'm dying anyway, Gabriel. Let it at least mean something."

"How will you deliver the sticks?" Shëlin asked. "You can't even light them."

"The torches," Phyllis answered. "Put a few around me for protection and lay the sticks on my chest. Take some torches for yourselves, and when you're ready, light the sticks and run like the devil himself is after you. My being here will distract some of the wildmen while you fight your way through the rest. Then the explosion should allow you to escape."

"But Mother, you'll be dead," Joshua said, hugging her limp body.

"And you'll be alive, dear, and that's a far better trade."

"It's a sound plan!" Ivan shouted over the roar of the wildmen. "The woman speaks wisdom."

Gabe and Joshua struggled for words and ultimately clung to Phyllis, sobbing. Joshua didn't want Phyllis to die. He pretended to be strong as he fought the wildmen and defended his tribe, but he couldn't face losing his mother. He just couldn't.

"You can't do this, Mother," he whispered.

"I have to, baby," she whispered back. "But I'll always be with you."

"No you won't."

Shëlin and Trent collected three torches, leaving Ivan alone to hold back the wildmen that tested their border.

"Pull the cart over her," Trent said. "That'll offer additional protection until..." He couldn't finish the sentence.

Joshua screamed for them to stop, but there wasn't time. Gabe pulled him away as Trent and Shëlin moved the cart. Then they set the torches around Phyllis and checked the flames.

"Anyone who would give their life in exchange for another will find passage into the kingdom of Heaven," Trent said reassuringly as he placed the sticks on her stomach. "Take comfort in that biblical promise. May God bless you in what is to come. Our prayers are with you."

Then he lifted Debra, who had been lying in the dirt nearby, and joined Ivan and Shëlin near the eastern border.

Gabe took the sticks from Phyllis' chest, and with a heavy heart, lit the fuse.

"I love you," Phyllis said, her fear pouring forth now. "I love all of you."

"I love you!" Gabe shouted as he set the sticks on her chest. "I love you so much!"

Joshua screamed for his mother as they raced from the cart. He heard the wildmen howl. He felt the heat of a torch swung by his father and the blood of a wildman as it was slain, but all he saw was his mother. Even as wildmen crowded the cart, obscuring his vision, he saw her.

He saw her dancing with his father beneath the stars. He remembered how she would tell him stories when he was little and how she held him after every bad dream. And then he heard her voice. She sang while doing laundry in the stream. Was she singing now? Was it really her voice? He wanted to go back. He called her by the name he'd given her a child, the name he always reverted to when he was afraid. He shouted it!

"Mommy!"

But his voice was drowned out by the chaos around him.

And then the fire came.

Randall screamed.

He and Tramin had been making their way east, searching for a weak point in the crowd of wildmen, when the explosion erupted, throwing them to the ground and deafening them. A faint ringing could be heard as Randall forced himself to stand. He saw some broken fragments of a radio nearby. How did it get this far from the medical tent? What happened? He was stunned, unsure of what he was doing, but then Tramin took his arm and pulled him behind a tree.

Wildmen screamed and ran by them. Some looked right at Randall, but they didn't stop. They were fleeing. Some were on fire.

"Randall, look!" Tramin shouted.

Tramin's brother, Trent, appeared shaken as he lifted Debra from the ground.

"On me!" Trent shouted.

Randall and Tramin ran to him, much to Trent's surprise, and Ivan and Shëlin joined them soon enough. The last were Gabe and Joshua, both of whom were sobbing.

"Is this all that's left?" Tramin asked. "Where are Kris and Orlan? We thought…"

"We have to go!" Gabe shouted through tears.

They ran for what felt like hours, unsure of where they were going until a shadow passed over their heads. It caught Randall's eye, and he glanced up to find Nikiatis flying east. The birdman faded in the distance, but they saw where he descended, so they headed toward that portion of the forest. Nikiatis wasn't hard to find; they just followed the sound of falling water.

A steady river ran through the Greysong Forest, and it fell over a wall of stone, cascading into several long waterfalls before continuing south. Nikiatis had laid Fagunol and Vetcalf near these falls and was now attempting to feed them fish. He drew his sword upon the tribe's arrival.

"I thank you," Randall said before the birdman could threaten them, "for saving my life."

Nikiatis snickered and sheathed his sword.

"I sought only revenge."

Randall nodded and dipped his hand in the river. The others did likewise and drank their fill.

"How are they?" Shëlin asked of Fagunol and Vetcalf.

"They are my concern now," Nikiatis barked, "not yours."

"Then they will die before long, and you'll be alone."

"Perhaps that is how it should be."

"Perhaps not," Randall said. "We were searching for two of our own when you found us. They had been missing, and we thought that perhaps you had rescued them."

"A foolish assumption," Nikiatis said.

"Is that so?" Tramin said bitterly. "It was foolish to believe a birdman saved our people when a birdman's print had been left in the soil?"

This got Nikiatis' attention. He stared at Tramin and Randall, hopeful at first, but then he shook his head and grew angry.

"You never found your missing people, did you?" he asked.

"No," Tramin answered.

"Then they were taken."

"By a birdman?" Randall asked.

"By Giyavin," Nikiatis said. His feathers ruffled, and his fist tightened on the hilt of his sword, "The birdman who betrayed my people to the elves."

"You think this Giyavin took Orlan and Kris?" Trent asked. "Then help us! God willing, you'll have your revenge, and we'll get our children back."

"If you do this," Randall said, extending a hand, "you will have repaid your debt to us. Were you not a birdman of honor once?"

Nikiatis grimaced, but then he peered at Fagunol and Vetcalf, and his features softened.

"The blood of an entire race cries out for vengeance," he said, "and as their king it falls on me to answer their call. I need not your help in finding Giyavin—I will hunt him to the grave—but I will aid you still, provided you nurse my kin back to health."

"We would have helped them regardless of your decision," Shëlin said.

He reluctantly took Randall's hand.

"Then I will help you find your children."

"And you will have your revenge."

The man in the black hood knelt and drank deep from the river. He had been disappointed that Randall's journey to Uuron Plauf bore no real fruit, but that opinion was beginning to change. The hint of a stem was beginning to poke through. His plan had taken a curve, but this new scenario was far better than the one he had originally conceived. Fate, it appeared, was an even better schemer than Ivan Shaymolin.

Part IV: Captives

Angela groaned and tried lifting her hand so that she might address the pain in her neck, but she couldn't because her wrists were bound behind a tree. Squinting through a headache, she saw that she was still in the forest and that she wasn't alone. A wildman was perched on a fallen tree, and it seemed to be scanning the forest in her direction. It grunted when its eyes fell on her. She looked away.

The quick glance revealed that the beast was large and muscular and that it had a plethora of scars covering its body. Two sharp teeth protruded from its lower jaw like inverted fangs, and it appeared as if it wanted nothing more than to feast on her bones. She held back an urge to cry out for help. Instead, she began scanning the forest herself and spied Benjamin tied to a nearby tree. His face was covered in mud and blood, and he seemed understandably upset.

"Are you alright?" she whispered as loudly as she dared.

Benjamin looked at her with red eyes but gave no answer. Of course he wasn't alright. They were bound to trees by cannibals.

"Do you see anyone else…" she began, but the wildman grunted again, angrily this time.

Her eyes went to the dirt, but then Benjamin caught her attention with a slight nod. He was motioning with his eyes, and when she followed them she saw what he wanted her to see. Pillar lay on the ground near him. His mouth and legs were bound, and he was quietly whimpering. It broke her heart.

Then something else caught her ear. She thought it was Pillar's whimpering at first, but she was mistaken. Someone was crying.

"Oh, Jillian," she whispered to herself.

She couldn't see Jillian but knew the girl's cry. She was somewhere behind Angela, just past Benjamin, and she wondered who else was back there. The wildman grunted again, loudly. Angela looked up and saw that it was looking beyond her. It didn't like that Jillian was crying. It grunted again, angrier this time, and then it howled. It took a step forward and grunted again. Jillian only cried harder.

"Leave her alone!" Orlan shouted from somewhere near the wildman. "She's a little girl!"

The wildman leapt at a nearby tree, and she could hear a strong fist colliding with flesh. Orlan cried out. The wildman hit him again. She couldn't see Orlan, but a third hit and a cry of pain told her that he was hurting. The wildman grunted and howled as if yelling at Orlan for speaking out of turn, and then it looked back to where Jillian's cries echoed.

"Stop crying, Jillian!" Angela shouted, risking attack herself. "Right now!"

The wildman grunted but then paused as Jillian's crying ceased. It waited a moment, peered at Angela and the trunk that hid Orlan, and finally returned to its fallen tree.

Angela could feel the tears flowing now. She was afraid and helpless with no means of escape. She told herself that her father would come, but she didn't even know if Randall was alive or dead.

These four could very well be the last surviving members of Refuge, and that wasn't likely to last much longer. If only her father hadn't intervened in Uuron Plauf, hadn't acted on Ivan Shaymolin's warning. Then perhaps Silus Rook's dream would have lingered a while longer. She could have at least hugged her father one more time.

Orlan spat the growing pool of blood from his mouth. His body ached, but his heart ached more. He thought he was alone, that perhaps everyone else had gotten away, but then he heard Jillian and Angela. The idea of Angela being captured—being used in whatever disgusting way these wildmen used women like her—it terrified him. He wished he could free her somehow, save her, but he couldn't even free himself. And Jillian—how could they have taken her? She was just a child, an innocent little girl for the love of God. She didn't deserve this. None of them did!

He could hear the quiet grunts nearby. Just beyond the wildman with the scarred body was a huddle of others. There were maybe twenty, and they were all kneeling in a circle, quietly grunting among themselves. In the center was a wildman that seemed older than the rest. Its hair was gray instead of black, and it was frailer. It led them in some sort of quiet chant, and it seemed to Orlan that they were sad. Were they mourning their losses? Did wildmen mourn?

They stopped chanting when other voices sounded in the forest. These voices were human.

"How many prisoners?" one was asking.

"I've not counted," a second answered. "They were still bringing them in last I saw. I'd guess four or five. I was surprised by how resilient the tribe was. They were stronger than we expected."

"And how many of their number did you kill?"

"Only one body so far, a woman we think. She was caught in the explosion."

Orlan was both excited and devastated by this news. It sounded like most of the tribe had survived, but then, one of their women didn't. Who was left? Phyllis. Debra.

Shëlin. He pushed the thought from his mind. They were nearly all alive. He focused on that.

They stepped through a patch of trees to where the wildmen were huddled. One man wore a long coat and a hat. The other was dark skinned and wore robes far too eloquent for the woods. It struck Orlan that the green birdman, the one who had captured him, was nowhere to be seen.

"Only one death?" the man in the robes said. "Mathew will be displeased, Maximus."

"Mathew failed to provide me with adequate forces."

"An army of wildmen was inadequate?"

"They fought because they were forced to, Mondel," Maximus the hunter said. "There was no heart in it. No craft or calculation. They were animals attacking as animals do."

"That's Advisor-Mondel to you," the man in the robes corrected, "and what of the other hunter?"

"Lobos? He was as useless as the wildmen—slain by an old man and a dog."

"A small loss then."

"They have birdmen with them," Maximus added, "at least two, possibly three. I personally saw their king, so we know he survived the extermination. A golden one was also seen, though it seemed badly hurt. A blue one might have been dead."

"Is that so?" Mondel said curiously. "Were there any females?"

"I wasn't informed one way or the other."

"Then I'll advise Mathew to arrange another assault, a better prepared one. We O'lors are already hated; no sense in making it worse by leaving a job unfinished."

"Worried that you'll lose favor with the elves?" Maximus asked.

Mondel laughed. "Trust me when I tell you, I care not what the elves think of me."

"Not even Kïer?"

"Especially Kïer."

The two men neared the large wildman who kept watch over the prisoners. The beast eyed them cautiously, a slight growl rumbling in its throat. Orlan wondered what Maximus meant when he mentioned the wildmen being forced to attack. The rest of the wildmen were silent now, watching Maximus the hunter and Adviser-Mondel. They did not trust these men, obviously. Beyond that, Orlan had no idea what they were thinking.

"Will Mathew send more wildmen?" Maximus asked.

"No, we've seen enough. General-Dägin-Bok infected them with a virus that he hoped would spread through mankind, but the human prisoners have shown no sign of illness. The virus is ineffective. Furthermore, the wildmen's failure to decimate this tribe shows how useless they really are. Dispose of them, and I'll see to it that you're paid for the effort."

Maximus smiled and pulled something from his coat. Orlan broke into a sweat when he saw it. It wasn't a stick like the one that killed his parents, but it was similar. His heart began to race.

"That tribe isn't the only one with dynamite from the old world," Maximus said, and the wildman guard suddenly eyed him worriedly.

"On second thought," Mondel said, "make sure a few survive."

Maximus nodded and lit the fuse. The scarred wildman howled in fear for only a second before Maximus backhanded it. Then he tossed the explosive into the huddle of wildmen and ducked.

Angela couldn't hear the two men very well, but she could see them. Her eyes widened when the man in the coat pulled the explosive from an inside pocket, and she recoiled when he tossed it somewhere beyond her line of view.

The explosion deafened her for a moment as a warm wetness splattered the forest. She screamed and could hear Benjamin screaming as well.

"Orlan!" she shouted.

He wasn't close enough to be affected by the blast, but a stick like that had killed his parents. She couldn't imagine what he must have been thinking. She heard wildmen screaming somewhere beyond Orlan. It sounded like the man in the coat was fighting a battle somewhere beyond the fallen tree trunk, and the man in the robes simply watched, seemingly pleased with what he saw.

"Orlan, are you alright?"

She looked around and saw that Benjamin was frantically tugging at the ropes, trying to pull his hands free. Then she noticed something very strange.

"Benjamin!" she shouted. "Where's Pillar?"

Benjamin stopped and looked around. His eyes were wide.

"There!" he shouted, nodding a short distance away. "His ropes!"

"What?" Angela whispered.

Had the dog chewed his way free? Could Pillar have escaped on his own? Then Benjamin screamed, and she could see that he was looking behind him. He began whispering, and she could faintly hear another voice. She wanted to question him but didn't want to draw the robed man's attention.

The man in the robes turned toward them a moment later and smiled. Benjamin faced him, and Angela did the same. He stepped forward, studied Orlan, and then moved on. The man in the coat came up beside him a moment later. He was cleaning blood from a sword.

"I see only three prisoners, Maximus," the man said.

Maximus scanned the trees and then pointed toward Benjamin.

"Looks like one's tied up behind the boy."

"So four then. Each the perfect age to have loose tongues and be made slaves of labor afterword, and that is why I asked for the young ones to be taken." The man took a few steps closer to Angela and studied her. Then he offered a rather disgusting grin. "What a lovely girl. I think I'll advise that Mathew let me have her when he's finished. I can think of a few ways in which she might serve me."

Angela could do nothing but spit. The man in the robes, however, laughed. He apparently liked a challenge.

Orlan fought his ropes; Advisor-Mondel's desire infuriated him. He wanted to break free and hurt the man with the lustful grin. He wanted to help Angela and the others escape, but the ropes were too tight.

"You won't touch her!" he shouted.

"What's it matter to you?" Mondel asked as he walked by Orlan's tree. Then he knelt down, smiled, and placed a gloved hand over Orlan's throat.

Orlan couldn't breathe. He fought to break free, jerking his head back and forth, but the advisor's grip held firm. He began to panic. He kicked and screamed and strained for air, but then the Adviser removed his hand and lightly slapped Orlan's cheek twice.

"So weak," Mondel said.

Then he stood, and Orlan noticed the confused expression he suddenly wore. Following his eyes, Orlan saw the hunter sneaking into a part of the woods that he couldn't see.

What was he doing?

Angela watched as Maximus crept toward Benjamin, quietly, as if hunting. Benjamin was looking behind his tree now, unaware of the approaching threat, and Angela felt her stomach turn.

"What are you doing?" she asked Maximus, if only to alert Benjamin of his approach.

Maximus broke into a sprint. Before Angela could scream Benjamin's name, the hunter had shoved the boy's head into the tree and swung his sword somewhere beyond her view. She heard a clash of steel, and suddenly, Mondel was running to get a better view. Benjamin was trying to hold back tears and failing.

"Go!" she heard Kris shouting. "Find Tramin!"

"Kris!" she and Orlan shouted simultaneously, but his only answer was a scream.

He struggled as Maximus dragged him into Angela's view. His head was bleeding, but he was still breathing. Maximus held Kris' sword.

"Who did he yell for?" Mondel asked.

"A little girl," Maximus answered. "A girl and a dog."

"Jillian," Angela whispered to herself.

"Should I chase them?"

"No," Mondel said, studying Kris. "We're already behind schedule. We need to move."

"Aren't you worried that they'll bring others?"

Mondel laughed again, maintaining his ill-fitted humor. "A tiny girl and a mutt? They'll be dead by morning. Bring the rest, including the surviving wildmen and this boy. There is much Mathew can learn from them."

Maximus secured Kris as Mondel made his way to Angela and untied her wrists. She attempted to fight but fell into his arms instead, her head spinning. The Adviser held her against the tree, pressing his body against hers, and smiled.

"Let's not get ahead of ourselves, my lovely," he said. "That will come in time."

Orlan's lip had finally stopped bleeding, but with so much walking, his lip was the least of his concerns. His legs wobbled; his heart pounded; his head throbbed. His body ached, and he was hungry and thirsty. He couldn't recall ever feeling worse.

Hours had passed. He and the other prisoners were bound by a single rope that kept anyone from darting into the forest around them. Angela marched behind him and Kris and Benjamin behind her. Behind Benjamin were four wildmen, including the large, scarred one and the gray one who acted as the tribe's leader. They grunted here and there but, for the most part, remained silent.

The wildmen no longer concerned Orlan. He wanted to hate them for what they did, but they seemed to be nothing more than pawns in the elves' greater scheme. He refused to think of them as innocent, but they weren't to blame—Kïer and the human traitors were.

"It's late," Advisor-Mondel said, wiping his brow with a handkerchief. "Perhaps we should break for the night?"

Maximus, who had been leading the march, paused and looked at the moon as if just noticing it was out. Orlan noted the hunter's frustration, but then the man sighed and took off his hat.

"We'll rest for an hour, maybe less, and then we'll keep going. I want to reach the prison before dawn."

"Before—before dawn?" The very idea of marching all night seemed to exhaust the Adviser, but he didn't argue. He simply sat on a stone, slipped off his boots, and quietly grumbled while massaging his own feet.

Orlan collapsed and fought to catch his breath. He turned and found Angela studying the wound on Kris' head.

"How is he?" he asked.

"He'll survive," Maximus answered.

Orlan didn't reply, but Angela stared the hunter square in the eye.

"Why did you take us?"

"And suddenly you think you can speak?" Mondel said as he bounced a small rock off her head.

She spat at his feet, missing by a large distance, but this infuriated him. The Adviser leapt up and grabbed her by the hair. Orlan struggled to stop him, but Angela pushed with her legs and drove the top of her head into Mondel's chin. He screamed and held his mouth, muffling the curses that escaped his lips. Maximus simply laughed.

"Trouble with the ladies, Mondel?"

Mondel replied with a heavy slap across Angela's face. Orlan yelled and jumped at Mondel, but the Adviser was wiser now and slapped him mid-leap. Orlan fell, and Mondel fell right beside him. Angela had tripped the Adviser and was now kicking his head repeatedly.

"Knock it off!" Maximus shouted, and Angela did as she was told.

Orlan nestled beside her as Mondel stumbled to his feet and drew a knife. Blood poured from his mouth and nose, and he had murder in his eyes, but then Maximus grabbed his wrist.

"I meant all of you."

"You forget your place, hunter!"

Advisor-Mondel pointed a finger at Maximus' nose and was about to chastise him further when he felt the tip of a blade pressed gently against his throat.

"You pretend that I'm in some minor level of your hierarchy, Mondel, but let me remind you—I am not. I am a hunter with a reputation to maintain. If you come between me and my job, I *will* kill you, despite our distant O'lor lineage. Would you like to continue testing me?"

Mondel's eyes went wide, but no words escaped his snake-like lips.

"Thank you," Maximus said without smiling. He put the knife away and turned to go. "Up. Walk."

Mondel appeared as if he were about to protest but then thought better of it. Looking unsure of how to redeem himself, he faced the prisoners and kicked a wildman hard in the ribs.

"Up!" he shouted. "March you useless monstrosities."

Orlan struggled to his feet and leaned back to help Angela, but she was already helping Kris. A kick from Mondel motivated Orlan to move.

Angela wasn't sure if she would make it much longer. She felt weak, especially in her legs, but she refused to complain. It was as if liquid filled them instead of muscle, and the liquid just sloshed around inside, constantly throwing off her balance. The only redeeming factor in this long march was that the privileged Adviser appeared more tired than she was. She worried about Kris, having received a head injury and then being forced to walk so far, but he kept pace.

Benjamin was stumbling. Mondel had already kicked him once after tripping, but he was barely lifting his feet now. He seemed to be at the end of whatever strength he had. She was right there with him.

"Last break," Maximus said.

Angela and the others were pushed toward something metal protruding from the ground, and she was glad to rest against it no matter how uncomfortable it was. Kris fell limply beside her, and Orlan rested his head on her shoulder.

"How are you doing?" she asked.

"I'm good," he replied with a smile that showed he was anything but.

She wanted to sleep but didn't trust to. So instead of resting her eyes, she began to study their surroundings. They were at the foot of the Roclä Mountain it seemed, or at least a very large, jagged hill near the Roclä Mountains, but she couldn't see too far up it. The moon had long vanished behind clouds, and the forest was black. She felt the piece of metal against her back and noted the rust. There were other metal pillars. Some were lying in the dirt, others were embedded into the rock, but they were obviously old and broken—more artifacts from before the Fall of Man.

"What?" Orlan said quietly.

"I didn't say..."

"No. The beam—it's wet."

He was right. Parts of the beam were wet with a warm substance; honey or sap perhaps? Then she felt a drip on her cheek, looked up, and screamed. The beam was broken into a jagged point, and skewered on that point was a body. The clouds parted ever so slightly, and she could see that the body belonged to a speared wildman. She pulled the others away from the dead creature, and the wildmen howled a sorrowful lament.

"Jumped or thrown, likely," Maximus said. "Within the past few minutes I would guess, judging by the blood that's still running down the pillar. There are likely more lying around here."

"Jumped or thrown from what," Orlan asked, "the mountain?"

"The prison," Maximus answered.

He pointed upward, and far above them on the side of a stony hill, Angela saw a tall silhouette. It was definitely a building from the old world, but it looked unfinished, or perhaps partially destroyed. She realized that these beams must have fallen from that structure at some point in its past.

"It's a long march up the path," Maximus told them as he sat down and removed his hat. He looked over to where Mondel was sleeping and shook his head.

"Is Kïer up there?" Angela asked.

Maximus laughed.

"You're joking, right? Kïer doesn't leave Amon-Göl, his being a higher being and all. He works through his Generals and the Kïen. One of the Generals is up there now."

"Which one?" Kris asked.

Angela was glad to hear him speak.

"Devin-Brek," the hunter answered, "from Vlörinclad. He didn't like the idea of Mathew running things."

"Mathew?" Angela asked, if only to keep the man talking.

"Mathew is Räthinock's Dömin of Intelligence. He stepped in after Dägin-Bok died."

"Dägin-Bok? The General of Räthinock is dead?" Angela asked. "How? When?"

"He was killed by a group of men just prior to the attack on Uuron Plauf. You'll meet them when you get up there."

"There are humans in the prison?" Orlan asked. He was obviously astounded at the idea of seeing more humans. It had been years since they'd seen another human outside of their tribe, not counting Ivan and the two who currently held them against their will of course.

Angela looked up at the structure, which was quickly vanishing in the diminishing moonlight. She wondered who up there could have killed one of Kïer's Generals. They were notorious for being powerful and ruthless.

"What would it take for you to free us?" Kris asked.

"We're all human," Orlan added. "We can work together."

Maximus laughed and leaned against a tree.

"Get some rest," he said. "We head up in an hour."

The hour had come and gone, but Orlan's legs were still aching. The rope stung his wrists, and the others weren't doing any better. He didn't complain though. He didn't cry and he didn't scream. He focused on the stone path ahead of him and just kept on walking. He'd tripped once already and took Angela and Kris down with him. Advisor-Mondel gave them all strong kicks for it, so he was determined to not fall again. He focused on the rocks at his feet.

The path had originally been a forested trail but eventually turned to rock with boulders rising on either side of the prisoners. The boulders grew closer together until they seamed into two stone walls that severed all connection to the outside world. Up to that point, their party had been the only travelers walking the stone path.

"State your name," someone demanded from up ahead.

Orlan's stomach dropped. He had come to terms with being a prisoner of two race-traitors. This voice, however, was not human. It was crisp, educated, and dripping with superiority. Orlan peered around Maximus and saw an elf standing with an arrow nocked and pointed at them. He had pale, olive skin and shoulder-length black hair—all elves had black hair—and it was slicked back as if wet. He seemed young. With the long lives of elves, however, *young* could have easily been a hundred years.

"I am Maximus, a hunter on Mathew O'lor's payroll. I bring prisoners: four humans and four wildmen."

Mondel cursed as he passed by Orlan and pushed Maximus aside, something that likely would have cost him an arm if they were not in the presence of the superior race.

"I am Mondel, Adviser to Dömin-Mathew O'lor. Step aside!"

"It is nice to officially meet you, Adviser." The elf did not sound as cordial as his words would lead one to believe. "My name is Elya-Ecshelï, and you certainly outrank my post as Captain of the Guard, but having been appointed to this path by General-Devin-Brek of Vlörinclad, who outranks Dömin-O'lor, my words have gained a higher authority." Then the elf's face grew stern as he tilted his chin and eyed Mondel wearily. "And you should be cautious of the tone in which you refer to your master race. Advisors are quite replaceable you know."

Mondel deflated but did not withdraw. Instead, he cleared his throat, lifted his chin in a manner that matched Elya's, and attempted a more regal approach.

"Let us not bring race into matters, Captain-Ecshelï. Might I travel ahead and inform Dömin-O'lor of our approach?"

Elya smiled slightly. "The Dömin of Intelligence is in council with General-Devin-Brek and is not to be interrupted. You may go on up the path, however, if for no other reason than that I find your company detestable."

Orlan watched as Mondel's face glowed red. He shook but said nothing. Instead, he lowered his eyes, walked around the smug elf, and stomped up the path until he vanished around a nearby corner.

"That was fun to watch," Maximus said with a chuckle.

"Do not think that I hold hunters in any better regard than self-important Advisers."

"What runs through that porcelain head of yours is no concern of mine." Maximus said. "I fulfilled a contract, and I want paid. When will Mathew be free?"

"When General-Devin-Brek decides it." The young elf gave no indication of faltering.

"Alright, I'll wait. What of the prisoners?"

Elya whistled, and two elves who had been hiding in the crevices of the stone walls stepped out. They were similar to Elya in appearance but with longer hair.

"Go with them. They will lead you to the holding cells."

Maximus tipped his hat, and Elya studied them as they passed by. Orlan looked back and saw that the other prisoners were keeping their eyes lowered. Kris glanced up and motioned for Orlan to face forward, and so he did. This did not last long, however, for as they turned a sharp corner and rounded a hill, they saw what Orlan assumed to be the prison.

On the edge of a cliff stood the broken remains of a building that had likely been very tall in the old world. Chunks were missing now, likely through time and neglect, possibly destroyed during the last wars, and metal beams jutted out in various directions.

Orlan assumed that Dömin-Mathew O'lor and General-Devin-Brek were housed in the more complete portions of the structure, but then he noticed movement on one of the levels that was exposed to the elements. These, he assumed, were other prisoners. He couldn't make out their races, but he was surprised by the number. At least one thing was certain: they were going to have company.

Angela shook violently as the elves led them toward the building's entrance. She tried to steady herself, but her fear was far too great.

"It'll be alright," Kris whispered.

His words didn't help.

Two elven guards stood at the base of the building with their eyes trained on the approaching party. One stepped forward and greeted his brethren, and they spoke privately in the elvish tongue. Then the guard nodded and waved them through.

The building was old. It looked as if it had been cleared of debris and cleaned, but the damage was obvious. Walls were missing, and makeshift furniture had been brought in for the guards to use.

Elves stood about talking, some laughing, but most stared at Angela and her friends, repulsed. She eventually dropped her eyes and stopped looking at them altogether.

They made their way up a winding staircase but got off when it ended in a jagged display of wreckage. They entered a door that, according to a sign hanging on the wall, led to the eighth floor. There wasn't much to this level, and they soon found another flight of stairs to climb. They exited on the thirteenth floor. Angela felt a breeze as the door opened.

"Follow us and do not speak," one of the elves said. Then he looked at Maximus. "That goes for you as well. You'll get your pay once we have them on the ledge."

Maximus nodded, and so they passed through a covered hallway with no walls. They had obviously crumbled sometime in the past, but the ceiling was supported by round pillars and naked metal beams along the edges, like those embedded into the ground below. A large metal gate had been erected to cordon off the far end of the thirteenth floor. There was no ceiling beyond the gate, merely a ledge exposed to the elements. This, Angela realized, was a prison without bars.

The elves approached more guards who unlocked the gate without a word. Seven elves drew swords, daring any prisoner to approach, and the gate was opened. First Orlan, then Angela, and then the rest were led inside, but the elves did not close the gate.

Angela turned and saw the elves circling Maximus.

"You're kidding," he said. "I'm a hunter! I'm exempt!"

The elves attacked, and Maximus defended himself. He injured one and landed a few well-placed kicks before being tackled to the ground. They held the hunter while the two elves who had escorted them up the stone path pulled the long coat from his shoulders. Maximus struggled, nearly freeing himself, but he was shoved through the gate, which was locked behind him.

"I'm exempt!" Maximus shouted as he kicked the fence.

"Not anymore," one of the two escorts said. "You spoke rudely to Captain-Ecshelï, and your traitorous status does not exempt you from that sort of crime."

"Get me Mathew," Maximus demanded.

"We'll see what we can do," the elf said. He smirked, and Angela doubted that the hunter was going to get his audience.

Maximus faced the other prisoners and showed no fear.

"Welcome to prison, hunter, and the rest of you," a stranger said.

Angela turned and found a group of four men huddled together. An older man, the one who spoke, offered a weak smile and looked away. She scanned the ledge and saw other prisoners, other races, but they did not speak. It was dark, and she couldn't see them clearly.

It was Kris who made the first move. He approached the four men, so Angela, Orlan, and Benjamin followed.

"May we join you?" Kris asked.

"Of course," the man said. "I think that'd be your safest bet." Then the man looked over to where Maximus was standing. "Would you care to join us as well, hunter?"

Maximus cursed and sat alone.

Angela watched Maximus, who was obviously upset, but then she heard Benjamin whisper something beneath his breath.

"What was that?" she asked.

"He didn't come," Benjamin said. Tears were streaming down his cheeks. "My father didn't come."

It was true. Trent and the others hadn't come, and Angela never really expected them to. Too much had happened. Those who were left, if any, needed time to recover. No, she and her friends were prisoners of the elves now, and there was no help to be had. They were alone.

Part V: Broken Tribe

Randall Whitaker rolled restlessly. In the dark corners of his dream he could see her. Her skin was pale, her hair auburn and curly. She was the most beautiful woman he had ever seen, and he loved her. Her family had come to Refuge only a short time before the elves destroyed it, but she had survived. He made sure of that.

He had crept through his blood soaked home after clinging to his dead parents, trying not to sob too loudly. Then he saw her through a window, crying beneath a table his father had built. He was young, and he didn't understand why the elves were killing them. What he did know, however, was that he didn't like seeing the girl cry, so he found his courage and went to her. He took her by the hand and they ran.

They were nearly caught. Two elves were preparing to sever their heads when a third intervened and slew his two kin. Randall could barely remember the elf, but he stood over them, his face grieved, and then he pointed toward a trail in the woods. It was the first time Randall had seen an elf who didn't hate him.

"Go," was all he had said.

The elf ran off, and Randall took the girl's hand and led her into the forest. Others were waiting.

"We'll be alright, Bethany," Randall had said. "There's Rand Medair'yin. We're almost free."

Years went by. Randall and Bethany matured, and she was still the most beautiful woman he'd ever seen. She agreed to marry him. They became pregnant.

"Angela," Bethany said. Her belly was swollen, and she glowed. "Let's name her Angela after my grandmother."

Angela was in Bethany's arms; she was such a beautiful child. She had her mother's skin, though her hair was light like his. Randall's love had always been reserved for Bethany alone, but now he found it divided.

How could a child he'd only just met mean so much to him?

"Why did you fail her, Randall?" Bethany asked as she rocked the baby to sleep.

"I'm sorry?" he replied.

"You failed her!" Bethany screamed. She was angry. Black pupils filled her eyes as bloody tears streamed down her face.

"I didn't mean..." he began, but she sobbed and covered her eyes with the palms of her hands.

"The one who takes the throne shall strive to surpass the last."

"Please don't say that," Randall begged.

He cried and screamed and covered his ears, but a voice dug deep into his brain. The voice came from Bethany's mouth, but it was not hers. It was hideous.

"The one who takes the throne shall strive to surpass the last. The one who takes the throne shall strive to surpass the last."

Blood poured from her eyes like a river, and she rocked alone, crying as she screamed, "The one who takes the throne shall strive to surpass the last!"

"Don't make me remember," Randall pleaded. He ran away from the woman he loved. He sobbed and screamed, but her voice echoed nonetheless.

"THE ONE WHO TAKES THE THRONE SHALL STRIVE TO SURPASS THE LAST!"

Randall shot up in a sweat. The dream hung heavily, and he shook with the image of his wife bleeding from the eyes. The memory of how she had died was far too strong already; he didn't need the reminder. And Angela—his poor, sweet Angela. He cried for only a moment but then sobered and calmed himself.

"It was a dream," he told himself. "We'll get her back."

"Randall?" Trent called from the cave's entrance.

"I'm fine."

The falls poured down over the mouth of the cave, hiding their new home from the outside world. The falls that Nikiatis had found had been serving as a house of healing for the past few days. Small caves were worn into the stone wall, most covered by various waterfalls. The majority of the tribe slept in the largest cave where

Randall now lay. The birdmen slept in a neighboring cave beneath another waterfall.

He was healing at a slower pace than the rest of the tribe—due to his age he suspected—and that frustrated him. He ached and felt feverish, but his body *was* healing, and he was grateful for that. His heart, however, was another matter.

"How are you feeling?" Trent asked.

"As well can be expected. And you?"

Trent Bishop forced a smile, but it was hollow. He slumped and shook his head.

"I want my son back, Randall. The old lessons taught forgiveness, but those monsters took my boy. I should forgive them—I *need* to forgive them—but every inch of my being wants to run a sword through their little necks."

Randall felt the same, and he longed for Silus' old Bible. He could have searched its pages for an answer regarding how to handle this situation; but alas, it was gone, destroyed in the fire that took Silus' life. Since the original Refuge fell, they had been reciting the ancient texts by memory, and only certain portions of its teachings had been retained. Trent had been Randall's finest student, just as Randall had been Silus', but neither was perfect in their knowledge.

"Do you remember the old stories, Trent," Randall said, "how God ordered his people to topple armies?"

"I do."

"And do you remember the story of an eye for an eye?"

"Those were later changed. We must turn the other cheek. We must forgive."

"Our texts are incomplete," Randall stated. "We do not know what God would have us do in a situation like this. I suspect that we should pray and seek guidance."

"I have not stopped since the attack."

"Good," Randall said as Trent helped him up. "Now, where are the others?"

"Nikiatis is circling north, searching for the prison that Ivan told you about. Ivan himself has been accompanying Tramin and Gabe as they search for signs of pursuers. Shëlin and Joshua are watching over the recovering birdmen."

"And Debra?"

"I'm not certain," Trent answered with a sigh. "She's done nothing but sharpen arrows for nearly two days. She is threatening to march north herself if we don't leave soon. She wants Jillian back."

"As do I, Trent. I want them all back. Has Nikiatis uncovered anything new?"

"No, and Ivan remembers little of his wanderings through Greysong. If we're to find the prison, it won't be through him."

"We need to leave now if we're to find our children. How are the birdmen?"

"Recovering. Fagunol is mobile again. The blue one is showing signs of physical recovery but is yet to awaken. Shëlin fears for him."

"Any improvement is better than none. We must not forget him in our prayers."

Randall rubbed his eyes and sighed. Most everyone was rested, but were they well enough to aimlessly march through Greysong in search of clues? He didn't know, but they couldn't wait any longer. Their children needed them.

"Is Joshua well enough to run errands?"

"He can follow simple direction."

"Have him retrieve Tramin and Gabe, and then I want you to gather whoever's available so we can discuss what comes next. We'll meet here in one hour."

Trent nodded and left the cave. Randall lay back down. He had been sleeping off and on for the past couple of days, but he didn't feel rested at all. A sudden coughing fit sprung him up again, and when he removed his fist he found blood speckled upon it.

His body was taking too long to heal itself, but he refused to wait. The children needed him. Angela needed him. He promised Bethany that he would keep their daughter safe, and he would do just that.

Bethany's final words echoed in his ears again, words that he had never shared with another human being, words that he tried to forget. They were the ramblings of a mad woman.

"Upon broken ledge Refuge begins their descent, and war is soon to follow," Bethany had muttered with her last breaths. "The one who takes the throne shall strive to surpass the last. With a forked tongue evil is halted, but only for a while. It comes again. So speak the gri'ori."

The words, he knew, were not his wife's. But then, could they have really belonged to the gri'ori, a fairy tale that children used to frighten one another? He knew it was silly, but if the gri'ori didn't possess his wife, who did? Who could have possibly killed her with demonic visions of war?

Joshua filled the makeshift basket much slower than he would have a week ago. He did everything slower now. It was difficult focusing on such tasks given that the only thing he wanted to do was sleep, and he really wanted to sleep. He thought slowly, breathed slowly, moved slowly. He hadn't spoken at all.

He had been plucking berries for over an hour on Shëlin's order, and the basket was barely full. He sat and plucked them one at a time, but his thoughts were elsewhere. They were on the woman who had adopted and raised him. He missed his mother.

"Joshua?"

He turned toward the voice but didn't answer.

"Ah, there you are," Trent said a moment later. "Randall would like you to collect Tramin and your father. We're to meet at the cave in an hour."

Joshua considered this and then nodded. His father had gone north, but they'd been sticking to a fluid routine. He knew about where they'd be.

Trent didn't leave. He waited for Joshua to speak, but Joshua had nothing to say. Joshua looked at the berries, mustered up the motivation to pluck a few more, and then stood.

"She didn't feel any pain, Joshua," Trent finally said. His brows were furrowed in concern; Joshua had been seeing a lot of that lately. "And according to our faith, she is in the most wonderful place now, happy and free from the hardships of life. It will only be a small time before we see her again."

None of this registered in Joshua's mind. She was gone and that was all. Now he needed to find his father. He could only focus on one thing at a time. Gathering his basket, he stood and brushed by Trent, who studied him as he walked.

"We all miss her. And I'm praying for Benjamin as well, and Kris, Orlan, and the rest. You're not alone, Joshua. We're all hurting with you."

He kept walking. He could hear Trent following him, but he didn't care. Randall asked that he find his father. He had to go north.

A hand fell on his shoulder, so he stopped. Trent turned him around and knelt. His eyes were wet, and Joshua felt a pang in his gut.

"I'd known Phyllis since I was young. Most of us did. I cannot express to you how much we miss her—how much I miss her—but she would have hated seeing you like this, Joshua. She would have wanted you to be strong for her, and for your brothers and Benjamin. Benjamin's your best friend, Joshua. Can you be strong for him? Can you overcome your grief for Benjamin?"

Joshua thought of his friends. He missed his mother, but he also missed Benjamin and Jillian. He missed his brothers: Kris and Orlan. He missed Angela. He had overheard his father talking about rescuing them, but it was hard to imagine, so it slipped away. He struggled with it now. He missed his mother.

Tears streamed down Trent's face, but he did not talk. He simply waited, painfully, for a reply. Joshua felt for him, and for the first time since watching his mother die, Joshua showed emotion. He simply leaned forward and hugged his best friend's father.

"There we go," Trent said, and then he began to sob.

Joshua held Trent and felt a stirring in his chest, but he did not cry or speak. Trent, however, unburdened a great deal of grief. Then the man stood and dried his eyes with the cuff of his sleeve.

"You're a good friend," Trent said. "Benjamin loves you a great deal, and he's lucky to have you, but we all need to be strong for him now. Oh, but we should be gathering the others. Come on." Then Trent smiled and patted Joshua on the shoulder. "We'll be alright, Joshua. We'll always miss your mother, but God will see us through."

Joshua kept hearing those words. He had a hard time believing them—they felt so hollow—but Trent seemed to believe. Trent had faith. Perhaps Joshua could have faith too. Faith wouldn't bring his mother back, but perhaps it could save his brothers and friends. Joshua tried clinging to this, but it was difficult. It was slippery, and he could already feel it slipping from his mind.

Arrows lay in bundles along the river's bank. Debra had been sharpening stones from the riverbank all morning, and now she was fastening them to sticks to replace the arrows lost during the wildman raid. The tribe needed to be ready if they were going to retrieve Jillian and the others, but Debra was getting impatient.

She had once been second-in-command of the medical tent, and that required a great deal of patience. Even Shëlin, the great elven healer of the tribe, served under her leadership, but those days were gone. She lost her drive to heal after Payson died, and it felt like she was reverting to something older.

In truth, it was Payson who domesticated her. She had once lived alone in the forest, always hunting, always hiding. It was by sheer chance that she stumbled upon Payson as he gathered herbs. She nearly shot him with an arrow, but she was taken aback by his handsomeness. He was older than her by a decade, but he still mesmerized her. She made the choice in that moment to cease living like a vagabond and to accept someone else into her life. She didn't realize that Payson would connect her to the first family she'd ever known or that they would create something as marvelous as Jillian. But Payson was dead now, and their daughter was missing, in the hands of cannibals and elves. Suddenly Debra felt the need to hunt again. So why were they not hunting?

"Debra?"

"Over here," she answered.

Trent passed beneath a low tree branch and stopped to survey the arrows lying in bundles.

"Good work," he said quietly. Then he motioned toward the waterfall with a thumb. "Randall's called a meeting. It'll start in about forty minutes."

"Have the others found something?"

"Not that we've been told, but Randall doesn't want to wait any longer."

"Good," Debra said as she stabbed the ground with the stick she had been sharpening.

She laid out a tarp and, with Trent's help, gathered the bundles of arrows, wrapped them together, and headed toward the waterfalls.

Fagunol wondered what the red-haired woman and the second-in-command were discussing. He had been testing his wings when he spotted them, but they were gone now, hidden beneath the branches of the forest.

The strain was great, but at least his wings were functioning. He found, however, that he couldn't stay airborne for long. He turned and glided on the wind until he saw the smaller of two waterfalls that hid the cave where he and his kin had been resting. The larger of the two hid the humans' cave. He contemplated splashing through the falls, to bathe in its cool water, but he wasn't strong enough for that yet and would have likely been bashed upon the rocks below. So he landed on the small walkway that connected the two caves and entered from the side.

"How was your flight?" Shëlin asked.

The golden birdman stretched his sore wings and tested them for pain.

"I am perhaps slightly better than I was before your tribe was attacked, an improvement. And how is Vetcalf?"

Shëlin had been kneeling beside the blue birdman when he arrived. She seemed to linger by his side more than any other. He was, after all, the gravest of them all.

"Improvement," she said. I've removed most of his stitches, and he does seem to be improving, but I worry about the damage done to his throat. My biggest concern is whether he'll awaken at all. This coma could be permanent."

"Can nothing force him awake?"

"Not with the medicine available to us, no. If we were members of the Elven Nation perhaps, but…"

"Why did you leave?"

It was a question that had been burning in Fagunol's mind since he first laid eyes on Shëlin. Elves hated mankind—this was common knowledge—yet Shëlin had betrayed her kin to join a tribe of humans. He thought he might be able to deduce the reasoning for himself in time once he had gotten to know her better, but his burning curiosity had gotten the best of him.

Shëlin sat back, studied the birdman, and then sighed and left the cave. Fagunol followed her. She stopped just outside of the waterfall where it was noisiest and pointed into the distance.

"I once lived in an elven community in the far east. I had a great amount of pride in my race and served Kïer boldly. I embraced every opportunity to defend my tower."

"Defend?" Fagunol questioned. "Were you not a healer?"

"No. I knew nothing of healing then. Debra's husband Payson taught me how to use medicine. He had been a young man when I first arrived, but I learned a great deal from him and came to the conclusion that I would rather heal than spill any more blood."

"So you were a warrior in the Elven Nation?"

"I was a guard of Olergöl, the Northeast Tower."

"And why did you leave?"

"I was exiled."

"Interesting."

Shëlin laughed, but there was no humor in it.

"I commonly guarded gateways, fought would-be invasions, and kept Olergöl safe. Then I was transferred. I was told it was a promotion, but I was not fond of my new position. I stood in a small hallway in the belly of the tower and guarded an old, unmarked door. I knew not what the room contained as I was never permitted to enter, but I now believe it concealed old records; I suspect documents from the old world and recordings from our recent past.

"High ranking elves were the only ones with clearance to enter the room—Generals, Dömins, Advisers—and one evening, the Dömin Adviser came. He unknowingly dropped a small scroll as he latched the door and left it lying on the floor. Like you, I was a curious creature, so I took the scroll and hid it away.

"That scroll, as it turned out, was a detailed report on the original Refuge community. It explained how their belief system threatened the Elven Nation, detailing the rate at which the community grew. Even elves were discussing the topic of faith, having been influenced by the humans at Refuge. The scroll explained how serving any besides Kïer was forbidden and how Refuge could potentially result in an uprising. The extermination order was detailed, and the scroll explained how that order had been carried out to completion, or so the elves thought. I was intrigued by what I learned from the scroll but chastised myself for having taken it."

Fagunol found this all very interesting. The very notion of the elves having rooms full of ancient texts filled his body with anticipation.

"Do you still have the scroll?" Fagunol asked.

"No, of course not," she replied. Her tone made the wise birdman feel silly. "I couldn't bring myself to destroy the scroll, so I hid it away, but my daughter Kära found it. She was a young child at the time and knew not what she was doing. She showed it to my husband, and he alerted the authorities of my crime."

"Your husband?" Fagunol questioned. "Birdmen have never entertained the notion of marriage, but we understand the bond it creates. Were you not in love?"

"My hand was given, not offered. Most elven unions are arranged, and no, we were not in love. I was the least of seven wives, merely a fulfillment of his physical desires, nothing more."

"I am sorry to hear that. Your kindness and beauty deserve a far greater passion than what he had to offer."

Shëlin smiled, and Fagunol realized what he had just said. Never in his life had he complimented an elf. It was disturbing.

"Thank you, Fagunol. To finish the story, I stood before the General and his two Dömins and explained to them how I had come by the scroll. They beheaded the Dömin Adviser who dropped it and exiled me from the Elven Nation."

"And you found your way here?"

"Yes, eventually. Remember, the scroll detailed the fall of Refuge; the elves knew nothing of there being survivors. I made my way to the river where Refuge once stood and saw that its destruction was complete, and so I made its ruins my home. I defended it from trolls and elves, and even a human or two, but then I saw a man standing in the grass just outside of the ruins. I threatened him, but he meant no harm."

"And who was that man?"

"His name was Rand Medair'yin, Kris' grandfather, and it was he who led the people of Refuge to safety after its fall. He had come looking for sojourners who might have come looking for Refuge, but there were none. I had scared them all away or killed them. He introduced himself, but my trust of mankind was lacking in those days. I threatened him, and he left. He returned six months later, however, and continued to do so every year.

"He always found me there, and against my better judgment, we became friends. I began to wonder if perhaps I should leave with him, join his people, but I was accustomed to living alone, and in secret, I missed my kin. I still clung to their ways, their bitterness and pride, and to join a tribe of men was a far worse crime than theft.

"Rand had been middle-aged when we first met and aged more rapidly than I was used to seeing. As an elf who had never been in the presence of a human, I found it jarring. Rand would eventually introduce me to Damian, his son, and Damian began visiting me in Rand's stead. Then after a couple years of seeing only Damian, Rand came with him. He was withered and pale, and he could barely speak, but he cared enough to visit me one last time. He offered me a place with his people, but I was afraid and refused. It didn't take long for me to regret that decision. My elven pride had diminished, I realized, and I was lonely.

"When next I received a visitor, it was Damian alone. Rand had died, and his son now led the tribe. I mourned for my friend and accepted his son's invitation. I feared what the humans would do when they saw me, but I needn't have worried. I was accepted into their family without question."

"You seem to have embraced their ways," Fagunol stated. "I have never met an elf so accommodating."

"Refuge has a way of changing people."

"And I am beginning to believe it." Fagunol smiled as he spotted Gabe, Tramin, and Ivan below. "It seems the trackers have returned."

"Randall's meeting should be starting soon. I will return when it is finished." She took a step but then stopped and turned to face him. "You are invited to join us."

"Thank you, Shëlin-Vin, but I trust the judgment of your tribe."

Shëlin nodded and descended the walkway toward the next waterfall. Fagunol watched her leave, surprised by the fondness he felt toward her, and then entered his own cave. He sat beside Vetcalf and examined the scar along his kin's throat. Seeing no change in the birdman's condition, Fagunol lay back and closed his eyes.

He had never trusted anything beyond the caverns of Uuron Plauf, and even then, a birdman's status had to be considered. He wondered what the Aerie would say if they saw him now, living among humans and communing with an elf. He had to admit that there was a certain level of shame in it. Then he cursed himself.

The birdmen had built Uuron Plauf above every other race and deluded themselves into believing it was where they belonged. Fagunol cursed his brethren. Why had his ancestors been such pride-driven idiots? How could he and his fellow scholars have been so foolish as to follow their ancestors' lead; but then, how could they not? The birdmen looked down upon the whole world, but the Aerie was far worse. The world was not enough for them; they belittled their own kind. Such ignorance and pride.

Fagunol sighed with a realization that he could barely fathom.

Uuron Plauf had received the punishment it deserved, the Aerie especially, and he should have died along with them. He was undeserving of this new life. They all were.

"We've found more trails, but they lead us in circles," Tramin said. "They overlap too heavily."

Randall rubbed his eyes and felt the never-ending ache in his chest. The weight of what he'd been through was bone crushing, and he felt unbelievably tired, but there was no time to nurse such things.

"Were you able to find anything concrete?" Shëlin asked. "Were there no human prints?"

"In several of the trails, yes," Tramin said quietly. "They looked about Orlan's size, but there were hunters with the wildmen, so we can't be too sure. That's where I'd recommend continuing our search, though."

Randall simply listened as Shëlin and Trent questioned Tramin and Gabe. He took in every word, but his mind had trouble holding on to them. The very idea of Angela being held by cannibals drove him mad. He wanted to act. He needed to act! They should be out there rescuing their children now, but to act hastily would only make things worse. So he kept a steady breath and merely listened.

"And what of Ivan?" Debra asked from near the cavern's entrance.

"What about him?" Tramin asked.

"You've spent the better of two days with him," she said. "Do you trust him?"

Randall watched with interest as Tramin and Gabe exchanged a curious glance.

"He's not given me reason to question his loyalty," Tramin said, "but I'm not convinced his stumbling into our camp was an accident."

"And why do you question this?" Randall asked.

"It was too convenient, and there's a strange foreboding that I get in my gut when he's with us."

"I feel it as well," Gabe said. "He doesn't serve Kïer, I don't think, but there's more going on in his head than we know. He thinks a great deal."

"Could he be a hunter?" Debra asked.

"He wouldn't have defended us against the wildmen if he were," Tramin answered. "He would have claimed the bounty for himself."

Randall understood their unease; he'd been feeling the same since Ivan invited himself into their tribe. He didn't trust the man, but to deny him a place in Refuge would go against everything Silus had taught them.

Debra continued, "And he remembers nothing of his wanderings through Greysong?"

"He has no memory of how he reached our camp," Tramin replied, "though he remembers the prison vaguely."

"He *claims* to have no memory," Gabe clarified.

"It is possible for him to lose a day or two of time," Shëlin stated. "He'd lost a lot of blood, and his fever was frightening. He was lucky to have found us when he did."

"What if it wasn't luck?" Debra asked.

"Then we will deal with that when the time comes," Randall said before anyone else could answer. "Refuge is a home for all who find it, Ivan included. He came to us a wounded man and fought alongside us when we needed him. Until we have justification to question his motives, Ivan Shaymolin is to be treated like family."

Debra stared at the waterfall, obviously not caring for Randall's opinion. He wasn't sure that he liked it himself, but acceptance was their way. He couldn't change that without changing Refuge, and that was something he refused to do.

"And what about Nikiatis?" Trent asked. "Have you spoken with the birdman much during your journeys?"

"We speak to that birdman as little as possible," Tramin blurted out. "Fagunol seems pleasant enough, but Nikiatis speaks only insults when spoken to. I swear he would kill us all if our backs were ever turned to him."

"Do not make assumptions," Randall said. "Like Ivan, the birdmen are all welcome here regardless of their temperament. Nikiatis has gone through a great tragedy. Give him time."

"He was their king," Shëlin said.

Randall had not forgotten this fact. As leader, he blamed himself for Payson's death, as well as Bethany, Fredrick, Danielle, and everyone else who had died under his watch. To feel as Randall did after losing so few, how must a king feel having lost so many?

"I have been speaking with Fagunol," continued Shëlin, "and he claims that Nikiatis had once been a loving king. The birdman that he's become, however, is unrecognizable. Until the day comes when he remembers his true self, Nikiatis must know that he has a family with us. He is not our enemy."

"We must forgive the things he says," Trent said, "as difficult as that may be."

Debra snickered sardonically.

"Ivan, Nikiatis," she said, "all I care about right now is our children. What are we going to do about them?"

Randall nodded and walked toward the waterfall. Ivan and Nikiatis were difficult distractions, but what the tribe needed to do was plan for their children's recovery before it was too late.

"Are we healed enough to begin our search?" he asked.

"Those of us in this room are," Shëlin answered. "Vetcalf is not. I promised Nikiatis that I would care for his kin, so I should stay behind with him. Fagunol is recovering nicely but should decide on his own whether he will help us or not. Nikiatis has already vowed to help find our children. Joshua…"

"I would prefer that Joshua stay behind," Gabe interrupted. "He is still dealing with Phyllis…" His voice broke, so he dropped his eyes and covered his mouth. Tramin put an arm around him.

"As are we all," Shëlin said, "and I agree regarding Joshua. He is physically well, but mentally, that's another story."

"Very well," Randall said with a nod. He studied his men. Trent, Tramin, and Gabe were for the most part strong. Debra was a little too eager to act, and that worried him. He considered asking Shëlin to go in her place, but he couldn't ask Debra to stay behind with Jillian among the missing. As a parent, he understood why she was so eager to attack. "And what of Ivan?"

"He'll come," Tramin said. "He told me as much."

"Good," Randall said. He didn't know what went on inside that man's head, but he liked the idea of keeping him close. "Gather what you need. We leave in an hour."

The others left, and Randall tried stretching the soreness from his muscles. It didn't do much good, so he prayed silently and crossed from his cave into the next. There he found Shëlin caring for Vetcalf while Fagunol and Nikiatis argued in the far the corner. Nikiatis did not seem happy.

"You told them?" Randall casually whispered.

"I did," Shëlin replied. "Fagunol feels obligated to help. Nikiatis wants him to stay."

"Should I intervene?"

Shëlin smiled. "Not if you value your life."

Randall felt a pull at the corner of his own mouth.

"Despite the horrible things that have happened," he said, "it's good to see someone smiling again."

"I grow fond of these birdmen," she said, "even Nikiatis."

"You might be alone in that."

"Give him time."

"I know."

They washed Vetcalf's fur and changed his bandages. Bethany used to say that healing was the most rewarding method of serving God, and Randall agreed. It was certainly better than wielding a sword.

"Fagunol will be staying here."

Randall and Shëlin looked on as Nikiatis approached them. Fagunol stayed at a distance and appeared very flustered. His feathers stood out in places, and his hands were tightened into fists.

"If that is what he's decided," Randall said.

"What he decides is of no importance. It is what his king has ordered."

"I do not stay for the words of my king," Fagunol said sternly as he approached. "I stay because Vetcalf will need a friend when he awakens. I fear for Shëlin and these men if a warrior of Uuron Plauf were to awaken believing he was in the hands of an enemy. Believe you me, I stay only for him. If not for Vetcalf, I would be accompanying these people on their task—despite what my *king* says."

Nikiatis fluffed as if he were about to attack.

"Might I have a moment with you, Nikiatis," Randall interrupted, "before any more harmful words are spoken?"

Nikiatis deflated slowly but never took his eyes from Fagunol. Randall exited the cave and stood on the walkway that connected the two caves. Nikiatis followed a moment later, and Randall led him into the opposite cave.

"What do you want?" Nikiatis asked.

"First, I apologize for interrupting what would have likely been a chastising of your kin. Being that your people are only three, however, I felt that perhaps you would have regretted the coming strife. I intervened."

Nikiatis hesitated and finally nodded, "Very well."

"And for the record, I agree that Fagunol should stay for Vetcalf's sake."

Nikiatis did not reply, and so Randall began to pace.

"I have been considering things through my restless nights, mostly in regards to how you were a king."

"I am still a king," Nikiatis said sternly, "despite the disillusionment of some."

"I do not question it. We've invited you into our tribe. Whether you ultimately accept the invitation is up to you, but I will never claim to be above you. The truth is I could use your help."

"In what way?"

Randall sighed and rubbed his eyes.

"It was never my intention to lead Refuge. When our founder died, a man named Rand Medair'yin took the reins and brought us back from the ruin of extinction. We nearly lost everything. Damian, Rand's son, took over when Rand was no longer capable of leading, and we expected Damian's son Kris, or perhaps our founder's grandson Orlan, to lead when Damian's time ended. Sadly, we lost Damian unexpectedly, and neither Kris nor Orlan were old enough to take his place. I led out of necessity."

"Some of the greatest kings in Uuron Plauf's history were kings of necessity."

"The quality of my leadership will be determined after my passing, but for now, I lead through the teachings of my youth. We are a tribe of acceptance, forgiveness, and love. I understand if you do not agree with our morals…"

"I do not," Nikiatis interrupted.

"Very well, but they *are* our morals. One thing we are unaccustomed to, however, is war. We are a tribe of faith. We have strong warriors in our midst and defend ourselves when necessary, but I am no general. I do not trust myself to lead an assault on a prison without losing more men."

"You wish me to lead your people into battle?"

"We are seven against an unknown number. I do not ask that you lead, as I doubt many would follow you, but I ask for your advice. I lead the tribe, and Trent Bishop is my second-in-command. I would place you below him in the official rank, but we would benefit if you worked with us as an equal."

Nikiatis snickered. "You would make a king *third* in command?"

"I do not question your rank among the birdmen, but do remember that you are not *our* king. I place you third because the tribe respects Trent and me more and because they will listen to us. You've shown yourself to be a difficult creature who cares nothing for our wellbeing despite the sacrifices we've made on your behalf. Would you follow someone who's treated you as you've treated us?"

Nikiatis seemed to thoughtfully consider this and finally nodded. "I care not what your tribe thinks of me, but your elf has done well in nursing Fagunol back to health, and Vetcalf is showing improvement. For that reason alone I will aid you. As third-in-command, will I have say over those below me?"

"I will see to it that Gabe, Tramin, and Debra know to listen to you—provided you have their best interests at heart. I know little about Ivan Shaymolin, but he will be informed as well."

Nikiatis pondered this, and Randall could see some sort of internal struggle within the birdman. Then Nikiatis extended a hand. Randall took it.

"I will advise you, Randall Whitaker. I will be your third-in-command."

"Thank you, Nikiatis. And know that when this is over and our young ones are returned to us, I will consider your debt paid in full. You'll be free to come or go as you please, but our arms will always be opened to you."

"Do not hope for too much," Nikiatis said as he released Randall's hand. "It is unbecoming for a king to serve under a lesser race."

"Overcoming bigotries like that could prove the king's great wisdom in the face of a world saturated with such shallow mentalities."

Nikiatis merely grunted and exited the cave.

Randall couldn't help but smile. There was nothing humorous in the exchange, but perhaps he saw what Shëlin liked in the birdman. He was difficult and off-putting, but there was a jaded nobility to him. Given time, Randall could see Nikiatis becoming an asset to the tribe.

Debra and Tramin pushed through the overgrown trail with the task of gathering the arrows she and Trent had stowed away. Her mind, however, was elsewhere.

"Where is Ivan?" she asked.

"Resting on the river's bed." He pointed a thumb over his shoulder.

"I'd like to speak with him before we leave. Can you gather the arrows alone?"

"You've made quite a few bundles according to my brother, but I should manage. If you have business with Ivan, though, I'd feel more comfortable coming with you."

"No."

She turned immediately and vanished into the brush. She could feel Tramin's eyes on her, and so she lightened her step. There was a time when she could lurk in the woods without anyone hearing her comings or goings, but she had grown careless since Payson made her an honest woman. Perhaps it was time that she remembered her old skills.

She became mindful of her surroundings. She noticed the leaves and branches littering the ground. She didn't leave a print or snap a twig. This was how it used to be before Payson found her. This was how she hunted. The river was near—and there was Ivan.

He lay on the shore of the river, seemingly asleep. His head rested on a smooth stone with his hood pulled over his eyes, his fingers intertwined on his chest. She crept near him with her hand placed firmly on the hilt of her sword. She could almost touch him.

"There was a time," he said, "when I would have heard you coming long before you were close enough to slit my throat."

She waited as he sat up and threw back his hood. His disfigurement made his expression hard to read.

"I assume our next course of action has been determined?" he asked.

"I want to know why you sent us to Uuron Plauf."

Ivan paused, seemingly surprised by her demand. She could feel him studying her, and then he stood, favoring his side.

"You blame me for your husband's death," he stated quite plainly. "I do not fault you for that, you know? But remember, I did not send your people to Uuron Plauf. I simply mentioned the extermination order to your leader. It was he who elected to aid the birdmen. I forced nothing upon him."

"You keep too many secrets," she said. "We know nothing about you, and I question whether you have our best interests at heart."

"I was under the impression that your tribe offered second chances; that you weren't concerned with whom I was before entering your camp? I admit to feeling a bit disappointed. Your tribe must not be as united in your views as your leader led me to believe."

"I speak for myself. We'll be leaving soon, and I will know more about you before we go. Tell me this at least: how did you receive the four gashes on your side?"

Ivan eyed Debra wearily.

"The wounds I received from a whip—four lashes—and they were made worse upon my escape."

"You were not wounded by a whip."

"And how can you say that I was not?" Ivan asked with a hint of irritation. "Were you present?"

"The wounds are not consistent with those received by a whip. A whip leaves quick, clean abrasions unless the tails are barbed..."

"They were indeed barbed."

"...and if the whip was barbed, then the tearing of your skin would have been messier. No whip still in use can hurt the ribs in a way consistent with your injuries."

"The four lashes..."

"Your four lashes began to the left of your abdomen and were ripped backwards for roughly five inches, the deepest of each wound being at your belly, revealing four separate entry points. A whip does not leave an entry point, and the lashes would not have been so evenly spaced. You were not lashed four times but struck once in the abdomen by something four-pronged, and it was dragged along your side and ribs. Now what other lies have you told?"

One of Ivan's hands tightly gripped the hilt of his sword while the other pointed accursedly at Debra. He shouted, "I did not come here to be accused of...!"

"It is my gut feeling," Debra interrupted, "that you've come to our tribe by accident but stay for an ulterior motive, something selfish that will only end in the second fall of Refuge. Randall may be forgiving, but I was not raised with his mentality. I see through your lies, Ivan Shaymolin. Remember that as I ask you this next question—where have they taken my daughter?"

Ivan's face glowed red, and Debra prepared to defend herself. Then he smiled.

"Very well," he said while drawing his sword, "let's play a game. We duel. For every blow you land I will answer you a specific question. For every blow I land I will state a question that cannot be asked. Do we have a deal?"

"A game?" she asked disbelievingly. "I have no interest in such childish..."

"You do seek answers regarding your daughter, do you not?" he asked with a slight smile at the corners of his mouth. "Then let us duel."

She was admittedly curious about where this was going. Would he honor his word? Would he tell her the truth about everything? She knew of only one way to find out. She drew her sword and took a step forward.

"I'm not sure about this, Randall," Trent said.

Randall had informed Gabe and Trent of his decision to make Nikiatis third-in-command for their upcoming mission and neither appeared to appreciate the notion. Their reactions weren't unexpected.

Gabe groaned and rested a hand on the hilt of his ax.

"We've accepted him into our tribe," he said, "but he is not one of us. He has much to learn, and his guilt weighs too heavy. Could he control himself when confronted by elves? Would he endanger the lot of us? It's my opinion that he will only make things more difficult."

"Are you certain of that?" Randall asked. "It was for two reasons that I asked for his help. The first is that we need someone familiar with warfare, not just battle, but true warfare. The wildmen tore us apart, and the elves are a far greater threat than those cannibals could ever be. The second reason is that Nikiatis is losing himself to grief and thoughts of vengeance. It is my hope that if given a new people to lead, he would find a new sense of worth and draw away from his madness. Then we might be able to help him."

"A mission to rescue our children is not the place to test theories," Gabe said, angry now. "We're in enough danger as it is."

He began to pace, but Trent remained still, his fist to his lips, lost in thought.

"We should put our faith in God, not this birdman," he said.

"And what if this birdman was brought to us by God with the purpose of helping us get our children back?"

Trent gave this more thought.

"I suppose it's possible," he said. "Do you feel led in your spirit that we should obey Nikiatis' tactics?"

Randall hesitated before answering. "I feel strongly that we should do this, but whether it is of God's volition or my own I cannot say. I fear to admit that my mind and perhaps my judgment have been a bit clouded of late."

Trent laid a hand on his leader's shoulder.

"You've been through a lot, Randall, with Bethany's death and now this. The burden you carry is heavy. If the time has come, if you need to relinquish your position, know that I would be willing to step in."

"Thank you, Trent, and you would do a fine job, but this burden is mine to carry. Just be vigilant in the event that I make a mistake."

"And this thing with Nikiatis," Gabe said, "is that a mistake?"

"The call is already made," Trent replied. "We will hear what he has to say. He is only third-in-command, remember. If need be, Randall and I could overrule his strategies."

"He won't like that," Gabe said. "I don't see the two of you overruling him going over very well."

"Then you'll be there to clip his wings," Trent replied, "but hopefully it won't come to that."

Randall did not like this talk. He brought Nikiatis into the midst of their leadership for his expertise and for healing, but here were Trent and Gabe discussing undermining the birdman. Somehow, he felt that Silus would be displeased with them. He was about to correct his friends when someone new caught his eye.

"You have company, Gabe," he said.

Joshua entered the cave without a word and stood a few feet from the falls.

"I'll be leaving soon, Joshua," Gabe said. "I'll bring your brothers back, I promise."

"Don't leave," Joshua said in almost a whisper.

Randall's heart broke. He looked at Trent, who nodded, and together they left the boy and his father alone. Standing out on the walkway between caves, Randall took a breath of the cool air and sighed. With Gabe distracted elsewhere, Randall began to feel the weight of his decision. Was he wrong to include someone as bitter as Nikiatis into their circle of leaders?

"I fear I've made a mistake, Trent."

"Address your fear with prayer and ask God to use the situation we've created. That is the best advice I can offer."

"I will do that." He hesitated a moment more and then spoke words that pained him. "I will lead us through this mission, but your words have merit. I acknowledge that my leadership has been lacking since Bethany died, and it's only getting worse. I pretend to be bold like Nikiatis, but I feel as fragile as poor Joshua in there. I'm barely holding on."

Trent put an arm around Randall's neck. "There is no shame in admitting when your time has come. You've been a good leader, Randall, and none will fault you if you choose to step down. All you have to do is speak the word and I will unburden you, but until then, share the weight you carry with me and with God."

Randall wanted to be strong, to shake Trent's hand, but a sob rose up from his chest, and his countenance faltered. Trent held his leader as the burdens Randall had been carrying broke through. Randall was not one to cry on another man's shoulder; in contrast, he was often the one offering a shoulder, but he had little control over himself at the moment. He was too tired. He unburdened himself of all the things that had been weighing over him as Trent prayed. Then he shared Bethany's final moments and the dreams that had been plaguing him ever since.

"I'm sorry, Randall. I had no idea."

"No one did," Randall replied heavily. "I sometimes wonder if I've dreamed the whole thing up, but the terror I felt was far too real to question. Then again, the mind and memory can play tricks on someone as lost as I was in those days."

"I don't know what to say. I wish I'd known earlier so I could have helped you through this."

"No, I didn't want you to know. I didn't want anyone to know. Bethany was beautiful. She was special. Those horrible final moments were not how I wanted people to remember my wife. She deserved better than that. I wanted them to remember her for how she lived. Please Trent, promise me that you'll keep this secret. I don't want others to know that she died bleeding from the eyes and speaking nonsense."

"I promise, Randall, for as long as the secret can be kept without endangering the tribe."

Randall sighed. "Fair enough."

"I'm here for you," Trent said mournfully, "and once we've returned with our children, I think it's safe to say you've earned your rest. Leave the tribe to Kris and me. He's old enough to serve as second-in-command now. Let us carry the burden."

Randall hesitated and then reluctantly nodded. Trent was right; it was time. One more mission, and he could rest—just one more mission.

It almost hurt getting the words out. Joshua had been outside by the river when Tramin shared Randall's announcement with him. While he liked the idea of getting his friends and family back, the one overpowering thought was that his father was leaving. He understood the need, but his broken mind could not fathom the possibility of losing his father as well. Without Phyllis; without Benjamin; without Kris and Orlan; and without Gabe, Joshua would truly be alone no matter who else survived.

"Please, don't leave," he said again, and this time a sob broke through. "Don't leave me."

He tried to move forward but fell. He struggled to stand for a brief moment, but then his father lifted him into his arms and held him firmly. Joshua did not hug his father or cry into his shoulder. He felt dead, but Gabe's hold comforted him and made him feel safe. He knew, however, that it would not last.

"It's alright, Joshua," Gabe said. His voice was heavy and unsure. "I wouldn't leave unless I had to, but I have to get Kris and Orlan back. I promised your mother that I would take care of them, and if that means marching to my death so that the three of you can be together, then so be it."

"No," Joshua said quietly, "no, no, no, no."

"I'm sorry, Joshua, but I have to do this. You will stay with Shëlin. She will take care of you and will probably need your help in caring for the birdmen. Can you do that for me? Can you keep them well until I return?"

Joshua shook his head. He grabbed his father's neck with as much strength as he could muster and held on tight. He would never let go.

Gabe sat and leaned against the wall with his broken twelve year-old son nestled in his arms. They sat in silence for some time until Gabe quietly laughed. Joshua looked up at him, wondering what could be so funny.

"I was thinking about your grandfather."

Joshua had never met any of his grandparents. The truth was most people didn't live long enough to become grandparents, and so Joshua had never met anyone else's either, not that he could remember, anyhow.

"I was thinking about the time when I asked his permission to marry your mother. Your grandfather told me that he'd hunt me down himself and skin me alive if I ever hurt Phyllis. He was very protective. He couldn't bear the thought of losing her, not after losing so much in Refuge, but it was what she wanted. It hurt him, but he gave her to me anyway, and do you know why?"

Joshua simply looked up at him. His words were slowly sinking in.

"He gave her to me because he wanted what was best for her. I never really understood that until we took you, Kris, and Orlan in. Sometimes you have no choice but to do what frightens you. I don't want to leave you, Joshua, but I have to do what's best for our family. Phyllis understood that, and that's why she did what she did."

He paused a moment, and Joshua noticed the tears building in his eyes. Gabe cleared his throat a moment later.

"Your brothers need to come home," he continued. "The idea of dying and leaving the three of you behind frightens me, but it's better than leaving Kris and Orlan to the elves. Phyllis' father sacrificed for her, and now I must sacrifice for your brothers."

"I don't want you to sacrifice," Joshua said quietly.

"It's a risk I must take for the sake of my children. It will be your task to prepare this place for when they return." Gabe lifted Joshua's chin and smiled. "And prepare a bed for me too. I did reroute a whole river with only my ax after all."

Joshua felt a strange pull at the corners of his mouth. He remembered the story.

"No, you didn't," he said.

"No," Gabe said with a sigh, "but I would if it meant putting our family back together. It'd cut the whole world in half if I had to."

"I know you would, Father," Joshua said as he clung tighter to Gabe's neck. "Please, come back."

"I'll be back with your brothers and the rest. We'll bring them home—all of them. I promise."

Joshua didn't reply; he simply held his father. Gabe cradled him as if he were still a baby, and they stayed like that for as long as they were able—as father and son.

Sweat fell from Debra's brow as she blocked a blow half-heartedly swung. Ivan laughed as their swords clashed. She had long since become angry, yet couldn't land a single blow.

"Are you warmed up yet?" Ivan asked with an almost sadistic smile.

She attempted another thrust, but he dodged it easily.

"How about a little motivation?"

He sidestepped a third attempt at a jab and smacked her in the neck with the flat of his blade.

"By the rules we agreed upon, you may not ask me about any wound on my body."

She charged him, but he ducked and touched her neck with the flat of his blade yet again.

"You may not ask why I was imprisoned. Come now, woman. If we keep this up the most you'll learn is what I had for breakfast this morning. Cut me!"

He swung hard and she ducked. She faked a lunge but then rolled left and tagged his calf.

"Very good!" he laughed. "I could have pinned you to the ground through the ribs if I'd wanted, but I thought I'd let you catch your breath. Your question?"

"Where is my daughter?" she asked.

"I can't say for certain, but I would hazard a guess that she is in the same prison from whence I escaped, somewhere to the north. That is all I need to answer, but I'll give you a bit more. The prison is a building from the old world, partially destroyed and susceptible to the elements. Your daughter is likely on an open flat."

"Would she be alone?"

Ivan held up his sword and smiled.

"Earn it," he said.

Their swords clashed again, and Debra was shocked by the force in which he pressed her. He seemed to have been toying with her before but no longer. The point of his sword dug into her shoulder, not deep enough to cause damage but enough to make her jump back.

"You may not ask if she is alone—if for no other reason than that there are better questions to ask."

He swung his blade hard and she dove into him, pushing against his chest so that he lost his balance and fell. She ran the edge of her blade along his hand with the precision of a doctor. He jumped and pushed her away.

"Going for the sword hand? Foul play, my dear."

"Do you..." she stopped herself. If he'd been lying about not knowing the way to the prison, he'd only continue to do so. What else could she ask? "What dangers await my daughter in that prison?"

"The elves obviously, and hunters. There were human-sized lizards that blended in with the fence. A fall from the prison's ledge would be horrifying, that is if the cannibals don't get to her first. There's also the possibility of torture, being that..."

She dove at him again, having heard enough. The idea of any of those things being a threat to Jillian made her feel sick and panicked. She wasn't sure what to ask or if Ivan would give her anything of value, but she was losing interest in this game. Her anger was getting the best of her.

"I've let you have two, take another!" he shouted.

He sounded angry, and every blow that he deflected felt like a hammer on brittle bones. Debra stood her ground, however, with Jillian remaining foremost in her thoughts.

"Why have you wasted two questions on your child? There are more important questions to be asked here."

"What could be more important than my daughter?"

She screamed these words and nearly lost her head as he swung the edge of his blade and just missed her scalp. He merely shook his head and attempted another thrust. She spun along his blade and drove an elbow into his cheek. He pushed her away and laughed. Blood trickled from his lip.

"Impressive."

"What questions are you talking about?"

Ivan eyed Debra and smiled.

"The questions that made you target me in the first place. It was because of me that your Payson died, remember? Would you like to learn more about that?"

Debra's eyes filled with tears. To hear this man speak her husband's name was like daggers of ice driven deep into her veins. He laughed again and motioned for her to raise her sword.

"Come on then," he said. "Show me how much you blame me for Payson's sacrifice. Seek your vengeance!"

She screamed her frustrations in a string of curses, and then she charged. Their swords clashed and concern registered on Ivan's face. That was because Debra fought without restraint for the first time since the game began, and she was a far better swordswoman that Ivan could have possibly imagined.

Fagunol sat up. Nikiatis and Shëlin had both frozen, listening to the wind that blew in from the falls.

"What do you hear?" he asked.

"I am uncertain," Nikiatis said.

Shëlin did not answer. She departed the cave, listening. Birdmen were gifted with excellent hearing in their youth, but their ears were nothing compared to those of an elf.

"Stay with Vetcalf," Nikiatis ordered.

Fagunol watched curiously as Nikiatis joined Shëlin on the walkway. He couldn't hear them over the roar of the falls, but he saw them pointing down toward the river where the trees hid its path from their view.

"Are we under attack again?" Fagunol shouted, but again, they gave no answer.

Nikiatis lifted from the walkway and flew toward the river as Fagunol joined Shëlin, his curiosity getting the best of him.

"Where is he going?" Fagunol asked.

"Debra was screaming profanities, which is quite unlike her. Then I heard the clash of steel. She is fighting someone—Ivan I think—but I hear no other movement in the woods."

"Should I alert Randall?"

"No," she said. "Nikiatis gave you an order. I won't overrule it. I'll go."

She descended the walkway and disappeared into the neighboring cave where the human members of Refuge had been preparing.

Fagunol listened to the wind but heard nothing. Curse his old age! But then he heard something else and his heart jolted.

"Vetcalf?"

He peered into the cave and saw the blue birdman coughing lightly into a fist. Joy erupted through Fagunol as he sprinted to his kinsman's side.

"I am here, Vetcalf."

The blue birdman shakily touched his throat and then opened his eyes ever so slightly. He attempted to speak, but a convulsion of pain waved through his body.

"Do not speak, my friend. You've sustained serious injuries. I must go find help, but I promise to return momentarily. Just stay awake."

Fagunol sprinted from the cave and followed after Shëlin.

"Stay awake, Vetcalf," he whispered to the wind. "You are going to be alright, just say awake."

Payson had once told Debra that to give in to your hatred was to do yourself a great disservice. It was one of the lessons that helped shift her from a savage woman of the forest to a respectable lady of Refuge. His words echoed in her memory now as she did everything in her power to wound Ivan Shaymolin. She jabbed, parried, ducked and rolled. He was just too good.

He was no longer laughing. It took his complete concentration to deflect her fury, but she didn't revel in the skill of her assault. She wanted to wound him. She wanted to avenge Payson by making him bleed. But Debra was angry and losing focus. Frustration distracted her enough so that Ivan eventually pulled her close, pinning her back to his chest.

"You're better than this. Your swordplay is impressive, but…"

She drove the back of her head into his mouth, and he shoved her to the ground, wiping away the blood that began to flow from his lower lip.

"We were at a parlay, woman!"

"Parlaying was never mentioned in the rules. Now tell me, did you intend for my husband to die?"

"I caught you first, and I say that you may not ask that question. Try another."

Debra gritted her teeth.

"Fine, did you intend for anyone to die when you sent our people to Uuron Plauf?"

"The answer is simple. No, because I did not send your people to Uuron Plauf. I merely relayed what I knew about the extermination order. Your husband left of his own accord and did a noble thing. You should be proud of him."

She thrust with her sword, and the battle continued. His answer was not enough. There was more. There had to be more! It was very much in Randall's character to aid others, but Uuron Plauf was suicide—they all knew it—yet he led them there anyway. Why?

She attempted to break his knee with a kick, but he jumped aside. Her foot, however, did manage a brief tag of the shin.

"How did you convince Randall to go? What are you not telling me?"

"I have no magical powers, woman. Your leader did what he thought was best."

She felt the tears before they fell from her eyes. She wanted to hate Ivan Shaymolin, to hurt him. She needed to exact revenge for how Payson died, but she could find no reason to firmly place her grief on Ivan. It frustrated her. She strained her brain to think of something that could make Payson's death Ivan's fault, but there was nothing. Randall had made the call to intervene in Uuron Plauf, and Payson had volunteered to go with him. If the fault was anyone's, it was Payson's for making the conscious and noble decision to help a needy people.

Payson Harlow died because he was selfless and because helping those in need was his calling.

She stepped back and lowered her sword. Ivan stood ready for another attack, but then he relaxed and sheathed his weapon.

"Have you gotten it out of your system now?"

"What do you mean?"

"I've lost a lot of people through the years. I know how grief can eat away at you, and yours was eating you alive. You needed to vent, if not at Randall or the birdmen, then at me. I was doing you a favor."

"Do you even feel remorse for his death?" she asked with tears streaming.

"I've felt remorse every day since they returned from Uuron Plauf, and I willingly shoulder a small piece of the blame. Without me Randall would never have known about the extermination order. I accept that portion of the blame and am reminded of it whenever I see you or your daughter mourning. And for that, I am truly sorry."

Debra simply stared as the scarred man hid his deformity beneath his black hood.

"I am not foolish enough to think that you will ever come to me with your grief," he said, "but do know that I would have died in his place if it were possible."

She did not have time to respond. Just as he turned to go, a great white blur collided with him and carried him into the trees above. He screamed and fell back to the ground, somehow managing to land on his feet. Drawing his sword, he quickly turned toward the trees and faced the white blur, which Debra now saw was Nikiatis.

Shock stilled Debra from acting or even speaking. It was when Nikiatis screamed a terrifying screech that she came out of her stupor. Ivan did not wince at the warning, and the birdman dove from the tree's upper branches. Swords met, and Debra ran to get help. She was tired and worried that she would be killed if she were to step between them. She heard the sound of footsteps a moment later.

"Debra!" she heard Trent yelling through the forest.

"Here!" she shouted back.

Randall and Trent raced to her, and Gabe arrived just behind them with Joshua on his heels.

"They're killing each other! Ivan and Nikiatis!"

"Did Ivan attack you?" Trent asked. "Shëlin heard you shouting."

"What? No," She shook her head. "It was a misunderstanding. I was being stupid."

Randall looked at her incredulously, making her feel small; then he rushed ahead with Trent at his side. She ran after them alongside Gabe and Joshua.

Ivan and Nikiatis were circling each other. They were both bleeding a great deal as if hate poured black from their wounds. Ivan gracefully attacked, and Nikiatis leapt over him with a flap of his mighty wings, but then Ivan leapt and caught the birdman's heel, pulling him back to the ground. He was about to sever the birdman's leg when he was knocked to the ground by Tramin, who had exploded from the other side of the forest.

Nikiatis stood and faced his foe. Tramin had Ivan pinned to the ground, but Nikiatis didn't seem to notice. He swung his blade with enough force to kill Ivan and Tramin both, but it was deflected by Randall's sword. The powerful blow threw Randall off balance, but Trent and Gabe were there to back him up.

"At ease, Nikiatis," Trent said. "Shëlin sent you to help Debra, not to kill our own tribesman."

Hatred filled Nikiatis' eyes, which remained trained on Ivan. It appeared to Debra that the birdman wanted to destroy every inch of Ivan Shaymolin despite Trent's order, but then Nikiatis lowered his blade and took a step back. He took a few deep breaths, composed himself, and pointed his sword at Ivan, who was standing beside Tramin now.

"I've seen how you move," Nikiatis said, "and I know how you fight. You, Ivan Shaymolin, are an elf!"

It was as if the woods had stopped breathing. Debra had trouble registering the accusation in her already tired mind, but then she looked at Ivan. Elves had pointed ears; Ivan's had been burnt off. Elves were terribly beautiful, but Ivan's body had been disfigured. He had demanded that she not ask him about his wounds during their fighting game. Why was that? She thought about the lithely way that he fought and how he often crouched and moved about without sound. Had he ever claimed to be human? She couldn't remember.

"Is this true?" Randall asked.

Ivan spat blood and covered his head with his hood.

"There may be some truth in it," he finally said, "I have elven blood, yes, but I am no longer counted among their ranks. I am a member of Refuge now, am I not?"

"Our people do not attack each other," Tramin said firmly.

"Is that so?" he asked while stealing a glimpse of Debra.

"I attacked him," she confessed. "I thought he was hiding something about, well, everything. I just... I didn't..."

It was as if every fiber of her being broke down. The strong woman she had been gave way to the desperate mother she'd become, helpless to save her own little girl. She attempted to speak, but no audible words came out. Her knees gave way, but she did not fall. Gabe caught her and held her close.

"I know, Debra," he said sympathetically. "I know."

"You have much to explain, Ivan," Randall stated.

"I'm sure I do. It was my understanding, however, that our past was to remain in the past. I will hold you to that for just a little longer, Randall. I simply pray that you trust me when I tell you that I mean your tribe no harm."

"No," Randall said. "I cannot accept only that, but I will do you the favor of hearing your confession privately.

For the safety of this tribe at a time when elves wish us dead, I will hear the truth about who you are."

"I suppose I can agree to that," Ivan said.

"I will be present as well," Nikiatis broke in.

"Nikiatis..." Randall began, but then he stopped.

Everyone grew still. There was a sound, movement, from deeper in the wounds. It had not come from the direction of the waterfalls but from the part of Greysong that extended northward. Weapons were drawn, and they waited. The sound grew closer. Was it a wolf or a man? An elf would not make such racket, but something did indeed approach. Then it barked.

"Pillar?" Tramin said with a forbidden hope in his voice.

The dog limped through the trees, and Tramin ran to him. They thought they'd lost Pillar lost during the wildman raid, and Debra couldn't believe that he had somehow followed their scent. Then Tramin shouted and leapt into the woods.

Debra watched, unsure of what to expect. Then Tramin returned with a battered and famished little girl in his arms. Life shot through Debra as she ran to them and wrapped Jillian in her arms. They sobbed together, their nightmare finally over, but others were not so fortunate. She could hear Gabe, Trent, and Randall tearing through the woods, shouting the names of their children, but they received no reply. Nikiatis was somewhere above them, scanning the trees.

Debra was suddenly aware of a second person clinging to her. Joshua was crying, holding onto Jillian's sleeve, and so she pulled him into the hug as well.

"Thank you. Thank you," she heard him repeating as if it were a prayer. Perhaps it was.

Jillian was desperately grasping the heart-shaped stone that Payson had engraved for her. Debra was already overwhelmed, but the view of Jillian clinging to her father's last gift was nearly too much for her to bear. She squeezed her daughter even tighter.

"How did you escape, little one?" Ivan asked.

He knelt beside Debra, who felt uncomfortable in his presence, but at least they weren't alone. Tramin stood beside him, holding Pillar as if the large dog were a child.

Jillian pointed at Pillar. "Kris saved us. Then I followed Pillar through the forest."

Tramin laughed and held the dog tighter.

"That's a very good dog," he whispered into Pillar's ear.

"And what of the others?" Ivan asked.

"I don't know," she answered.

"Was Kris able to save them?" asked Tramin.

"No," she answered. "They were taken."

Ivan was about to ask another question but Debra stopped him and stood, still holding Jillian in her arms.

"She needs food and water."

Ivan nodded reluctantly.

"Let's get Jillian and Pillar taken care of," Tramin said. "Then we can follow their trail to where Kris freed them, and from there we can look for a proper path to the prison. We can still save everyone if we hurry."

Debra headed for the falls and prayed with every step. She thanked God for His favor and held Jillian tighter than ever before.

"It's alright," she whispered into Jillian's ear. "I have you. Mommy has you."

"I love you, Mom," Jillian mumbled through tired lips.

Debra held back the tears that nearly overwhelmed her again.

"I love you too. Now rest, baby. You're safe."

Fagunol watched Shëlin curiously. She had been studying Vetcalf's condition while keeping an ear to the wind when she suddenly shouted and ran from the cave. He found her standing on the walkway overlooking the trees. She was crying.

"Shëlin?" he said softly.

She whispered something that sounded elvish. She faced him after he called her name again, but then she looked over his shoulder to where Vetcalf rested. She laughed and wiped away the tears that flowed.

"I am sorry, my friend," she said while composing herself.

She was often so serious that Fagunol found himself stricken by her laughter. It was beautiful. These were happy tears.

"What has happened? What have you heard?" he asked.

"Jillian's back. Pillar led her home," she pointed a thumb toward the cave, "and Vetcalf has awakened." She took a breath and wiped more tears from her eyes. "It is a day of miracles, my golden friend."

Then she said something softly, just barely loud enough for Fagunol to hear.

"I am not alone."

What did she mean by this? He had never seen a more unified people than these. None were belittled or looked down upon. None were cast aside in favor of the more superior members. He was curious what she meant but decided not to delve into it.

"Should you go to them?" he finally asked.

"Debra and Tramin are bringing them here. Vetcalf is well enough for the moment. They'll need food and water."

She began to cry again, and without thinking, Vetcalf wrapped his arms around her and held her close. He was gentle, and she smiled when he released her.

"Thank you for that," she said before turning away.

He watched as she made her way to the other cave, and then he turned his attention toward the river. He saw Debra and Tramin walking along the shore a moment later with a little girl and the dog in their arms. They were both crying. Joshua was with them. Nikiatis was on his way back as well. He took a breath and rejoined Vetcalf, who watched him curiously. The blue birdman held up a weak hand, so Fagunol took it.

"Vetcalf, my friend," he said as Nikiatis entered the cave and froze at the sight of them. "We've awakened in the midst of the most amazing people."

"So you are an elf?"

Randall leaned against a tree, watching as Ivan tended the wounds given to him by Debra and Nikiatis. The mysterious hooded figure did not answer at first. He finished what he was doing, washed in the stream, and then considered Randall's question.

"I was born an elf, yes."

"And why did you not tell us this?"

"I've kept my heritage a secret for decades. There was no reason to reveal it to you. Do know, however, that my kin and I have rejected each other and gone our separate ways. I am merely a vagabond now."

"And why were you rejected?"

Ivan took a deep breath and seemed to deeply consider his answer. Randall wondered if he was concocting a lie.

"I fear you would find the whole story unbelievable, but I can share the portion that you would believe."

"That might be for the best. We don't have long before our meeting with Nikiatis regarding the mission. Be as brief as you can."

"I will try." Ivan paused a moment, considering how to begin. "I've never shared the opinion that elves were a superior race, and because of that I was labeled a threat." He took a breath. Randall sensed that Ivan was skipping a large portion of the story. "It wasn't that I had any great love for humanity—I was as disappointed by their actions as any other—but I worried for my kin. I feared that their hatred would lead them down a path similar to the one that nearly destroyed the world, and I wished to stop it."

"I can understand that," Randall said.

"I'm sure you can. Anyhow, I wandered alone for a time but eventually found a home, surprisingly, amongst men. I'm sure you remember that I was familiar with Silus Rook's death."

The memory struck Randall. "You belonged to Refuge?"

"Yes, when it was young. Silus Rook could be quite persuasive. He found me and brought me in, though I did not share your faith, and I remained there in secret as to not cause panic among the people. Silus kept me busy with new ideas and intellectual debates. I found him interesting." He took a breath and lowered his hood. "I tried to save Silus. I fought off the elves and dove into the pyre that killed him, and I was lit aflame for it. As you can see, the scars last to this day."

"You were disfigured by the fire that killed Silus?"

"I was. The flames burnt away my elven flesh, so I swore off my heritage and became my own person apart from any race. And so I have wandered alone for forty-some years as you see me now, having adopted the name *Ivan Shaymolin.*"

"And your given name?"

"Is irrelevant."

Randall began to pace. He considered an old memory, one that he had long questioned the authenticity of. Having heard Ivan's story, he no longer questioned it.

"You saved my life," he said. "I remember being rescued by an elf while Refuge burned. You pointed me toward Rand Medair'yin."

Ivan laughed humorlessly.

"It's possible. You would have been a small boy at the time, but I did lead one or two to safety."

"Thank you."

Ivan did not reply. The words seemed to hit a nerve, but he shook it off. He replaced the black hood and looked out over the trees toward Uuron Plauf.

"I was recently found by another man. His name is Arick Kasdan. He stumbled across my camp not too long ago, and I nearly slew those with him, but Kasdan was persuasive. He wasn't as simple as most men are or pompous like the birdmen. Like you, he thought I was human, and I allowed him to continue believing that.

"He talked about reunifying the race of man. I explained that such a goal had been attempted before, referring to your Refuge, and that it had failed miserably. But there was just something that attracted me to Arick Kasdan's dream. He was a stronger leader than Silus Rook for one, and he had a clearer vision. I demanded that he and his men leave, but after further consideration, I saw that Kasdan had the potential to achieve his dream. If the race of man were to unify, then they could potentially overthrow Kïer. His oppression would be lifted. The world could grow again as it had when the elves first came, before their hatred blinded them."

Randall felt a sudden pang in his gut, and sweat beaded on his forehead. He heard an old, horrible voice echoing in the back of his mind.

"And so you joined his tribe?" he asked.

"No, but I tracked him to this forest and gave him the opportunity to persuade me further."

"Arick Kasdan lives in Greysong?"

"I gathered that he was visiting the forest, but I know not where he lay his head. We were discovered by elves soon after I'd found him, and we were all imprisoned."

"Were Kasdan and his men executed?"

"Not as of my escape. A guard had boastfully informed me that we were to be dealt with after Uuron Plauf's fall. That was how I discovered the extermination order. I later fought my way to freedom and ended up in your camp."

"And you stumbled across us by sheer chance?"

"No, not chance," Ivan confessed. "The prison is on the ledge of an old building in disarray. I have the eyes of an elf, remember, and saw smoke rising faintly in the distance. I knew not to whom the campfire belonged, but

I wandered in the smoke's general direction after my escape."

Randall nodded. This was all very interesting, but was it the true?

"Why didn't other elves see our campfires?"

"They were too focused on Uuron Plauf to notice anything else, and I got the impression that they hadn't been there long. The prison ledge faced south, and there wasn't much more for me to do than stare. Even so, the distance and the smoke's faintness nearly escaped my notice as well."

"And this Arick Kasdan... he is still there?"

"That is my hope, yes."

"Then Angela and the rest might not be alone."

"It is hard to say, but for the sake of your tribe, for your entire race, Arick Kasdan must be saved."

"Why for the sake of my race? Is Arick Kasdan that important?"

The pain in Randall's stomach was intensifying. The voice was growing louder.

"Mankind will be lucky to see three or more generations before disappearing altogether. If they do not unify and defend themselves, many of today's elves will witness the last fall of man—and they will cheer. But that time has not yet come. If mankind has any hope of surviving, of rising up, it will be under the banner of Arick Kasdan. He must…be…saved!"

Randall's stomach lurched, and he vomited. He felt ill, but that alone hadn't caused him to be sick; rather, it was because everything in Ivan's story felt so horrifyingly familiar. Randall's body shook, and with despair he recalled the words spoken by his late wife as blood ran from her eyes. The voice that proceeded from her mouth screamed in his memory.

"Upon broken ledge Refuge begins their descent, and war is soon to follow. The one who takes the throne shall strive to surpass the last. With a forked tongue evil is halted, but only for a while. It comes again. So speak the gri'ori."

Part VI: The Prison Ledge

Orlan rolled over with hopes of finding some as of yet unfound comfort, but it was no use. Sleeping on this hard, flat floor just wasn't happening. He sat up with a groan and rubbed his neck.

"If you think the floor's hard now, try sleeping on it at my age," said the elder man sitting beside him.

Palin Marick was one of the four men who had already been imprisoned by the time Orlan arrived and the one who kindly welcomed them as they stepped through the gate. He was short of stature with a gray ring of hair from ear to ear. Despite his obviously deprived diet, his spirits were high.

Palin was kind enough to use some sort of ointment, which he had hidden in his belt, to treat their wounds. The ointment, grëoform, was apparently made from a plant found in Kïer's northern territory, Amon-Göl, and it was amazing. Palin didn't explain how they got ahold of the plant, but all four men had a pouch hidden somewhere on their person.

Kris and Angela were still sleeping, her snuggling next to him. Orlan had accepted the fact that she was in love with Kris and that he would never be more to her than a dear friend. This was becoming more apparent as their imprisonment dragged on. He wondered if Kris saw what he saw. Was he aware of Angela's advances, or was she just throwing her emotions to the wind?

Benjamin didn't look quite asleep, but he was close enough to not disturb. The boy had been awfully quiet since their arrival, speaking only when spoken to, and seemed to be praying a lot. Trent would have been proud.

The other three men were scattered about. Two who Palin introduced as William Danes and Jon Profit sat on the ledge of the prison, constantly watching the forest below. They were hoping for assistance, though in what form Palin would not reveal. They didn't trust the ears of the elven guards and were wise not to do so. The fourth man introduced himself as Arick Kasdan, though he spent most of his time speaking to the giant.

Yes, there was a giant in the prison. Orlan couldn't believe his eyes when he had seen it.

It was believed that giants had descended from the tallest mountains after the Fall of Man and took humanity's side in their war against the elves. The elves feared the giants' strength and destroyed them before they could truly unify, stunting any other aid that might have come to humanity's defense. Rumor had it that the giants had since become extinct, but Orlan never believed in giants to begin with. He considered them myth like the gri'ori and the legendary Tröbin-Dur. He believed now.

There it sat, gray and bald with indentations where its eyes should have been and no nose, just as the stories described them. This one was a stone giant, the reason being that its skin was made of dense rock. And it was huge. He couldn't determine the creature's full height, as it hadn't stood since their arrival, but he guessed it to be about ten feet or more, maybe taller, and full of muscle. Orlan could stand beside both Kris and Angela and they still wouldn't be as wide as the creature's chest and shoulders. It was an intimidating beast. Orlan could see why the elves would have feared them.

The giant would not speak to them, only to Arick Kasdan who had apparently been building its trust since he first arrived. Orlan had no idea what the creature and Arick discussed, but he was certainly curious. Besides the giant and the four men, the prison ledge also held the four wildmen, several lizard-like creatures that Orlan wasn't familiar with, and Maximus the hunter.

Maximus remained apart from the other prisoners and never seemed to sleep. His eyes never closed. He watched every inch of movement that took place on the prison's ledge, but he hadn't spoken since they first arrived. Jon Profit eventually cursed him and invited the wildmen to eat him in his sleep. Jon seemed snippy like that.

But honestly, the past two days were rather uneventful. He had seen Adviser-Mondel once, who yelled at the guards for imprisoning Maximus, but they laughed and threatened to throw him in as well. Mondel left but not before offering Angela another lustful glance. That was hours ago.

And now Orlan watched as Mondel returned for more verbal sparring.

"Can we help you, Adviser?" the Master of the Guard asked.

"You know why I'm here, Master-Sölva," Mondel replied. "I've come for the hunter on Dömin-Mathew O'lor's order."

Sölva laughed. It was obvious that Sölva, like most elves, had no respect for mankind, not even for those in Kïer's service.

"I am sorry," he replied, "but the Dömin's orders do not overrule those given by the General of Vlörinclad. General-Devin-Brek has ordered that the hunter remain until further notice."

Orlan turned his ear a little closer. He had noticed that there were two different emblems on the guards' armor, one a blue flame—the symbol of the Northwest Tower of Räthinock—and a green fist that he didn't recognize. It was now apparent that the green fist belonged to Räthinock's neighboring tower, Vlörinclad. Both towers had apparently been involved in Uuron Plauf's downfall.

Mondel smiled, but his nervousness was apparent.

"You are aware," he said," that Maximus is an O'lor?"

Orlan caught Sölva's hesitation. He had heard the O'lor name but didn't know whether what he'd heard about it was true or not. He wondered if perhaps it was.

Sölva looked at his guards, all of which seemed bewildered, and then he looked at the cage separating the partially covered wing of the prison from the open-ended ledge. Orlan followed his eyes and found Maximus staring at the ground with a wide, closed-lipped grin.

"I..." Sölva stumbled, "I was not aware of his lineage."

"He is Dömin-Mathew O'lor's cousin, and as you know, we O'lors are protected by Kïer Law."

So it was true. Orlan had heard a little of how Kïer kept one family of humans, the O'lors, as a servant slave class. They were looked upon as the ultimate traitors to their race for serving Kïer willingly, though Orlan was led to believe that the O'lors were a mistreated people. If this Mathew O'lor had somehow attained the high-ranking position of Dömin, then perhaps Orlan hadn't heard the whole story.

Sölva stuttered a few words and finally cursed in elvish. He nodded to the nearest guard and refused to look Maximus in the eye as the gate opened. Maximus, however, just tipped his hat and motioned toward his coat. The elves gave the coat and all the weapons they had removed from it back to its owner.

"Thank you for your cooperation," Mondel said, and they turned to go.

Sölva screamed at his guards once the two men had gone, and it was obvious that he was both furious and frightened.

"Where is Captain-Ecsheli? I need to speak with General-Devin-Brek immediately. Get Elya up here now!"

Several elves vanished through the door and down the stairway.

"Well that was interesting," Kris said.

He and Angela sat up. They had apparently awakened during the exchange. William and Jon joined them from the ledge.

"So the hunter was an O'lor," Jon said spitefully. "I should have thrown him over the ledge when I had the chance."

"What's an O'lor?" Benjamin asked. He had also been awakened by Sölva's yelling.

Palin was about to speak but then paused and motioned for William Danes to explain. William grew excited which struck Orlan as peculiar.

"As the story goes," William began, "O'lor was the name of a powerful leader from before the Fall of Man. He was one of those responsible for leading the world to ruin, and he grew bitter when the elves reversed the damage he and his fellow leaders had caused. He felt that the elves' intervention made humanity's remnant appear weak, so he challenged the elves with the intent of proving mankind's superiority. He and his meager forces were defeated, and as a means of punishment, Kïer made O'lor his servant and readily abused and humiliated him.

"Though he had a hand in the Fall of Man, O'lor still had a great amount of love for his people and watched in horror as they were hunted down and killed. He grew old and frail, but he never let go of his pride, resisting Kïer as often as possible. Due to this, Kïer decreed that his punishment be made generational so that all O'lors would suffer their ancestor's fate. O'lor died, and his oldest son became Kïer's servant. His other descendants were divided among elven officials and were equally humiliated, as were their children and their grandchildren. And now to this very day, the O'lor line serves Kïer as a slave class, punishment for their ancestor's unwavering pride and resentment."

"But why would Kïer enslave the O'lors for so long?" Angela asked. "Why not just kill them?"

"It was a part of Kïer's original decree," William answered. "The O'lor line must serve the elves until their natural end. Now, as we know, elves live three times longer than humans, so generations of O'lors mean as much to them as generations of dogs to us. They were eventually bred and distributed until O'lors served the entire elven race."

Olan held up a hand.

"If they were meant to serve, then how did Mathew O'lor become a Dömin?"

"Or Mondel an Adviser?" Kris added.

William smiled and leaned into the story. "That's because things changed, to the bewilderment of many. Sometime after his celestial ascension, Kïer made a new decree. The O'lor line was to remain servants, but he would occasionally promote one or two above the elves in such roles as Captain or Adviser. Now, I've never heard of an O'lor reaching the rank of Dömin Adviser, which is Adviser-Mondel's official rank, or even Master of the Guard, let alone a full-fledged Dömin. But I suppose it's possible."

Orlan found William's story fascinating, but it still didn't answer his question. Not really. Why would Kïer issue such a decree? He was about to ask this when William continued his tale.

"The elves, of course, were infuriated by this, but they feared Kïer and dared not question him. It is rumored that he places O'lors in positions of power to keep the elves on their toes, to keep them from getting lazy. Imagine the mindset of an elf having to serve under a human; they would do everything in their power to surpass the O'lor. It is believed, and I believe, that Kïer placed O'lors in positions of power to keep his elves angry."

"Angry?" Angela asked.

"At mankind. O'lors rising in power fuels the hate that the elves feel toward humanity, but they were ordered never to harm an O'lor. Therefore, the elves must overcome in other ways such as surpassing them in rank through discipline and deceit."

"And what if they do harm an O'lor?" Orlan asked.

"Kïer sends the Kïen after them. That's why Sölva was so furious after learning about Maximus' lineage. He was afraid."

Orlan didn't need to hear about the Kïen. They were Kïer's personal subjects and the only ones worthy enough to stand in his celestial presence after the ascension. They were his voice and hands. Some believed that the gri'ori myth was based on the Kïen, but Orlan tried not to think about it.

"Why should Sölva worry?" Kris asked. "Maximus left his lineage behind when he became a hunter. I can't imagine he'd still be protected under the O'lor name."

"Perhaps," Palin broke in, "but he serves an O'lor who is very important. We have been watching a great deal since being imprisoned, and it is obvious that Mathew O'lor favors his cousin."

Kris and Orlan exchanged glances. This was all very interesting, but Orlan felt very far out of his depth. Kris, however, seemed to be drinking in every word.

"So," Kris asked, "what can you tell us about this Mathew O'lor?"

"I can tell you this," Jon piped in, "if I ever find him while I have a sword in my hand he'll be half the O'lor he once was."

"You, my friend," Palin said with a faint smile, "are of little help. And sadly, that is all the help I will be in answering your question. What I do know is that Mathew O'lor served just below General-Dägin-Bok as his Dömin of Intelligence."

"And Dägin lost his head when his people attacked us," Jon added with a prideful grin. "I held it in my own hands."

"Yes," Palin agreed. It seemed to Orlan that Palin was becoming tired of Jon's fiery interruptions. "With Dägin-Bok dead, that left a gap in Räthinock's leadership. His Dömin of Forces, an elf named Vlö-Bek, was killed during the raid on Uuron Plauf, so Mathew O'lor has been acting as General ever since. I assume that his being in charge is what brought General-Devin-Brek to the prison. You see, as neighboring towers, Räthinock and Vlörinclad must work closely together, and Devin-Brek hates all humanity, especially O'lors. The idea of an O'lor being his Räthinockian equal likely spurned Devin-Brek to action. I suspect that he's come to assume leadership of the whole operation as his rank would allow."

"And who ranks above Devin-Brek?" Kris asked. "Who would be the one to assign a new General to Räthinock?"

"The Kïen serve over the towers, and as I said before, they are Kïer's voice and hands. So Kïer will ultimately decide."

"Should we expect the Kïen to show up?" Orlan asked.

Palin sighed, and Orlan saw the weariness in his tired expression.

"I do not know," he said, "but I certainly hope not. I fear our lives would become forfeit if one of the Kïen arrive, and I long to kiss my wife one last time."

It was a lonely place for an O'lor being above so many. His superiors hated him, and his subjects longed for his death but feared to supply it. For this reason Mathew O'lor had sent his Adviser, a distant nephew, to retrieve Maximus.

Mathew and Maximus had known each other since childhood when their fathers served together under the General of Dësinbok. While they learned how to serve the elves, they also found time to play, as O'lor children often did if they were crafty enough. When Mathew wasn't playing with Maximus, he was learning from his father, Nathan O'lor. Mathew's father was often mistreated by his master but never bowed to the elves; he challenged them, just as that stubborn O'lor had centuries before. Aaron O'lor—Nathan's brother and Maximus' father—had done the same. Mathew and Maximus adored their fathers for their strength and loyalty to each other.

It wasn't until Aaron O'lor died at the hands of their master that Nathan's will finally broke. Fearing for his life, Nathan begged the Kïen named Sheligog to take him as a servant. Sheligog slew the General of Dësinbok for his crime against the O'lors and left with Nathan in tow, leaving the two boys orphaned and abandoned.

They carried Aaron O'lor's body from the tower under the cover of darkness and buried him beneath a tree in Dësinbok's southern territory. There were no songs or prayers, only bile and venom. Mathew had attempted to reason with Maximus, but his cousin was far too angry to keep playing the elves' game, and so after a brief argument, Maximus rebelled against his O'lor heritage by declaring himself a hunter. The cousins said their goodbyes and Maximus left Dësinbok, forgotten in the confusion of his father's death and the General's punishment.

The hatred that Mathew felt following his father's desertion motivated him to become more than a slave. He vowed to embrace the true strength of the O'lor name, a strength that he had once seen in his father, but he would not rebel. He was far too wise for that. Mathew grew strong, not in arm or pride, but in reason. He became an invaluable help to the elves and was eventually rewarded by becoming the lowest of Advisers. That was only the beginning. He had moved himself through several promotions since then; from Adviser to Dömin Adviser to Dömin of Intelligence. He had further aspirations.

Maximus the hunter found tutelage and gained notoriety by the strength of his arm. Despite the hatred he felt for elves, he played the hunter game properly, and many found his talents admirable. Having heard of his cousin's success, Mathew searched out Maximus, and they were reunited again after a fifteen-year separation. At that moment they made a pact to protect each other, to be the friend that each needed in a world that wanted them dead.

Truth be told, if Maximus wasn't under Mathew's thumb, he would have likely been killed long ago. The hunter's tolerance for the elves was waning, and his tongue had become far too loose. Fortunately, the cousins had an agreement. Maximus was to work for Mathew, being paid handsomely in the process, and Mathew kept Maximus safe, as Maximus was no longer protected by the O'lor name. This was a fact apparently forgotten by Sölva, Master of the Guard. Mathew expected as much. Sölva was an idiot.

"General-Mathew O'lor," a guard called from the door.

"Dömin will suffice. I am only acting as General until a proper replacement can be found."

"A you wish, Dömin. Adviser-Mondel has arrived, and he has the hunter with him."

"Good, send them in and leave us."

The elf bowed, and Mathew could see how much it pained him. The two O'lors entered a moment later.

"Thank you, Mondel," he said. "And try to be more careful, Maximus. I cannot save you if you continue treating elves in this manner."

The hunter grunted as he inventoried his replenished coat. "I'll see what I can do."

"I am serious!"

"Listen, Mathew," Maximus said sternly. "We have a deal. I kill or capture whoever you ask, and you keep your little elf friends off my back."

"And if you continue speaking rudely to them," Mondel chimed in, "we'll all have our spines handed to us on plates."

Maximus laughed loudly and plopped himself into a chair. "It's ironic that you would mention spines, Mondel, as you seem to lack one. I will not cower as you do."

"It is not cowardice to...!"

"Enough of this nonsense," Mathew said before Mondel's quickly reddening face emitted words he'd likely pay for. "Let's put this behind us and move forward. I'm told that there was only one confirmed death in the wildman raid. I am displeased by this, but enough damage was done to drive the point. We have their children, we killed one of their women, and we sent them fleeing for their lives. What of the birdmen you saw?"

"I only saw one," Maximus answered, "the white king. The wildmen claimed to have seen an injured golden one as well. A blue one was also spotted, but it might have been dead. They weren't sure."

"Only three?" he asked.

"That was all. Three birdmen will not regrow the race. The extermination was a success."

"Good. I'll need this information. Devin-Brek is seeking to deface me, and I need to show good numbers if Sheligog arrives."

"He is coming here?" Mondel asked timidly.

"Devin-Brek seems to think it's a possibility. If I am to become General, then we will need to exaggerate our success. So we tell them that the tribe's number was greater than it was, nearing seventy by the wildmen's count, and that we killed an estimated ninety percent of them. We took several young prisoners to learn why they interfered in Uuron Plauf and sent the few who survived fleeing for their lives. And there were no birdmen there. The extermination of Uuron Plauf was complete."

"Very well," Mondel replied.

Maximus simply nodded.

"Now, bring me the newest human prisoners one-by-one, beginning with the two men, then the woman, then the child. He will unknowingly reveal the others' lies."

"At once," Mondel said and left the room.

"So how long do you plan on keeping them alive?" Maximus asked.

Mathew simply shrugged. "Until I've learned enough. Then the elves can have them."

"I might not be as *wise* as you and your little Adviser," Maximus said with mild sarcasm, "but a little piece of advice: be quick. You've already kept the other four alive for far too long. Save these and you'll look like a human sympathizer."

"I am aware of what it looks like. I have no desire to keep these new ones alive beyond today, but there's just something about the original four. They're hiding something, and I *will* learn what that secret is. Until then, let's just focus on this newer group. I want to dispose of them quickly."

"Good man."

Devin-Brek would work hard to hinder his promotion, Mathew knew, just as General-Dägin-Bok and Dömin-Vlö-Bek had tried to do. They hated him, and the feeling was mutual. Mathew had advanced further than any O'lor before him, and he wasn't finished yet; he wanted the General title. Only then would he be content—possibly.

Vlö-Bek, Räthinock's Dömin of Forces, had challenged him daily and attempted to slay him in the confusion of Uuron Plauf. Mathew survived, and the elf reaped what he had sown with a knife through the throat. Mathew surmised that Dägin-Bok had arranged the assassination attempt but couldn't prove it. Fortunately, Arick Kasdan and his men had taken care of the General for him. He owed them a debt which would never be repaid. General-Devin-Brek was sure to bring the prisoners to Sheligog's attention, and so they had to be dealt with sooner rather than later.

There was no room for error, he knew. Not in the presence of the Kïen.

"Are we going to be okay, Kris?" Angela asked.

She was a strong young woman, but her strength was fading and she needed reassurance. Kris, however, sat beside her, drawing circles and squares on the dusty floor, completely lost in his own thoughts.

"Kris?"

"Not right now, Angela."

She wanted to get into his head, figure out what he was thinking, but he was too focused on other things to pay her any attention. She typically hated when he got like this, but he was likely coming up with some plan of escape, so she forgave him. Deciding that it would be best to give him space, she scooted closer to Orlan and listened in as he spoke with Palin Marick. She was surprised to find that they were whispering Ivan Shaymolin's name.

"Ivan?" she asked, joining in.

"I was telling him about all the things leading to our capture," Orlan said, "and he recognized Ivan's description. He's one of theirs."

"Well, somewhat," Palin said. Then he began to whisper so quietly that Angela had to lean in to hear. He was obviously afraid of the elves overhearing. "He was bringing us through Greysong, searching for an old friend of his."

Angela looked across to where Arick Kasdan sat with the giant.

"No, not the giant," Palin said, "though the rumor of a giant sighting was what drew us to this part of the forest. It had been captured already by the time we arrived, and we likely wouldn't have found it at all if not for fate bringing us all together. No, Ivan was leading us to a willow."

"A what?" she asked.

Orlan seemed just as unsure.

"They aren't well known in this day and age, but the willows were integral in the salvation of our world. They worked with the elves for a time, but what's become of them since then no one knows; though, William has some related stories that he likes to tell. As you saw earlier, William fancies himself a storyteller. Worthless talent if you ask me. I'll take fact over myth any day."

"Did you find the willow?" Orlan asked.

"Surprisingly, yes, just as the elves attacked us. I don't know what became of the willow, but I assume she fled. We never even got a chance to speak with her."

"What is a willow exactly?" Angela asked.

"A woman of the forest was how Ivan described her. William's told stories of how they control trees with lullabies, but it sounds like rubbish to me. She was an interesting sight, though."

Angela shook her head in amazement. Giants. Willows. What else would she discover in this prison?

"And what about those lizard people by the fence?" Orlan asked.

"Ah, those. Tell me, how many do you see?

"Four," Orlan answered.

"There are seven by my count."

Angela was confused at first, but then she saw them. The back foot of one creature seemed to be missing. She could barely make it out, blending in with the gray floor, and that revealed the others. Three more lizards clung to the fence, their skin matching the rusted zigzag pattern of its links.

"They blend in with their surroundings," she said to herself, "like chameleons."

"And that is precisely what they are—chameleons. It is my belief that they were engineered by human scientists from before the Fall of Man, as weapons of war perhaps. William thinks that they're the product of old world radiation. No one knows for sure."

"Are they dangerous?" Angela asked.

"Yes. Keep your distance. I assume they are prisoners like us, but you never know. They are a mystery to me, and they do not speak as we do, so I cannot learn from them. For now, we must treat them as if they were in league with the elves."

Angela studied the creatures and felt a slight chill. They were ugly, very ugly. She couldn't determine their true color, as they were all different shades, but she could see their claws, which were long and sharp. One looked at her, and she turned away.

"So Ivan," Orlan said. "How did he escape?"

"I'm not sure to be honest. He was taken from the ledge and never returned. We assumed he'd been killed until Jon spotted him weaving through the trees below. His escape brings us hope, though hope must hasten if it is to do us any good. Devin-Brek's arrival quickens our fate, which is why Jon and William keep watch. If we are still here when the Kïen arrive, and I believe one is coming, then all will be lost."

"Are there other members to your tribe?" Angela asked.

"There is hope there too."

Palin's answer was vague but enough. Angela and Orlan exchanged a glance, and they seemed to be thinking the same thing: there were others who could rescue them, even if their own tribe could not. There was still hope.

"Was Ivan injured when he left?" Orlan asked. "Was his side gashed?"

"We were all hurt when we arrived, though it was nothing a little grëoform couldn't handle. He was whole when last I saw him."

"Then he must have been wounded during his escape or soon after while in the woods," Orlan reasoned.

"Perhaps," Palin said with a shrug. "Now..."

Footsteps preceded Adviser-Mondel's arrival. Elya-Ecsheli and several other dark-haired elves arrived with him.

"It's about time," Sölva said. "You're in charge, Elya. I have to find General-Devin-Brek."

Elya gave Sölva a curious glance. "Why go to a Vlörinclad General when you are an elf of Räthinock? Is Dömin-Mathew O'lor not our General now?"

"Not yet, and even if he was, I would die before serving an O'lor. I'll skewer him myself." Sölva spat and ran from the prison as if Kïer himself was after him.

"Then to you, Captain," Mondel said. "Dömin-Mathew O'lor requires an audience with one of the two young men."

"I see."

The elf peered at the prisoners and smiled, motioning for someone to come forward. Kris and Orlan glanced at each other, unsure of what to do.

"You," he said, pointing at Orlan.

"No," Kris said. "I'll go."

He stood and willingly came to the fence. The guards opened it and let him out as the chameleons hissed. Angela watched as Kris was led from the prison, and she began to cry.

"He'll be fine," Orlan said, putting an arm around her.

"We don't know that."

Orlan's composure broke a bit, so he held her close. He had always been a good friend, but she needed more right now. She needed Kris.

Mathew stood in the room that he had been using for interrogations and breathed deeply. Days-old smoke rose from the ruins of Uuron Plauf, and it felt good knowing that he had helped achieve that victory. It felt even better knowing that he could and would claim the victory as his own after the deaths of General-Dägin-Bok and Vlö-Bek, Räthinock's Dömin of Forces. He watched the smoke through a window and imagined how his improbable but well-deserved promotion to General would infuriate the Elven Nation. Their imagined displeasure brought him a certain amount of joy.

Then he felt the hollow ringing in his ears. It was dim at first, barely noticeable, but the ringing soon blared and his head felt as if it could explode. He was not excited for what was to come. He closed his eyes as the sensation built, and then they went cold. Sheligog of the Kïen had broken through his mind.

"I am here," Mathew said plainly.

"Good," spoke a voice in his head.

Mathew built his reputation through hard work and determination. He was not fond of the magic that Sheligog studied, and he hated when the Kïen used it to see through his eyes. He kept his thoughts guarded in case the Kïen was listening to more than just his words.

"I have sent my servant ahead to prepare for my coming," Sheligog said. "We will discuss Räthinock's affairs when I arrive. But first, what is the latest regarding Uuron Plauf and those who infiltrated it?"

Mathew held his head high and spoke with as much pride as he could realistically muster.

"The extermination is complete; no birdmen were left alive. We are letting their corpses rot as a sign to others who gather in too great a number. As for the men who aided them, based on reports from the wildmen, their number was northward of seventy, but we killed perhaps ninety percent of them. We've taken several captive for informational purposes, and the few who survived fled to spread word of what happens when you interfere with Kïer's will."

"Very good," Sheligog said. "What have you learned from them thus far?"

"The first is on his way up now. I will keep you posted."

"See that you do."

The coldness faded in the silence that followed. He rubbed his eyes. They always burned after being violated by Sheligog's mind. When he opened them again, he saw Mondel in the doorway with one of the prisoners.

"Come in," Mathew said with a smile. "What is your name?"

"My name is Kris Medair'yin, sir," the boy answered without hesitation.

"And why was it that your tribe chose to hinder the work of Kïer's hands?"

"Because it was the right thing to do."

"And who is to say what is right and what is wrong?"

"Thou shall not kill," he replied.

"What?"

Mathew was dumbfounded. What did the young man mean by this statement? Was it a command? Was the boy threatening him? Mathew didn't like being threatened. He marched forward and smacked Kris with the back of his hand so that Kris fell to the floor. Then Mathew unsheathed his sword and pressed its point against the back of Kris' head and pushed down just hard enough to make the boy squirm, barely piercing his scalp.

"Threaten me again, boy, and I will pin you to the floor for the next to see. Do you understand?"

"I was not threatening you," Kris said through clenched teeth.

"Attempting to give a Dömin an order is just as punishable a crime."

"I gave no such thing. You asked a question, and I answered it."

Mathew gave a pause and looked at Mondel, who seemed just as uncertain. He sheathed his sword and backed away. His hand, however, remained on the hilt.

"To your knees and explain yourself."

Kris did as he was told and began quoting a series of commands, most of which beginning with the word *thou*.

Mathew had never heard of the word but gathered that it meant *you*.

"Stand up and explain these rules to me."

Kris stood, looked at Mathew and Mondel wearily, and nodded.

"They are the premise of our tribe. We have no intention of challenging Kier, but we feel that it was wrong of you to exterminate the birdmen. We wanted to save as many as we could."

"So the commands are a code that you live by? Then why did you kill so many wildmen? Why not let them kill you and keep your integrity?"

"We were protecting ourselves, but I now mourn their passing as it is obvious that they were merely pawns."

"My, my—how soft-hearted of you," Mathew replied, uninterested in Kris' compassion. "And how did you come up with these ridiculous rules?"

"Through the teachings of our elders, recited from a book long ago destroyed."

"And the name of this book?"

"The Holy Bible."

Mathew paused. That title rang a bell somewhere in the recesses of his mind. He'd heard of it. Had he seen its spine in the archives?

"The old religious book?" Mondel asked, sparking Mathew's memory. The Adviser began to laugh. "So they are not rules; they are your religion!"

Mathew couldn't help but smile himself. Religion was discarded long before the Fall of Man. The thought of this boy embracing one of those old world fairytales tickled Mathew. He laughed alongside Mondel O'lor. "So you worship a god then?"

"We do."

"And it told you to interfere in Kïer's business? Your god certainly is a brave one. Isn't that right, Mondel?"

"Certainly," the Adviser answered with a sarcastic grin.

"We simply live as the teachings instruct. We have no conflict with Kïer."

"That is all good and well, but your statement is flawed. When you challenge an order given by Kïer himself, Kïer suddenly has conflict with you. In fact, Sheligog of the Kïen is on his way here as we speak, and he will likely deal with you personally. You can thank your god for that by the way."

"So be it."

Mathew studied Kris. The boy did not shake or scream as most did when threatened with the Kïen. He simply looked Mathew in the eye and accepted what had been said to him.

"Do you not fear the Kïen?"

"I do not fear death. How it comes is irrelevant."

"Oh, I disagree with that a great deal. But tell me, why do you not fear death?"

"Because I believe in life after death."

What an odd thought that was. It was intriguing to be perfectly honest, this idea of eternal life, but he couldn't allow the boy to leave with such a brave face. Kris needed to be broken as an example to the others.

"Is Maximus near, Mondel?"

"He is resting, I believe."

Mathew cursed beneath his breath. He was going to have to get his hands dirty, but then he had another thought.

"What of the birdman?" he asked.

"Giyavin has returned to Uuron Plauf."

"Feeling regret is he?"

"Perhaps, but officially he is searching for signs of survivors."

"Is Giyavin the green birdman?" Kris interrupted.

"Yes," Mathew replied, "the one who betrayed his people. I suppose I feel a kinship with him for that. Tell me, boy, what do you know of his people? How many did you rescue?"

He could see that the boy was hesitant to answer. This Medair'yin boy had no qualms risking his own skin, but to chance someone else's life was obviously a chore.

"A number, boy."

"Three," he finally said. "Though, it is likely that at least one of them died during the attack. He was already gravely injured."

The white king and the golden one that the wildmen had seen accounted for two. Maximus had mentioned a blue one that might have been dead. The boy was likely telling the truth, as disappointing as that was, but nevertheless, an example needed to be made.

"Very good," he said. "Your cooperation has made what is coming much easier on you. You will live to see your companions again, if only for a little while, but please, bring them this reminder that they are to cooperate as well."

Then he slid the knife into Kris' side.

Kris screamed and fell. Then the boy sobered, half-picked himself up again, and removed the blade. Mathew wondered if he was going to fight back, but he simply set the knife at Mathew's feet and stood as straight as he could. He had tears in his eyes, and sweat beaded his brow. Despite the pain and fear that registered on his face, Kris merely looked into Mathew's eyes and nodded.

"Is that all, sir?" he said as blood ran from his side.

"What a strange young man," Mathew replied, and he motioned for Mondel to take him away.

Kris seemed to slump a bit as he was led through the door. Mathew looked down at the small pool of blood and the drips that led toward the hall and decided to leave them. *Such a sight will loosen the others' tongues.*

The next boy should be along soon.

***

Angela leaned against Orlan as the sky grew dark. The setting sun created a pink and orange sky over the forest, and she wished more than anything that she could be enjoying the view with her father. She wondered how he was handling things. Thinking about her father was the first break she'd taken from worrying about Kris. She was concerned for them both.

"It's pretty," Benjamin said.

He had been lying quietly on the floor beside them. In fact, he had been so silent for so long that she was startled when he spoke.

"It is," she replied.

"I wish we could enjoy it under better circumstances," Orlan said.

"Do you think we'll die here?" Benjamin asked.

Orlan stole a nervous glance at Angela and shook his head.

"No," he whispered. "I think Randall will save us, if not him then maybe Palin's people."

Benjamin considered this before sighing.

"I'm trying to be realistic," he said. "I just don't see it."

"Don't think like that, Benjamin," Angela said pleadingly. She scooted toward him and held him close. "Someone will come. We'll find a way out of this, I promise."

Benjamin nodded, but he could obviously see through her hollow promise. She struggled to believe it herself.

"Who we need," William Danes said, drawing their attention to where he lay, "is Tröbin-Dur."

William had been resting nearby after finishing his shift on the ledge, but now he laughed, sat up, and scooted next to them. He couldn't be much older than Kris, yet there was a youthful vigor to him that Angela found refreshing. His mentioning Tröbin-Dur, however, led her to believe that he might be a tad naive.

"Have you ever heard of Tröbin-Dur?"

"Some," Benjamin admitted.

Nearly everyone had heard of Tröbin-Dur, the legendary elf who betrayed his own kind to save humanity. He was, in essence, the very architect of mankind's continued existence. There were so many different variations of the Tröbin-Dur stories that Angela had never heard the same story told twice, at least, not in the same way. Shëlin knew a few good renditions; Gabe did a good one as well. Unfortunately, stories were all they were. As everyone over the age of ten knew, Tröbin-Dur, like the gri'ori, was a myth.

"Well," William continued, "I fancy myself a bit of a storyteller, so I know a few tales, and since we have nothing else to do I thought I'd share. Would you like to hear one?"

Benjamin shrugged, and Angela couldn't help but to smile just a little.

"He was once left to die in the desert south of Rinwood. Have you heard that one before?"

"No," Orlan said, and Angela laughed. He smiled shyly. Orlan always did love a good story.

"None of us have," she said almost playfully. "You may continue."

"Very good!" William rubbed his hands together in anticipation and made himself comfortable.

"Great," Jon Profit said from the ledge, "someone who hasn't heard this idiot's stories."

Palin, who had taken William's place on the ledge, gave Jon a disapproving glance.

"We could all use a good story," Arick Kasdan said from his place beside the giant. It was one of the few times that Angela had heard him speak.

She scanned the area and saw that several wildmen watched William, though she was certain they couldn't understand what was being said. The chameleons and the giant ignored him completely, but the elves peered at him through the fence. While some seemed curious, the majority grimaced and looked as if their only wish was for the man to stop talking. William paid them no mind, however. He seemed oddly excited.

"It happened long ago while the world was still rebuilding," William began, but Angela interrupted him.

"You forgot to say 'once upon a time.'"

"Oh, I never begin with 'once upon a time.' I feel it cheapens the story, lending to the possibility of it being a fairytale."

She gave him an odd look, but he just shrugged.

"You never know," he said. "What I like most about the old folklores is that we never really know how much truth they're steeped in. The Tröbin-Dur stories are likely myth, but somewhere in those myths are bound to be some form of truth."

Then William smiled and looked over Angela's shoulder at the elves.

"Have any of you met Tröbin-Dur?"

The elves laughed at his stupidity, and Elya merely shook his head.

"Keep your silly stories inside the cage or you might lose your tongue," the Captain said to the mocking approval of his kin.

"See, even the elves aren't sure what to think of the old stories. So I begin my tales as if they were true, because you never know which ones might actually be."

"Then tell the story already and stop risking our lives by making friends with elves," Arick chastised.

Angela caught Elya smiling. The elf apparently found Arick's comment humorous, though she was fairly certain it wasn't intended to be.

"As I was saying, it was long ago, shortly after the elves had come to power. This story, however, takes place in the south before the Elven Nation had reached that far. Therefore, everyone in the story are human men and women.

"As we all know, mankind attempted to rebuild after the wars, before the elves decreed that they be exterminated, and there was one such community just north of what we now call Rinwood Forest. They had lost everything in the war and were rebuilding, but in their hearts, they wished for revenge. They wanted to fight back, to rebuild humanity, and to once again rule the world, but they were much too weak."

"I like this story," Elya said quietly to his fellow guards, and they laughed. William ignored him.

"Then the deaths came," he continued. "Every so often they would hear the howls of a beast in their camp, and when they searched for the howls' origin they would find puddles of blood and missing tribesman. Often they were children but sometimes adults of various ages. They hunted for the creature, believing it to be a wolf or bear, but they never found it.

"By the time Tröbin-Dur had wandered that far south the camp was terrified and exhausted. They were too afraid to move north for fear of the elves, and they feared what hid beneath them to the south. They had lost ten people to the mysterious beast over the course of a year, seven of them children, and never once did the beast leave a clue as to where it came or went. The people didn't hunt; they didn't sleep. They were terrified, and Tröbin-Dur took pity on them."

William gathered a large handful of pebbles that had fallen from the cliffs above and positioned one closed fist above an open palm. The pebbles began to fall one at a time from his fist to his palm like sand through an hourglass.

"The days sweltered—the nights froze—and Tröbin-Dur began earning the trust of the people. For nearly two months he earned their good graces, and then he began training them. Their home was a simple farming community as that was the best they could accomplish in their day, but Tröbin shared with them his wisdom, and they began to flourish and grow prideful. And then the howls returned.

"Tröbin-Dur met with the town's leader in the home of an elder who had gone missing. Blood speckled the wooden walls, but there were no other signs of conflict nor clues as to where the beast had come or gone. For the next three months Tröbin-Dur taught them the art of combat, but despite their training, fear filled their bones.

"And the howls came again. This time it was a child who had gone missing, and Tröbin-Dur told them that they were to hunt the beast to the ends of the earth so that they might save their child, and the men of the tribe agreed. Tröbin-Dur took every able-bodied man who could defend himself into the Rïnwood forest, and night after night, they searched."

William began throwing the pebbles from one hand to the other with a great force, emphasizing his next words.

"At first they were *ready*, they were *angry*; they were *furious* and *thirsty* for the blood of a creature that would snatch children from their beds. But as the days dragged, on they began to lose that focus and grew tired."

The pebbles slowly fell from William's hand, pouring onto the floor, and he gathered them into a pile. Then he ran his finger through the pebbles in a circular motion and continued to do so as he told the story.

"Then one man spoke to his leader and said, 'Why do we follow this elf? Do we not know what he knows? Are we not now his equal? Think, my lord, of what we could do with this knowledge instead of wandering in the woods at night, searching for some little wolf. We could raise an army! We could train soldiers and reclaim what is ours. We could overcome the elves!'

"And the leader asked, 'Who is to say that this Tröbin-Dur isn't the monster we've been hunting all along, only in disguise, making fools out of us?' And then the leader began to contemplate his kin's words.

"As the hot summer days burnt on, more and more of the tribesman took to this way of thinking, and Tröbin-

Dur was unaware of their scorn. Then at the very moment when Tröbin-Dur found an old bloody print, a true sign of the beast, the tribesmen betrayed him. They attacked from behind and beat him with sticks and swords. He was rendered unconscious, and they dragged him to the desert south of Rïnwood. There they dug a hole, stripped him of his garments, and tossed him in. They cursed him for tricking them, for slaying their loved ones, and then they left him there to die without food or water."

Angela looked down and noticed that the pebbles William had been running his finger through were now in a perfect circle, piled about two inches high with a large white stone in the center. He scooped up a few more pebbles and began tossing them into the air so that they fell on Benjamin. Benjamin protected his head with his arms, and Angela could see the faint outline of a smile on the boy's lips.

"Tröbin-Dur stayed in that hole for days," William continued, "baking in the sun and eating any bug that was unfortunate enough to pay him a visit, but he had nothing to drink. He was dehydrated. He was dying, but he still had hope that help would come. None did. And then, when he could stand no more, he shouted to the heavens with a broken, dried voice—and the sky opened."

Suddenly Angela knew why William had chosen this story. She glanced at Orlan, who watched with his mouth slightly ajar. He hadn't put it together yet.

"At first it was just a few drops of rain," William continued, "but then it began to mist. The water cooled his skin, and he opened his mouth to drink and it refreshed him. The mist hardened to a drizzle and then to a steady fall. Before long it was a full-on downpour, and the hole began to fill. Tröbin-Dur was weak, but he clung to his prison's muddy walls until the water lifted him clear to the top. Dehydrated and famished, beaten and bruised, Tröbin-Dur crawled from the hole. He was naked and burnt, but more importantly, he was alive."

William threw what was left of the pebbles into the air, and they fell down on Angela, Orlan, and Benjamin. He did not gather more; he simply smiled and watched Benjamin as he concluded the story.

"He dressed himself in the clothes that had been scattered, and he made his way back to the forest where he hunted and found food. He gathered his strength and returned to the small community only to find that the men who had betrayed him never returned. Some say the beast ate them, a demon in the form of a giant black bear, others believe that it was the gri'ori who hunted those early survivors, but in the end, it was their own pride and stupidity that led to their downfall.

"None can say for sure what became of those men or that southern community, but that doesn't matter, because they were not the story, nor was the beast. The story was Tröbin-Dur and the will he had to make the desert skies break open and carry him to his salvation." William dropped to a whisper. "The moral of the story, young Benjamin, is that you must never give up hope—because you never know when the rain is about to fall."

A chill swept through Angela, and she couldn't help but smile. Orlan actually gave a cheer and then composed himself, seemingly embarrassed by how engrossed he had been in the story.

"What a wonderful tale," Elya said mockingly from his seat, "but expect no rain this day." He laughed, and those with him followed suit.

Benjamin was lost in thought, so Orlan pulled him close. Angela simply nodded and thanked William.

"It truly was a good story," she said. "Thank you for sharing it."

"It was the most uplifting and fitting one I could think of. I've been going over it a lot these past few days."

"And now I will too."

They turned at the sound of more feet. The joy that Angela had received from William's story dissipated when she saw Kris. He was being prodded, stumbling under his own weight, and his left side was covered in blood. She and Orlan rushed to the gate, ignoring the hissing chameleons.

"Back, animals," Elya demanded, and the chameleons did as they were told.

They tossed Kris in, and he collapsed in Orlan's arms. Orlan and Angela dragged him to where the story had been told and began surveying his injuries.

"The other one," Elya said, "your turn."

Orlan ignored the Captain.

Palin and Arick attempted to give Kris grëoform while William and Jon stood guard, but Kris fought them. He grabbed the pebbles that William had been using and pushed them into a jagged little line. Then he hastily drew a series of circles in the dust surrounding the pebbles. He jabbed his finger into a corner of the diagram.

"There," he said weakly. "Orlan... there..." but then his voice fell away, and he began to shake.

Palin and Arick applied the powdered medicine called grëoform as Elya angrily shouted for Orlan to come forward.

"He was stabbed," Palin said. "The grëoform should take care of any infection, but the wound is deep, and he's lost a lot of blood."

"You better go," William told Orlan. "We'll keep him safe."

Angela watched Orlan as he pulled himself away and walked backwards toward the fence. The guards pulled him through as William, Jon, and Arick stood in a triangle around Kris, Angela, and Benjamin. She followed Arick Kasdan's gaze to where the wildmen were crouching. Their eyes were black, and they licked their lips. It had been days since the cannibals had last tasted flesh, and now the smell of blood was in the prison. Even a chameleon or two turned its head at the scent.

Tears filled Angela's eyes, and she heard Benjamin, so much like his father, beginning to pray. She prayed alongside him, helpless to do anything else.

A tribe of faith. Such a thing was unheard of in the modern day world, yet Mathew found it fascinating. The boy Kris didn't seem to be lying, not until he hesitated regarding the birdmen—even then, Mathew was pretty sure he was telling the truth—but why would any sensible creature believe in a god? If nothing else, they should know that God, if one existed, had deserted them, left them to their misfortunes. It was silly really.

"We have a visitor," spoke a chilling, elven voice.

Mathew turned to find a tall, menacing elf standing in the doorway. His head was buzzed, making his ears seem all the pointier, and his features were chiseled and strong. He seemed to have taken up the old world tradition of piercings as pieces of metal lined his ears and eyebrows, reflecting the black and green of his Vlörinclad armor. The thick, royal cape of the same colors, however, marked him as more than the common elf.

"Devin-Brek," Mathew said plainly.

"Rather disrespectful."

"General-Devin-Brek. My apologies."

"Better."

Mathew cursed himself. He could not make that mistake again. Devin-Brek was the type of elf who made it a game to rid the world of O'lors. He came to the prison with hopes of degrading Mathew in the presence of Sheligog, whose coming was not unexpected following Dägin-Bok's death. Disrespecting Devin-Brek's rank was certainly a way to draw the Kïen's ire. Mathew must also remember that although the elf hailed from another tower, *General*-Devin-Brek was still in every way his superior.

"So," the elf said as he strolled into the room, "I was informed that another of your kin has arrived."

"Sheligog mentioned one would."

Devin-Brek paused and eyed Mathew. Then he continued, unfazed. "The Kïen contacted you as well, I see. Then know that your father is preparing Sheligog's quarters as we speak."

"So be it."

Devin-Brek studied Mathew with a toothy, chilling, grin. "Do you not wish to see him—your father, I mean?"

"I have other concerns at the moment."

"Ah, yes. How are your interrogations going? What have you learned?"

"They are a faith-based tribe. The first I've ever encountered."

The pierced elf considered this fact but then discarded it. His lack of interest did not surprise Mathew. Devin-Brek had only one interest in this prison and that was defacing the O'lor who was currently acting as his equal. The elf strolled to the window and admired the smoke rising black before the setting sun.

"It's beautiful, isn't it?" he said. "Watching as an entire race is destroyed. One more step on the path to total elven dominion."

For as intimidating as Devin-Brek could be, Mathew was not fazed. He already knew where the elf was taking the conversation and opted to reach it first.

"The remnants of humanity will be next."

Devin-Brek turned slowly, obviously disappointed. This pleased Mathew.

"How does that feel," the General asked, "to know that you will have a hand in the eradication of your own kind?"

"I serve at the pleasure of Kïer. I care little for the race that birthed me."

"And the man whose seed spawned you? Do you care for him?"

Mathew sighed. Devin-Brek apparently knew of the disdain Mathew held for his father. Why must he press that? What good would come of it?

"We each have of our own place in Kïer's kingdom," was his answer.

Devin-Brek simply grunted. He began to pace with his hands tucked behind him. He was desperate for a reaction of some sort, something that could be reported to Sheligog upon the Kïen's arrival. Getting nothing from the previous two attempts, Devin-Brek tried a third.

"You do remember that I am a General, and thus, your superior, do you not?"

"I do."

"Then why was I not included in your decision to discard the wildman project?"

"Because you had no hand in that project. General-Dägin-Bok spearheaded every step of the wildman experiment, but it was ultimately proven ineffective."

"In what way?"

"I continued the experiment after General-Dägin-Bok's death but found that the virus would not infect other humans. My guess is that the biology of each race is similar but not similar enough to spread disease. We had kept a handful of infected wildmen in the prison where they were in constant contact with the original four prisoners. The virus was supposed to have been airborne, but none of the four showed any sign of having contracted it. The virus was deemed ineffectual and the wildmen were disposed of."

"And who decided that the project was to be terminated?"

"I made that call in the absence of General-Dägin-Bok."

"You did not contact Sheligog?"

"Again, the project was Dägin-Bok's alone. I did not wish to burden anyone else with his failures."

The subtle insult of Devin-Brek's fellow General seemed to annoy him, but he held his tongue in check. He couldn't argue what was obviously true.

"And do we have any infected wildmen left?" he asked.

"The four that are on the ledge had been infected prior to their departure. I keep them to prevent the humans from resting comfortably. Prisoners become tired and more susceptible to my interrogations while in the presence of wildmen. It garners results."

Devin-Brek paced slow circles around Mathew. It was supposed to be intimidating, but Mathew was not amused.

"I've heard another theory."

Mathew knew it, but he opted to let Devin-Brek have his moment.

"And what would that be?"

"Why is it that you keep so many prisoners on that ledge?"

"Various reasons. The giant could be useful as a warrior or a slave. The lizards we caught stealing from our stores; therefore, we've begun skinning them to replace what they took. We've served six already with seven remaining. A feast will be in order once Sheligog arrives, and they will be the main course."

Devin-Brek flashed his teeth again.

"That's all fine and good, really, but what of the humans? There are elves, many elves, who wonder if perhaps you are a wolf in sheep's clothing. They wonder if you have sympathies for your brethren, and if perhaps *that* is why you delay their executions. Are they wrong?"

"I assure you they are. The four young people will be dead by morning, and the ones who killed General-

Dägin-Bok will be offered to Sheligog as punishment. If he rejects them, then they will be cast over the ledge to their deaths."

"So you say."

Mathew held Devin-Brek's glare. He did not fear this elf and wanted the General to know it. Devin-Brek seemed to read Mathew's thoughts clear enough. Then Mathew blinked, feeling a familiar tension behind his eyes.

"Your time will come, O'lor," the elf whispered. "Your cousin, the hunter, would already be dead if not for Master-Sölva's stupidity. O'lors have no place among the elves."

"So you say. Now if you'll excuse me, my eyes are feeling cold. You know the way out."

Devin-Brek stormed from the room, but Mathew couldn't enjoy the sight. Sheligog was listening.

"I am here."

Orlan fell down a small flight of stairs and cried out as pain shot through his body, but the elves that guided him showed no mercy. They kicked him down the next flight as well and threatened to do it again if he didn't find his footing.

"Don't injure him too gravely," Adviser-Mondel said. "He has questions to answer still."

Orlan's body throbbed, but he barely noticed. He was too focused on the trail of blood that Kris had left behind. His best friend and adopted brother was hurt, really hurt, but Palin said it wasn't life-threatening. He clung to that and mentally switched to the drawing that Kris had made. He was trying to show them something—but what?

It wasn't long before Orlan figured it out. Thinking about the angled lines and the circles, he began to notice that he was walking in the same path as the diagram. Kris had drawn a map. Orlan went over it in his head and tried to remember where Kris' finger was pointing. He looked over his shoulder to get his bearings and received a punch in the mouth for it.

"Eyes forward," an elf of Räthinock commanded.

He turned a sharp corner and then a more subtle one. Remembering the map, he knew a circle was coming, and as expected, there descended a spiral staircase. Whatever Kris wanted him to see was at the end of that staircase.

He began the descent and reached the bottom step after only three full circles. There, to his right, was a room. The door was shut and barred with a wooden beam, and there weren't any markings to tell him what was inside. He noticed that there was a strange draft at the bottom of the stairwell and it was coming from beneath that door.

Then Orlan slowed. He could hear something, like music and a child moaning. It might have been coming from behind the door, but he swore he could hear it inside his own head. The sound was by far the strangest he had ever heard.

"What is that?" he asked and was shoved for it.

He fell forward and hit his chin on the floor. Blood dripped. Then he was lifted to his feet and pressed against the door.

The elf that pushed him down the stairwell held a blade to his stomach and looked as if he were about to speak, but then he eyed the door and hesitated. A sudden nervousness overcame him, and he opted to prod Orlan forward instead.

"Walk," he said, "and no more questions."

The sound faded as they walked and was gone by the time they reached the last flight of stairs, these being angular. At the top was one single door. They opened it and led him through.

"Welcome," a man said. He was facing a large window with his hands tucked behind his back. He turned and Orlan startled. His eyes were entirely black.

"Come closer," the man said. "My name is Dömin-Mathew O'lor, and looking through my eyes is someone who has taken a great interest in your party. You are a tribe of faith, yes?"

Orlan hadn't time to think; he simply nodded.

"And this faith comes from a book?"

Orlan nodded again.

"Use your words in the presence of the Kïen," Mathew said.

The Kïen! Could such horrors really be watching him through Mathew's eyes? Orlan's knees wobbled, and he felt as if he would be sick. He knelt quickly, unable to hold his own weight.

"Fetch a chair for the boy," Mathew demanded, and Adviser-Mondel did as he was told.

Orlan sat but refused to look Mathew, or the Kïen rather, in the eye.

"The... the book," he said. "It was called the Holy Bible."

"You have this book in your possession?"

"No."

"Did you have one at your camp?"

"No. We were taught through word of mouth."

"How long has it been since your tribe possessed this book? You did not pluck its teachings from the air."

"Forty-seven years."

Mathew paused. Orlan risked a glance and saw that the man's head was tilted as if listening to something only he could hear. Then Mathew looked at him again, and Orlan lowered his eyes.

"Your tribe was burned and scattered."

Orlan did not answer at first, but he felt the black eyes of the Kïen boring into him. He nodded.

"Refuge," Mathew said, and Orlan nodded again.

If he had any hope of misleading the Dömin or lying to him he was doing a horrible job. Orlan wasn't one to give in to fear, but there was something in that man's eyes that terrified him. No words came to mind, save the true ones, and he was too afraid to hold them back. It was as if he were under a spell.

"What does your tribe number?"

Orlan struggled with the answer.

"Twelve," he said, "fifteen maybe?"

Mathew gave a disappointed sigh.

"I was apparently misled, my lord," Mathew said. "The wildmen are not known for their arithmetic." He paused and then nodded. "My hunter has already killed all but the four wildmen in the prison. I will send word."

Orlan took a deep breath. Why was he so afraid? He hadn't been this frightened since he was a child. He concluded that it must have something to do with the Kien. Its presence must draw terror from the most primitive levels. Orlan fought the fear, and it subsided. Was it really that easy? Then he looked up and saw that Mathew's eyes were a normal shade of white and brown. The Kien was gone.

"Adviser-Mondel," he said. "See to it that the wildmen are thrown from the prison's ledge."

"At once," Mondel replied and left them.

Mathew sighed and circled Orlan, who simply stared through the window. Smoke still rose from Uuron Plauf.

"I'd like to apologize for that," Mathew said. "I would rather have done this without Sheligog's interference, but it garnered results. So you're the remnant of an old faith-based community? The elves thought it had been exterminated, but I'm not surprised by your continued existence. Religion had always been a stubborn thorn from what I understand. Foolishness is what I call it."

"We are proud of what we believe."

"Yes, I understand that, but it only heightens the need to be rid of you. The elves are the masters of this world, and they will not share it with some contrived fairy tale."

"Not every elf thinks as they do."

Mathew laughed and eyed Orlan curiously. He cursed himself for his loose lips. How could he rat Shëlin out like that?

"I hadn't heard of elves living in your tribe. Did my hunter miss that detail?"

Orlan shook his head, but Mathew seemed to detect his lie.

"Do you, a human, have elves for friends? Is it possible that a miniscule tribe of men have persuaded an elf to join their ranks? Tell me of this elf."

Orlan tightened his lips. He tried to concoct a lie, but Shëlin filled his every thought. Mathew's smile faded, and Orlan could see that the man was becoming annoyed by the delay. Then Mathew marched forward and took Orlan by the throat. He fell back into the arms of a guard.

"The elf's name," he demanded slowly.

"Tröbin-Dur," Orlan choked out, the name suddenly coming to him. Thank God for William's story.

"A tribe of fairy tales to the very end, I see," Mathew said, and he threw Orlan to the floor. "I am not a fan of liars."

Orlan stood but fell again upon seeing a knife in Mathew's hand, already blackened with Kris' blood.

"What marking should I leave you with?" Mathew asked. "Your friend's lie was uncertain, so I merely snipped his side. But you, you claim that a myth lives among you. Does the book you follow tell the accounts of Tröbin-Dur? Absurd! Such a misleading lie deserves a mark for certain, but where?"

Two guards grabbed Orlan as Mathew gently ran the knife from his stomach to his chest to his throat.

"Ah," Mathew said with a scowl, "a rumored tradition for marking liars. Smile for me."

He shoved the knife into Orlan's mouth and cut to the left. Blood flew. Orlan screamed and would have fallen if not for the guards that held him. He did not rebound as Kris had. He merely bled.

"I tire of these games," Mathew told the guard. "Bring me the boy."

"I can't even feel it," Kris mumbled with his head resting in Angela's lap. He was nearly unconscious.

"That would be the grëoform," Palin replied as he finished stitching the wound. "It has a certain numbing affect."

Angela was amazed by the resourcefulness of Palin Marick. Not only were he and his people able to sneak a powerful medical plant into the prison, but he had a needle hidden in the heel of his boot as well. He reminded her of an older Payson Harlow. The thought saddened her; Payson had been such a good man. She had been so worried about her father and Kris that she never mourned for Payson like she should have. How must Debra be feeling?

Thinking of Debra and Payson made her wonder about Jillian and Pillar. How were they? Was Pillar able to find the others? Angela couldn't possibly know that, and worrying about them would do no good. She focused on Kris.

Palin had no thread, but Kris' unraveled shirt provided that for him. She protested at the idea of using a dirty shirt for thread, but Palin assured her that grëoform would take care of any infection that might come. Kris would survive the knife wound. Unfortunately, that wasn't their only concern.

"Get back!" Jon shouted with a stomp.

The cannibals had been inching their way toward the humans little by little but haven't yet attacked. Angela assumed it was due to their being outnumbered.

"If I had my swords..."

"They are acting on simple instinct, Jon," Arick interrupted. "They are not the enemy."

Jon merely snorted.

Angela had learned a little more about Arick Kasdan since Orlan was led away. Not only was he proficient in speaking with giants, but he spoke the wildman language as well. He was currently speaking with Krom, the gray-haired wildman and leader of their tribe.

"What'd he say?" William asked.

"He is asking for Kris and is promising to leave the rest of us alone."

"Could we spare him?" Jon asked.

"I am offering another deal."

"The boy?" Jon tried again. "He's the least useful."

Benjamin startled, and Angela pulled him close. William elbowed Jon, who grunted and would have likely retaliated if not for the wildmen.

"No," was Arick's simple reply.

The conversation between Arick and Krom continued for several minutes. Then the gray-haired wildman motioned for his people to back away. The large, scarred wildman—Grot was his name—argued, but Krom put him in his place with a loud grunt. The wildmen retreated, and Arick's men relaxed.

"Thank you," Angela said.

"Don't thank me yet. This will likely cause us more grief in the end. William, Jon—be prepared for when the guards return with Orlan."

"You aren't giving them Orlan are you?" Benjamin asked.

"No," Arick whispered. "We're giving them an elf."

The pain was unlike anything Orlan had ever felt. He was panicked and terrified as any animal would be after receiving such a wound. Blood ran from his mouth, which was roughly two inches wider now due to his slashed cheek, and his head was throbbing. His clothes were soaked. He was beginning to sway.

He fell against one of the guards as he walked and clung to him. The elf yelled in the elvish tongue, but Orlan couldn't understand it. He just needed some help. He couldn't feel the floor as he hit it. He felt a kick, but it was faint. Then he heard some voices and realized that more elves had come.

Then he heard something else, like music, and there was a voice floating softly within it. It seemed to be coming from deep inside his head, and he wondered if perhaps his parents were coming to take him away.

"Pain," the voice said. "Unbearable."

Orlan didn't answer. He could barely focus.

"Different. Kind." The voice hesitated as if it were thinking. The music shifted just a little. "Good?" Then it waited longer, and the music grew more soothing.

Orlan wasn't sure who he was listening to, but it didn't sound anything like his parents. The music was calming though, so he closed his eyes and drank it in.

Then, lovingly, the voice said, "Better."

Orlan's whole body tingled. He jumped with the sensation, and his face went numb. His mind cleared, and suddenly he knew where he was. He was in the hall, surrounded by nine elves, and he was covered in blood. Then, carefully, he brought his hand to his cheek. It didn't hurt. He wasn't cut! There was a scar, roughly two inches long running from the corner of his mouth toward his ear, and it felt ugly, but the scar was tightly knit. He had been healed!

Orlan looked around and saw the stairs leading up to where the other prisoners were being held, and then he noticed that he was leaning against a door. The door! He had heard that same music before seeing Mathew O'lor. He could still hear it.

"Thank you," he whispered.

"Love," the tiny voice in the music replied.

"Who are you?" he asked but received no answer.

"Come on," a guard said, lifting him from the ground and pushing him forward.

Orlan clung to the stair rail as his legs regained their strength.

"Wait," one of the elves said. "Wasn't his cheek slashed a moment ago?"

An elf turned Orlan's face and studied his left side, then his right, and then his left again. Then he cursed and backed away as if afraid. The other elves began talking among themselves in their own language, and one of them pointed at the closed door. The lead elf shook his head and spat at it.

"The despicable witch," he said. Then he prodded Orlan, and up the stairs they went.

He was still in shock, not because of the pain that had left him or how healthy he felt despite having lost so much blood, but because he couldn't explain what had happened. Someone was behind that door, and they were like nothing he'd ever encountered.

Angela sat with Kris' head in her lap. The wound had congealed and looked better already thanks to the grëoform, but he had fallen asleep. She stroked his hair and sang a soft song. It was all she could do.

Benjamin sat beside her with his knees tucked up to his chest. He had been watching the skies for a while—they were growing dark due to clouds rolling in—but concern for Orlan drew his attention from the weather. His eyes were now focused on the gate. Arick Kasdan's men sat in a circle around the three captives from Refuge.

"How long has it been?" Benjamin asked.

"Twenty minutes give or take," answered Arick Kasdan. "Kris was gone twenty-five by my count, so Orlan should be returning soon."

"What if he doesn't come back?" Benjamin asked.

Arick studied Benjamin and then ruffled the boy's hair.

"Have faith, Benjamin. We have two tribes—yours and mine—who miss us dearly. One is sure to come. Find strength in that."

Angela wasn't so sure. She couldn't imagine Refuge having the strength to attack a structure like this. Not after the wildman raid. She knew nothing of Arick's tribe, but there weren't any strong tribes of men left in the world. She just couldn't see how either of their tribes could help.

"Our friend awakens," Palin announced.

Kris groaned, and Angela jostled his head in excitement.

"Oh, sorry," she said.

"How do you feel?" Palin asked him.

"My guts hurt," Kris replied.

"Even that will be gone when the medicine is finished. Just lie still. It won't be long."

Kris nodded and took a shallow breath. She ran her fingers through his hair, and when their eyes met, her heart broke for him. She had never seen him so helpless, not since his parents passed away when he was a boy.

"Orlan?" he asked.

"With them," she answered, "but he should be back soon."

He took her hand in his. She thought that maybe he wanted her to stop caressing his hair, but he threaded his fingers through hers and held tight. Her stomach leapt, but she suppressed a smile, pretending that his touch didn't make her feel weak.

"Thank you," he said.

She simply nodded and took his other hand as well. "You'll be alright, Kris."

"They're coming," Jon interrupted.

"We're going to have to move you, Kris," Palin said. "Bear the pain."

William and Jon grabbed him by the arms and dragged him to where the giant sat. Arick had gone to speak with the giant not long ago, but Angela didn't know why. Now she knew. If they were going to kill an elf for the wildmen, then they needed Kris out of the way. The giant would be his protector.

She knelt with Kris, but then the giant's stone features morphed into an angry grimace, making her stumble backwards. Jon pulled her away by the arm.

"Arick has gained its trust. We have not."

"But Kris…"

"Will be fine," he replied gruffly. "Arick has seen to it."

They rejoined the others, and Benjamin stood at Angela's side. She put her arm around him and watched as elves entered the room. There were four at first but then more came. Adviser-Mondel was with them.

"Where's Orlan?" Benjamin asked.

Angela had no answer. She waited, and more guards showed, but still Orlan didn't come.

"There are too many elves," Arick said. "Something's happening."

Mondel strode toward Elya-Ecsheli and pointed at the wildmen.

"Make them fly."

"On whose order?" Elya asked.

"Dömin-Mathew O'lor gave the initial order," Mondel replied, "though General-Devin-Brek agreed with it once I ran it by him. Here is his signet."

Mondel handed Elya an envelope, and the elf opened it. He read its contents and then nodded and spoke to the guards in elvish.

"And I might as well take the next prisoner while I'm here," Mondel said. He looked through the fence and grinned lustfully when he saw Angela staring at him. "The girl was next on Mathew's list if I'm not mistaken."

"Come forward, woman," Elya ordered.

"Where's Orlan?" Angela shouted, unmoving.

"You are to come forward alone," Elya demanded.

"Your friend is still with Mathew," Mondel said with a smile. "I'm sure they're laughing it up as we speak."

Angela felt Benjamin's grip on her arm, but then she heard something else. Arick was speaking in soft grunts and clicks, and the wildmen were answering.

The wildmen were suddenly irate and began to howl. The large, scarred one—Grot—beat his chest and screamed at the elves, challenging them.

"They don't like the idea of being thrown over a ledge," Arick said with a smile. Then he glanced at Angela and whispered, "And you've just become a lesser concern. Don't go to them. Make them come to us."

Mondel and Elya's eyes widened as the wildmen shouted and screamed. There weren't many of them, but they were loud and ferocious. Arick clicked and grunted, and the elder wildman—Krom—returned the odd sounds.

"Let's stand with them," Arick said quietly. "They recognize that we are not the enemy and that their numbers are few."

"Our numbers are few," Jon said.

"But where few come together much can be done."

"What about the chameleons," William asked. "Can we pull them together?"

"I am unable to communicate with them," Arick replied. "Be cautious."

The humans and wildmen stood as a tribe of ten. Jon Profit began to shout in a beast-like manor and stomped his feet like the wildmen. The others simply stood, staring defiantly.

"We will not come to you, Captain-Ecshelï," Arick declared, "but you are welcome to come for us. From this moment on—man and wildman are one."

Mondel looked nervously from Arick to Elya, but the Captain of Räthinock's forces showed no concern.

"Very well," Elya said with a grin. He did not appear worried at all.

The elves halted just shy of the last stairwell. More had joined them, and the group was being led by Master-Sölva, having completed his apology to General-Devin-Brek for having imprisoned an O'lor. A darkening bruise on the elf's porcelain cheek painted an image of Devin-Brek's frustration.

Orlan tried eavesdropping, but it was pointless. He didn't speak elvish. He did, however, hear howls and screams that he recognized. The wildmen were very upset, and he guessed that the elves were preparing to kill them as Mathew had ordered.

Then elves began to shout, and the elf who held Orlan's arm pushed him forward.

"Go," the elf demanded, "move."

Orlan was shoved through the crowd and handed off to Master-Sölva, who then led him up the stairs. He reached the top and was surprised by the number of elves who had gathered. Were four wildmen worth all this?

He saw Mondel and Elya, and then he glanced through the fence. The four wildmen stood side-by-side with Angela, Benjamin, and Arick Kasdan's men. All save Angela and Benjamin looked as if they were prepared to die fighting.

"Where's Kris?" he asked, but Sölva backhanded him for speaking out of place. He felt a sting in his cheek and tasted blood, but the scar held.

He was pressed against the fence so that he faced his friends. Angela immediately ran to him and panicked when she saw how much blood he'd lost.

"I'm alright," he said, but she didn't seem to hear him.

Then his head was yanked back by the hair, and a knife was pressed against at his throat. Sölva spoke from over his shoulder.

"Step back, girl. Boy!" he shouted, referring to Benjamin. "Step forward or your friend loses his head."

Angela stood and pushed at the fence.

"No, I'll ago."

"She's next in line," Mondel said, questioning the Master of the Guard.

"Dömin-Mathew O'lor changed his mind," said the guard who had led Orlan from the interrogation room. "He wants the boy."

Mondel seemed conflicted, and Orlan noted the lustful glare he gave Angela.

"Very well," the Adviser said, "the boy then."

Orlan watched as Benjamin bravely stood and walked forward. He didn't appear afraid, but Orlan knew better. He had to be terrified, and Orlan was terrified for him. Then Angela ran to Benjamin and stood defiantly beside him.

"Take us both," she demanded.

"Fine," Mondel stated eagerly.

Sölva gave him a disapproving glance but shrugged and motioned for the guards to open the gate. Angela locked onto Orlan's eyes as she passed through, and Orlan's stomach dropped. Then a thought occurred to him.

"The door at the bottom of the stairs!" he shouted, but then his head was yanked back, and the hilt of Sölva's knife collided with his nose. He felt it crunch and tasted the blood that immediately flowed. He was blinded by the pain and felt himself being dragged and thrown.

He fell on someone's boot—no, not a boot—a foot. He looked up, and through blurry eyes he saw a scarred face with black eyes looking down at him. Grot sniffed and saliva dripped from his fangs. The wildmen were still hungry, and Orlan, covered with old and fresh blood, lay at their feet.

"Let's find out how long this union can last," Elya said with a laugh. "I would advise that you humans kill the cannibals or risk losing one of your own, and I'd suggest doing it quickly. They do look so terribly famished."

Orlan attempted to crawl away but felt a powerful hand press down on his back. The wildman bent over him, savoring his ensanguined fragrance as a slow and menacing growl echoed from behind his lips.

Angela was sickened by Adviser-Mondel's grip. It was firm, but not too firm, and he affectionately rubbed the skin of her arm with his thumb. The touch was obviously a thrill for him. In addition to this, his eyes continually wandered over her form, and she wished she could gouge them out with her fingernails.

Benjamin was ahead of her, being prodded forward by an elf with a spear. He was maintaining his brave demeanor, but she wondered how long it would take for him to crack. He was just a boy after all. If she challenged Mondel now, Benjamin could possibly get hurt, and she couldn't allow that.

Then Mondel stopped.

"You go ahead," he told the elf. "Mathew has requested the boy, so he should go first. I'll wait here with the girl until her time comes."

Benjamin looked back, and Angela was surprised to see a lack of fear in his eyes. Was he really that calm? Was he so consigned to death that he no longer feared it? The elf led him away.

Angela studied her surroundings. She was in a long hall with twelve closed doors running along either wall. There were no windows and no obvious means of escape save the stairs at either end of the hall. As Benjamin disappeared down the stairs, she began to shake and feel panicked. She was alone with the lust-driven Adviser.

"Now," Mondel said. His grip was tightening on her arm. "I believe that I owe you a bit of a debt."

He smacked her, smacked her again, and then pinned her against a door.

"You nearly broke my nose before. Let's not do that again."

Then he kissed her. It was horrible. He pressed his body against hers and violated her lips so violently that she tasted blood. Her hands were pinned to the wall and useless. She couldn't break his grip. Then he pulled away, a disgusting, lust-filled grin on his face, and dragged her toward a nearby room. The door, she now realized, had his name scrawled on a plate.

He released one hand to open the door, and that was all she needed. She leapt at him, throwing off his balance, and drove the top of her head into his chin. They fell into his room, and as he lay on his back, holding his mouth and cursing, she drove her knee up into the midst of his robes, bringing another cry from his repulsive lips.

Then she ran. She didn't know where she was, but she knew where Benjamin had gone, so she followed. She descended the stairs and realized that they went down for quite a distance with multiple floors branching off of each landing. She paused. What floor would they be on? It couldn't have been too far down or they'd have still been descending, four or five levels at the most.

Then she remembered Orlan's words.

"The door at the bottom of the stairs," she said to herself. It wasn't much to go on but it was something.

She descended the stairs and saw that there weren't any doors on the next level, and so she kept going. Two floors later she found a door barred with a wooden beam. Was this it? Was this where they took Benjamin?

She approached the door but then paused. She heard something, like music or a whisper. She waited and realized with astonishment that the music was inside her head. She waited, unsure of what to do. Then she heard a voice.

"Friend," it said. "No. Orlan. Love."

She didn't understand, but Orlan's name confirmed her suspicion. This was the door he had been talking about. She removed the beam, tossed it aside, and slowly opened the door. Inside, Angela found a woman unlike any she had ever seen, and the sight stilled her.

The woman had hair of thorns and leaf-filled vines, and bark covered her extremities. Her skin was a dull tan color but lines of green showed through. Chlorophyll-filled veins perhaps? Her features were close to human, though slightly exaggerated, and her eyes were lime green on brown. Then Angela noticed the chains. Each pointy-fingered, bark-covered hand was bound to the floor by a four foot chain, and four more chains bound her waist. These were attached to the four corners of the room.

"Angela," the voice echoed, though the woman's lips never moved. "Orlan's love."

Angela hesitated. Then she entered the room and shut the door. This, she concluded, was Ivan's willow.

"Do not struggle," Palin ordered. "Struggling will only heighten their instinct to kill. They are hunters."

Orlan lay flat on his stomach feeling the weight of the scarred wildman on his back. Grot was sniffing his blood-soaked clothing but hadn't sunk his teeth in yet. Others were gathering.

Arick was grunting at the elder wildman with ferocity. He was adamant about the things he was saying, and then Krom grunted at Grot. Grot replied angrily. Orlan could do nothing but keep his eyes closed, anticipating the first bite. He could hear thunder crashing in the darkened clouds, but nothing was as deafening as the growl coming from between Grot's teeth.

"Come now!" Elya shouted. "Defend your little friend."

"Draw your fists, humans," Sölva demanded.

The other guards laughed and beat the fence in anticipation.

"Tell me, beasts," William said jovially, "who is more savage, wildmen or those who encourage them to eat flesh?"

The laughter stopped.

"You dare compare your master race to those disgusting cannibals?" Sölva questioned.

"No, no, no." It was now William's turn to laugh. "To do so would put shame on these pour creatures. You are not worthy to lick their dung-stained feet. At least they are attempting to show restraint. Perhaps *they* are *your* superiors?"

Orlan couldn't move enough to see the elves' reactions, but he could imagine based on their commotion. If he weren't in such a predicament, he'd laugh.

"How dare you, human!" Sölva screamed. "You, whose race is nothing but..."

"Cease, Master-Sölva," Elya said calmly. "Do not show them your anger, or they might feel they've won something."

"Do not order your superior!" Sölva snapped at Elya, who recoiled slightly from the bitter chastising. Then Sölva turned and pointed a finger at William. "None speak of the elves in such manner and live. No matter what Mathew O'lor says, that one's head will sit at my feet by sunrise."

William merely laughed.

"Only one person is qualified at beheading in this company," he shouted, "my friend Jon here. Why, you should ask General-Dägin-Bok about it; he seemed to enjoy his beheading a great deal."

Another eruption sounded as William theatrically ran a finger along his own throat.

Orlan hadn't originally understood what William was hoping to accomplish, but he saw it now. As the man mocked the elves, Arick and Krom were speaking more fervently, and the wildmen were beginning to back away. The distraction was saving Orlan's life while tightening a noose around the storyteller's own neck. He'd have to thank William if they both managed to survive this.

Master-Sölva was shouting again—quite an angry elf—and Elya was again attempting to calm the crowd. Krom argued with Grot now. He was the last wildman that still seemed to want to eat Orlan, but then with a loud grunt the wildman pushed Orlan away, and Jon dragged him to Palin's side.

"Snort this," Palin demanded, holding what was left of the grëoform to Orlan's nose. "We must prevent infection."

"Angela or Benjamin might need it."

"Do it now or those wildmen will be back. We need to staunch the blood flow."

Orlan hated to take the last of the grëoform, but he did as he was told and choked. It burned, and his discomfort was made worse when Palin suddenly grabbed his crooked nose and cracked it back into place. Orlan screamed.

"Be still and let it heal. We will need you alert in the coming moments."

"What is this, master elf?" William shouted. He was standing before the rest of his people and the wildmen with his arms outstretched. "The cannibals have denied their bloodlust? I suppose this proves something that I've always suspected. Perhaps it is *they* who should be called master, for they, it seems, are more civilized than even you."

"I have heard enough!" Sölva shouted. "Prepare for entry. We kill every man and wildman on that ledge. Make it bloody. Make it painful."

"Master..." Elya attempted, but Sölva shoved him aside. He tried again. "We do not have the authority. The wildmen are to die, but the humans..."

"Open the gate!" Sölva shouted, interrupting his inferior Captain. "Kïer will praise the elves of Vlörinclad and Räthinock for putting an end to such blasphemy. Sever their heads. Splatter their bodies upon the distant ground. And bring me the tongue of the blasphemer so that I may present it to Kïer as a trophy."

"We must wait for General-Devin-Brek's..."

Elya's protest was interrupted quite painfully as Sölva backhanded him and pressed his face against the fence so that the links dug into his porcelain skin.

"You are dismissed from this post, Captain of the Guard. Cower in the halls below."

Elya hesitated, so Sölva dragged him by his breastplate and threw him toward the stairwell. Elya disappeared down it, leaving Orlan and the others at Master-Sölva's brutal mercy.

Sölva stood before the rest of his people, their swords drawn, and he signaled for the gate to be opened.

"Slaughter them all!" he shouted.

Orlan stood as lightning parted the night sky. His nose still stung, but the bleeding had stopped. He was thinking straighter now, so he balled his fists and prepared to defend himself. At least Angela and Benjamin weren't on the ledge. They might actually see morning.

Then the gate opened, wildmen howled, and the elves of Räthinock and Vlörinclad stormed the prison's ledge.

Part VII: The Fight for Freedom

"The hunter," a dark-haired guard announced.

Mathew waved Maximus into the interrogation room and offered him a seat. The hunter waved him off as usual.

"Rested?" Mathew asked.

"Better than I was. I hear Sheligog is on his way."

"He contacted me himself. My father is preparing his room as we speak."

"Your father, huh? Have you spoken to him yet?"

"I try not to. He's not worth my time."

"He serves the Kien, Mathew."

"My father is a smear on the legacy of proud O'lors."

"Is that what I am?"

"No, you've molded your own destiny. He opted to be a slave." Mathew sighed and ran his fingers through his hair. The last thing he wanted to have to deal with was his father. "That aside, we have to be ready for Sheligog's coming. He invaded my mind during an interrogation and learned that the tribe's numbers were exaggerated. I blamed it on wildman arithmetic, but who's to say if he bought it. I've ordered them to be slain."

"Have you finished the interrogations?"

"The young men are finished. The boy is on his way up."

"And the girl?"

"Let Mondel have her."

"Have they given you no viable information then?"

"They come from a faith-based tribe, remnants of a dead community called Refuge."

"And that's all?" Maximus asked.

"So far."

"Have they any connection to the other four men?"

"Not that they've unveiled."

"Don't you think it's a coincidence that two separate tribes of men were found in such close proximity of each other?"

The thought had occurred to Mathew, but he couldn't find any real evidence that they shared a tribe. He was pondering this when the guard entered the room with Benjamin.

"Let's find out," Mathew said. "Have a seat, boy."

The guard led Benjamin to the chair and stood behind it.

"Your presence won't be necessary," Mathew said. "Maximus and I should be able to handle this one alone."

The guard removed himself from the room, and Mathew approached the chair.

"Your name?"

"Benjamin Bishop."

"And what is the name of your other companions?"

"Kris, Orlan, and Angela."

"And what is your connection to the other four men on the prison's ledge?"

Benjamin thought about this.

"You saw what I did to the other two, yes?" Mathew asked.

Benjamin nodded. Mathew was amazed by the boy's calmness. He expected terror.

"We've only just met them."

Mathew had a suspicion that the boy was telling the truth.

"Very well," he said. "Why were your people in Uuron Plauf, Benjamin?"

"We wanted to help the birdmen."

"Because your faith says it's wrong to murder?"

"Yes."

This was all old news. Benjamin was confirming what the previous two prisoners had said, but Mathew wanted more. Then he had a thought.

"How did you learn of the attack on Uuron Plauf? How did you know it was coming?"

The boy hesitated again, and so Mathew withdrew the bloodied knife from its sheath. The boy's eyes widened.

"Ivan told us."

"Ivan?"

Mathew looked at Maximus, who shrugged.

"Who is Ivan?"

"I don't know. He wandered into our camp. His skin was burnt."

"Oh, him!" Mathew had nearly forgotten about the deformed man. "I wasn't aware of his escape."

The deformed man was their fifth prisoner who, according to Master-Sölva, had been killed by the willow. This Ivan must have escaped, and Sölva, self-serving as always, thought it would be best to lie about it. Mathew gripped the knife tighter but then sighed and put it away.

"Maximus, do me the favor of retrieving Master-Sölva. We will be assigning a new Master of the Guard soon."

Maximus grinned and departed. After having been humiliated by the elf, Maximus would see to it that Sölva suffered a painful death. Mathew had no problem with that.

"Now Benjamin," he said while kneeling before the boy, "what are your beliefs exactly?"

The boy began quoting the same commandments that Kris had, and so Mathew motioned for him to stop.

"You children sound rather brainwashed. Tell me something different."

Benjamin thought for a moment and then smiled. "My father's faith is stronger than anyone else's. He taught me to love everyone despite our differences. For example, we do not hate the elves... or those who serve them," he quickly added. What a smart boy. "We hope that they will someday believe as we do."

"Is that so?" Mathew said. "I sent a pack of wildmen to kill everyone in your tribe, including your father. You do not hate me for this?"

"No. I forgive you."

Mathew wanted to laugh, but something about those words troubled him. Pain and hatred made Mathew strong and drove him to levels of success thought unobtainable by O'lors. To forgive was to embrace weakness.

"Your father is a fool."

"I disagree."

"You will learn that I am right... in time. All fathers disappoint their sons before the end. Trust me on this. Now explain to me why you show no fear. Are you not afraid to die?"

"I don't want to die, but I don't expect to live long enough to see my father again. Alive or dead, I am in God's hands."

"Such brave words coming from one so young. Your father should be proud of such an idiot boy."

A role of thunder echoed, and several droplets of rain appeared on the window. For some inexplicable reason, this made Benjamin smile. Mathew considered smacking the boy, but then he heard running in the stairwell. Mathew looked at the door and saw the dark-haired guard motioning for someone to stop, but Captain-Elya-Ecshelï pushed his way into the room anyhow.

"I am in the middle of an interrogation!" Mathew shouted. His face grew suddenly hot.

"Apologies," Elya said breathlessly. "General-Devin-Brek was not in his quarters, and I fear a grave misfortune is coming. It could not wait."

"Explain."

"Master-Sölva has taken it upon himself to slay every man on the ledge. He is leading an attack that I fear could unravel our hold on this prison."

"They are but a few prisoners. He was wrong to take matters into his own hands, but..."

"The men and wildmen have united. One of the human prisoners has befriended the giant, and I'm certain that, in his haste, Master-Sölva has forgotten about the chameleons."

"How many elves has your master recruited for this task?"

"Two dozen perhaps. Enough to deal with the men and wildmen, but not near enough if the chameleons and giant get involved."

Mathew cursed. The fool! Master-Sölva had been strong and fiercely loyal to General-Dägin-Bok, but his loyalty lessened when it came to serving an O'lor. His hasty decision, made without higher approval, could unravel the illusion of Mathew being in control. Devin-Brek would be pleased; Sheligog would not.

"Go," he said. "Intercept Maximus and however many elves you can find, and keep those prisoners from escaping. Once you've regained control, be sure that Maximus brings Sölva to me."

"Yes, sir."

Elya bowed and turned to go.

"And, Ecshelï?"

"Yes?"

"Thank you for bringing this to my attention. You are the Captain of Räthinock's forces, second to Master-Sölva, correct?"

"I am, sir."

"Kïer willing, you have earned yourself a promotion this day."

"Thank you, Dömin."

Elya bowed again and raced from the room. The dark-haired guard went with him. Mathew thought everything over and felt pressure building in his temples. If this goes badly, he will need an out. Where could he redirect the blame? In what way could he come out of this looking competent? He'd have to think this through.

Then he noticed the boy. For the first time since he arrived, Benjamin appeared frightened.

"You fear for your friends?"

Benjamin nodded.

"Why?"

"Because they're my family."

Mathew sneered.

"Family is a lie, Benjamin—as is your faith. Heed my warning and forsake them both."

Benjamin shook his head, and Mathew saw that the boy was trembling. This made Mathew smile. Having lost his courage, Benjamin was more susceptible to the threats that Mathew had in mind, but then a sudden clap of thunder rolled, and rain began to beat against the window. This caught Benjamin's eye and seemed to interest him a great deal. Why was the boy so fascinated by the rain? Mathew walked to the door and glanced down the stairwell. Though the sound of rain echoed through it, the stairs themselves remained dry and clear of any danger. The interrogation might as well continue.

"As I was saying…"

Benjamin collided with Mathew, and though he could normally have dealt with the boy, he was caught off-balance and lost his footing. Still, he tossed Benjamin aside easily enough and went for his knife—only to find that it was missing. Then he felt the pain in his leg.

Benjamin's footsteps were already echoing down the stairwell, having stolen the knife, and Mathew cursed his own stupidity. The wound was small, but the fact still remained that a mere child had gotten the best of him, had stabbed him. He cursed again, loudly this time.

He wrapped the wound with a handkerchief, drew his sword, and began his own descent. None could know that a mere boy had escaped him. Mathew grimaced. Benjamin would learn what fear really was.

<hr />

Angela's heart beat at a rate that rendered her breathless. There were already so many things to be afraid of in this prison, and now, standing before this willow, Angela felt as if she could tolerate no more. And yet, she felt drawn to this otherworldly creature.

The willow stared at Angela without speaking. Six candles illuminated the room and cast an eerie light on the creature, intensifying the strangeness of her being. The willow's hair of leaves and thorns moved about as if floating beneath water, though it did not move in cohesion with the breeze that made the candles flicker. That breeze confused Angela, however, because the room was entirely enclosed without a window or fireplace. Where then did the breeze come from? She could determine only one source. For as little sense as it made, the breeze had to have come from the willow.

"Love," she heard the willow say in her head. "What love? Familiar."

"I-I don't understand," Angela stuttered. She was shaking now. The willow was certainly terrifying, and Angela was beginning to wonder if she had made a mistake entering the room.

"Fear," the willow said, and for the first time she made a disapproving expression. "Fear me. Do not fear. Peace. Be still."

The breeze hit Angela so suddenly that her hair flew straight back, and her body broke into chills. As the wind passed through her, it was as if her fear grabbed ahold of that wind and was carried away by it. She felt calm. Her heart's intense beating slowed to a normal rate, and her hands stopped shaking. She had to sit due to the suddenness of it all.

"Better," the willow's voice echoed.

Angela studied the strange creature and shook her head in disbelief. The breeze was calming now. Nice.

"You control the wind?"

"Breath. Drawn to you. Love."

"I'm sorry, but I don't understand."

The willow tilted her head and then looked at the walls. The breeze whipped more violently now, and the candles suddenly blew out, making the room pitch black. Images invaded the room, or rather, as Angela quickly surmised, invaded her mind. She saw a forest. No. The trees were alive. They were willows, and they spoke to the cotton-like clouds that covered the world. She couldn't understand the willows' language, but the heavens obviously did. Rays of light shone through the clouds, changing in expanse and brightness as the willows spoke. The exchange was like nothing Angela could have ever imagined. It was beautiful. She could sense an immense love between the willows and the clouds; so immense, in fact, that Angela could barely stand to be in its presence.

"God," the willow's voice echoed in her mind. "Spirit."

Then the image grew darker, redder, and fire burned. Angela could feel an intense heat, and she turned away to protect her face from the blast. There was screaming. Her heart began to race again, but then the willow's calming voice returned.

"Peace. Be still."

Angela calmed. The fire passed, and the willows stood in a blackened, charred world. They mourned in what sounded like music—a song of anguish—and the sound tore at Angela's heart. The clouds were smaller now, gray and thin, but they seemed to hear the willows' lament. Then, when the worst of the willows' pain had passed, the clouds dissipated and were gone, leaving the willows alone in a dead world.

"The clouds..." Angela began to question.

"God. Spirit."

"The clouds receded. Was this when mankind deserted God?"

"Left mankind. Not willows. After the Fall. Left all."

Then there was movement in the image. A man approached the willows—no, not a man—an elf. He was young and handsome with white hair. Much more handsome than the dark-haired elves of the prison, and there was something inherently good about him. He spoke to the willows, and suddenly there were more elves, all with white hair. The willows taught them magic.

The willow screamed in Angela's head. "No magic! Corrupt. Magic."

"I'm sorry," she replied.

"Spirit," the willow said, calmly now. "Pureness."

The elves began using this pureness, and with it life began to grow again. The black became green. Joy returned to the willows. Then the elves began to leave, and it seemed to Angela that the willows mourned for them. The elves' hair became black, as if a great darkness had passed through them. Only one elf remained, the original elf, and his hair had dimmed to grey. Then he forsook them and left as well. The willows mourned again, but there were no clouds to hear them, and the image faded.

The candles did not flicker, but a dull green light filled the room. It seemed to radiate from the willow herself.

Angela considered the surreal scene she had just witnessed and drew a conclusion.

"You taught the elves how to save the world after the Fall of Man."

"Yes."

"And they somehow left you?"

"Forsook. Pureness denied. Greed. Anger. Hatred."

"I see. Who was the elf with the gray hair?"

An image began to form in Angela's mind, and her heart raced again. There weren't any calming words this time, and she instinctively knew that she was feeling the willow's wrath. She saw how this willow had recently been captured by elves. The willow's screams were horrifying, and then she was chained in a room. This room. A door opened in Angela's mind, and someone stepped through it. Angela couldn't see him clearly, but she could feel the willow's resentment. He lowered his black hood, revealing his disfigurement.

In her mind she heard the willow scream. She had broken through her chains and attacked the hooded man.

He escaped, but not without his side being ripped out by four extended, wooden talons. The door slammed shut behind him, and the willow's cries echoed in Angela's mind. The image faded, and still the willow mourned.

"Ivan? That was Ivan Shaymolin. But what does..."

"Not Ivan."

Then Angela realized the truth.

"Ivan is an elf?"

"The first elf. The last elf."

"Ivan was the one who convinced you to teach the elves your," she hesitated, "your pureness."

"Darkness!" the voice shouted in her mind. "Thieves."

"But they don't seem to have that sort of power anymore."

"Unworthy. Left them. Hunted. Alone."

Angela struggled to understand this, but then she saw an image of elves imprisoning willows. They demanded that the power be returned to them. Many willows died in the process. This willow had survived. She wasn't certain how many others had lived.

"Unworthy."

"The elves became unworthy. The power left them."

"Yes."

"They wanted it back and hunted you for it, but you couldn't give it to them?"

"Yes."

"I understand."

"God."

Angela hesitated.

"Faith," the willow said. "Love."

Then an image softly filled Angela's mind. She was a child. Randall was praying with her as she lay in her cot. The image changed, and she saw Orlan passing through the hall. She saw in Orlan's mind his concern for her, his love for her. She saw images of Kris plucked from her own mind. She saw the three of them together as children. Laughing. Playing.

"Pureness."

The image faded, and Angela realized that she had begun crying. The elves lacked the faith and love that she and her friends carried. The whole world, it seemed, lacked that love. It thrived instead on fear and the lust for power or vengeance. She never realized how different the people of Refuge were until now, how amazing they were.

"Leave."

"What?" Then Angela realized what the willow was telling her. "You want to leave. I understand. But you're chained, and I have nothing to…"

The chains fell as if they had never been latched.

"If you could…" Angela began. "But then why…"

"No reason. No faith. Found faith. Found you."

Angela couldn't help but smile.

"I have friends here. Three others, and there are other prisoners as well. I can't leave them."

"Have faith."

The voice in her mind was reassuring. She had heard these words all her life, but they meant something more coming from the willow. When her father told her to have faith, it was with the hope that something good might come of it; but when the willow told her to have faith, it was an absolute based on wisdom beyond Angela's understanding. It was as if the willow had a direct connection to God Himself, knowing things that no one else could.

Feeling comforted, Angela opened the door a crack but then shut it again as a small group of elves ran by. She waited a moment and then opened the door and peeked out. The hall was empty. She turned and found that the willow was directly behind her.

"I don't know the way," Angela said.

"Stay," the willow said.

Angela waited. She wasn't sure why she had to wait, but something about the suggestion felt right. Then she heard running. She backed into the room, but the willow stopped her.

"Stay."

She waited as the steps grew closer and then peered through the crack of the door as someone flew by.

"Benjamin!"

Benjamin nearly fell at the sound of his own name. He turned, saw Angela, and burst into tears. She ran to him and pulled him close.

"Are you alright?" she asked.

"I stabbed his leg and ran." He held up the knife. "He's after me."

Then Benjamin saw the willow and screamed, but then he stopped screaming and became tranquil. Angela didn't hear the words spoken into Benjamin's mind, but she could guess what they were: "Peace. Be still."

"She's with me," Angela said.

Benjamin seemed cautious but nodded.

"Follow," said the willow, and then she glided past them.

Her legs moved without her feet ever touching the ground, and Angela was astonished by the eeriness of the sight, but only for a moment. Then she took Benjamin's hand and followed after the willow. It was almost instinctual. They came to the stairwell, and the willow began her descent.

Angela stopped.

"But my friends are up there," she said, pointing up.

"Have faith," the willow reminded her.

Angela and Benjamin exchanged glances, took deep breaths, and followed after the willow. They had faith.

Mathew's leg was on fire, but he ignored it. The boy was fast. Mathew's chances of overtaking him were slim due to his leg slowing him down, and he cursed himself for allowing it to happen. He turned a corner and headed toward the stairwell, but then something caught his eye. He slowed his pace and glanced into the open room. It was dark and empty. He remembered what had been in that room.

"Benjamin," he called out. "Do not trust that witch. She is an evil, selfish creature. Benjamin?"

Had the boy freed her? Was he no longer alone? Mathew would be lying if he said he did not fear the willow, and the idea of it being free concerned him greatly.

Then he heard footsteps. They were racing down the stairwell, and Mathew raced to meet them. Mondel nearly ran him over. Mathew steadied his Adviser and was shocked to find his face covered in blood.

"What happened?"

"The girl!" Mondel said venomously. "That harlot attacked me."

"The willow?"

"What? No. The one from Refuge. She's escaped."

The girl? Benjamin and the girl had both escaped. The willow was missing. The prison ledge was likely in turmoil by now. A boiling rage built inside Mathew and culminated with a backhand that sent Mondel tumbling down the stairwell. He followed his Adviser and picked him up, pressing him against the wall by the collar of his robes. Mondel cried out and shielded himself from another blow.

"The boy and the willow are missing as well. You must find them and kill them all. No elf can know, and I say that with the threat of death. I can lay blame on Sölva for what happens on that ledge, but not this. Go."

"The willow?" Mondel whispered. His eyes were wide with fear, and his voice trembled.

Mathew would hear no more of Mondel's cowering. He launched Mondel toward the stairs, causing him to stumble down the first few steps before disappearing around a corner. Mathew watched him go and then cursed. Why did he tell Mondel that Benjamin had escaped? The Adviser was sharp enough to deduce that the boy had escaped *him*, the Dömin of Intelligence. Must he look so weak even to his closest allies? He cursed again, and his voice echoed through the stairwell. Other sounds echoed as well. He heard metal clashing, shouts, commotion. The prison had fallen to chaos, that was certain, but what could he do? How could he regain some semblance of control?

He knew. He needed to assert his strength and show Sheligog and Devin-Brek—all the elves—that Mathew O'lor was more than mere human. He was their superior. He tightened his grip on his sword and ascended the stairwell two steps at a time.

It was Jon who killed the first elf. The elves rushed the ledge, and Jon ran straight at them. Orlan couldn't believe the man's fortitude, but Jon managed to disarm the nearest elf just as the rest arrived. Then he killed the next in line and was lost in the madness. The last Orlan had seen him he had one sword in each hand and a smile on his face.

Jon Profit might not have lasted long if not for the chameleons. Orlan had nearly forgotten about them, but as the elves charged, and Jon drew their focus, the chameleons leapt into the crowd, breaking necks and clawing eyes. Their coloring made them hard to see to the point where Orlan was sure he saw an elf or two fighting each other in the madness.

By the time the elves reached Orlan, they were spread out enough so that he had room to maneuver. He dodged a sword and wrestled the elf who wielded it to the ground. He attempted to pry the sword from the elf's hands but was too weak. It had been too long since he last ate anything substantial, and the elf was overpowering him.

Then his foe screamed and fell aside. Orlan took the elf's sword, and Arick helped him to his feet. They fought back-to-back as elves poured forth.

It seemed that William and Palin had also found swords in the madness. Despite their obvious fatigue, Orlan noted how skilled they all were. Jon was obviously the strongest swordsman, but the others held their own. William's face was covered in blood, and Palin was favoring his left arm, but they continued to fight bravely.

The smallest wildman was dead and trampled, but the other three fought on. They bit and wrangled anything that came near them, and Orlan shuddered at the memory of their powerful grip. He had lost track of the chameleons but could tell by the elves who seemingly fought nothing that they were still present. Between the flying blood and chaos he could see the number of guards thinning. The chameleons had changed things.

Then more elves arrived. He saw a man in their midst: Maximus the hunter. Elya-Ecshelï arrived shortly after him but left again, assumedly to gather more forces.

Orlan screamed. A blade cut into his shoulder, and he turned away from it. Arick deflected another as Orlan regained his footing.

"Stay focused!" Arick shouted.

Orlan did just that.

It was then that he noticed who had attacked him. Sölva, Master of the Guard, had made his way to them and attempted a quick kill, and it would have worked if not for Arick's ability to hold off more than one foe at a time.

Arick focused on Sölva, but the elf was powerful. He separated Arick from Orlan, who was now struggling with two other elves, and set Orlan up to be the first human to fall. But then one of the elves lurched forward painfully, and William was pulling a sword from the dead elf's neck.

"That's two I owe you," Orlan managed to say between frightened breaths.

William was too focused to reply.

Palin soon joined William and Orlan, and Jon was with them soon enough. He was covered in blood. Orlan wondered how much of it was his and how much belonged to elves.

"We must stay together!" Palin shouted. "Where's Arick?"

Orlan pointed as William deflected another blade. Then Orlan cried out when he saw that Arick wasn't alone. Kris had left the giant and was now fighting at

Arick's side. He hadn't claimed a sword yet, but he was clinging to Sölva, hindering him as Arick struggled to find his footing again. Sölva shoved Kris aside and deflected Arick's blade, but Kris jumped at him again, weaponless. Other elves joined in.

Orlan could see the stroke before it fell, so he ran to his friend despite Palin's call for him to stay. Sölva swung his sword at Arick, and Kris threw himself at the blade. He screamed as the blade cut into his side, but he clung to the sword as Arick attempted to behead Sölva. Another guard deflected the blow and pulled Arick away. Kris was alone and defenseless, clinging to Sölva's blade, an unknown portion of it imbedded into his side. Then Sölva threw Kris to the ground, loosened his sword, and lifted it with murderous intent.

Orlan screamed as he ran, full of desperation. An elf had attempted to tackle him, but he wriggled free and slew it. Then he sprinted for Kris, despite the fact that his sword was still imbedded in the elf's ribcage. Sölva spotted Orlan out of the corner of his eye, and that distraction was enough to make his sword miss its mark, saving Kris' life, but Orlan was defenseless. He threw himself at Sölva, pushing the elf as far away from Kris as he could, but Orlan realized his mistake as the ground vanished beneath their feet. He had pushed himself right over the prison's ledge.

Sölva's terrified scream faded as he fell toward the broken mountainside below. Orlan, however, fell silently. Dozens of images flashed through his mind. He thought of Kris and Angela. He remembered how innocent Joshua had been. He remembered Tramin's dog, Pillar. Gabe. Phyllis. Randall. He remembered his parents vanishing in the midst of an explosion. He thought of Payson's cold body. He remembered the wildman pierced on the beam below. He remembered the blood. He closed his eyes and prayed.

Then the impact came.

All wind was knocked from his lungs, but the stop wasn't sudden. It was gradual. Then, between his failed attempts at breathing and his desperate grasping of white fur and feathers, Nikiatis spoke.

"I have you."

<hr>

Mathew raced through the doorway and paused before the carnage. He had been in Uuron Plauf on an advisory level, not to fight, and he only bore his blade once while defending himself against Dömin-Vlö-Bek. He didn't care for warfare and grimaced at its ugliness. He was no Dömin of Forces after all. No, but he *was* the Dömin of Intelligence. He was good at concocting plans of death and obedience; he simply watched as others did the dirty work.

But Mathew O'lor was no coward. He wasn't afraid to overcome an obstacle, and he certainly wasn't afraid to bloody a sword.

He ran through the gates, slick with rain, and challenged the first wildman he saw. The beast lunged at him, and Mathew skewered it through the stomach. It screamed and clung to him in death until he pried it off and tossed it aside. Then he saw Maximus fighting a man with two swords, Jon he believed the man was named, and so he joined him.

He expected Maximus to laugh at the idea of him joining the battle, but he didn't. That's what Mathew liked about his cousin. He was a man of business. Jon held his own against the two O'lors, but he was tiring. Mathew pressed him, but through the mist of distant rain, something caught his eye. A creature had come up over the ledge, carrying the boy whose mouth he had slashed, and then dove back down out of sight. He caught only a glimpse of the creature but recognized it immediately.

"The white birdman!" he shouted. The distraction nearly cost him his life.

Jon's sword cut into his neck. Maximus deflected the blade so that it cut only skin, but it was enough to sober Mathew of what he was doing. He could fight, but he was no warrior. He was what some might call a politician. He fought with words and thought, not with a sword. He backed away. Maximus preferred to fight alone, he knew, and he could tell that the hunter was relieved.

He left the ledge and headed back down the stairwell. If the white birdman had arrived, then it wasn't likely to be alone. The people of Refuge had become much more problematic than Mathew would have expected of them. Somehow, he would have to make this their fault. They would take the blame for his failures and learn what it meant to cross Dömin-Mathew O'lor.

He paused in the stairwell as the puzzle laid itself out in his racing mind: The disfigured man had been captured alongside those who killed Dägin-Bok, but he escaped and found the people of Refuge. Was it coincidence? The people of Refuge interfered in Uuron Plauf because of the disfigured man, ultimately leading to their imprisonment. Now the people of Refuge had come to rescue their own. It was becoming obvious that the original four prisoners had been members of Refuge all along, all of them were, and the disfigured man had arranged their jailbreak. Was he their leader?

The people of Refuge had rescued birdmen, unbeknownst to Mathew, and the birdmen plucked the prisoners from the ledge, resulting in chaos. Such a thing would reflect badly on the guards more so than Mathew. Master-Sölva would take the blame. Sölva's guards were weak, the guards that General-Dägin-Bok had assigned. Would Sheligog believe that? Would General-Devin-Brek allow it to be said?

Devin-Brek.

The General of Vlörinclad hadn't been in his quarters according to Elya-Ecshelï, but there was someplace else he might be. Mathew stormed down the stairs. Devin-Brek would want a hand in preparing for Sheligog's coming, and that would likely involve the subtle torturing of Mathew's father, Nathan O'lor.

Mathew didn't care about his father's wellbeing. What he cared about was how easily he could swing this disaster onto Sölva and the people of Refuge. Devin-Brek was the only obstacle. The elf would attempt to pin everything on Mathew, and that was one thing he couldn't allow.

Despite his being the Dömin of Intelligence, Mathew would have to get his hands bloody. There was no time for cleverness. This obstacle required a sword.

The white birdman dipped into the nearby forest and maneuvered through trees in order to throw off any who might be watching. He eventually came to a small, makeshift canopy where Debra and Gabe were waiting.

"He will live," Nikiatis said as he sat Orlan on the ground.

The boy seemed dazed at first, but the sound of his adopted father's voice brought him back.

"Gabe!"

It was hard for Nikiatis to see Gabe and Orlan hugging, just as it had been difficult watching Debra and her daughter reunite. It pained the birdman knowing that he could never again hold those he loved. He focused on that pain.

"The others," Gabe said suddenly. "Who else did you see? Was Kris up there?"

"It is chaos…" Nikiatis began, but then Orlan interrupted him.

"He's right on the edge. I fell trying to save him."

Nikiatis leapt into the air without another word. Rain rolled off his slick feathers and fell to the earth in drizzles. The ledge approached, but instead of plucking another prisoner from the air, he landed and fluffed his feathers and fur to their fullest extent—and he screamed. The screech echoed and thunder roared, and many of the elves fell back in terror. Let them cower. Let the abominations fear the last king of Uuron Plauf!

He took in the chaos. A new horde of elves was arriving. There were five, no, six men fighting, and at least two wildmen. He couldn't count the lizards, but there were many. Then he saw the stone giant. It stood to the side, watching the chaos. Nikiatis knew of these creatures, having seen a few in his lifetime. They were stupid and slow in their decision making, but this one was about to act.

Of the six men, only one looked familiar. Nikiatis fought his way toward Kris and then dove over the ledge with the young man in his arms. They were soon with the others. Kris was covered in more blood than Orlan but seemed to have his wits about him. He favored his side.

"Angela and Benjamin are somewhere inside," Debra told Nikiatis, repeating what Orlan had apparently told her.

"I've memorized the building's layout," Kris said. "I can find them."

"You're in no shape to..." Gabe began, but Nikiatis interrupted him.

"If he knows the building, then he's an asset. He knows the risk. Randall's group shouldn't be far."

The bearded man scowled at the idea of his eldest adopted son going back into the prison. Nikiatis understood his anger. Then Gabe grabbed his ax.

"If he goes, then I go."

"I understand," Debra said as she laid her bow beside her. "I can protect Orlan."

Gabe nodded and motioned for Kris to follow him. Orlan attempted to stand, but Debra held him down.

"You're staying, Orlan. You've lost too much blood. Kris shouldn't have gone either."

"These two are no longer children," Nikiatis said. "If you want to rescue the others, then that man's knowledge of the prison will be needed." He turned his attention toward Orlan, who still lay on the ground. "What of the birdman who took you?"

"I haven't seen him since we arrived. I don't think he's here."

Nikiatis cursed.

"Is there a Kïen or a General inside?"

"There's a man named Mathew O'lor who's the acting General of Räthinock. The prisoners up there killed the previous one. The General of Vlörinclad is in there as well. His name's Devin-Brek."

"No Kïen?"

"Not yet."

That was all the information Nikiatis needed. He'd done his part. He had devised a plan to rescue the captured members of Refuge, detailing how Randall's men should proceed inside the building while Nikiatis saved those who remained on the ledge, his appearance serving as a distraction. The prison erupting into chaos provided a much better distraction allowing Nikiatis the opportunity to rescue the tribe's captives without much resistance. Those who were still inside, however, were Randall's responsibility. Now Nikiatis could focus on what really mattered—revenge.

His wings carried him above the trees as he defied the pouring rain once more. He was searching for an entry point when he heard the roar. It was like metal grinding on metal, and it echoed through the air. The giant had made its decision. It leapt from the ledge, and Nikiatis had to swerve in the air to keep from being crushed.

The giant fell past him with a man in its arms and forged a crater with its landing. The man spoke to the giant, and then it leapt again, passing Nikiatis, and clung to the ledge. It pulled itself up, and Nikiatis followed. The giant crushed four elves as it made its way to the other bloody and exhausted men. It took two of them and leapt again. A man with two swords remained, and he was smiling despite the blood dripping from his chin and extremities. He fought an equally exhausted human that wore a long coat. The man with the swords had been fighting alongside the others, so Nikiatis grabbed him and dove over the ledge.

The man shouted as they plummeted through the air, cursing Nikiatis for removing him from battle, so Nikiatis screeched at the man. He cowered, but more importantly, he shut up. They landed near the giant.

"Are there more?" Nikiatis asked.

"Not on the ledge, no," one of them said. He was the first taken by the giant. "There were others, a woman and a boy..."

"Their people are searching for them. A woman with medical training can be found if you march straight into those trees. She will help you if you need it. They seem to enjoy picking up strays."

Then, not caring to hear a reply, Nikiatis lifted into the sky and returned to the prison's ledge. An elder wildman with gray hair ran toward him with terror-filled eyes. Nikiatis recognized the beast from when it had led the attack on Refuge. Then Krom howled and fell with a knife imbedded into the back of his head. The man in the long coat leaned against the fence, breathing heavily.

Nikiatis cared nothing for the beast at his feet, so he took the knife from its head and stepped over the body. The few elves who remained on the ledge cowered near the entrance. They held out their swords, but none seemed eager to advance.

"So there *were* survivors," the man said. His teeth were red with his own blood and his clothing damp.

"The Generals of Räthinock and Vlörinclad," Nikiatis demanded.

The man leaned his head against the cage and studied the birdman. Then he laughed softly.

"If revenge is what you're seeking, then seek Devin-Brek alone. Mathew O'lor had little to do with what happened to your people. He is merely a Dömin of Intelligence. General-Devin-Brek, however, was one of two elves who devised the plan to destroyed Uuron Plauf. He is still inside."

"And the other elf?"

"General-Dägin-Bok, but he's already dead. Killed by that man you just rescued."

"Traitor!" shouted an elf in Vlörinclad armor. He took a step forward but then fell dead with the knife that Nikiatis had claimed embedded in his neck.

"And who are you?" Nikiatis asked the man.

"I'm just a hunter, and the bounty on birdmen has expired. Just do me a favor. Kill these elves. I'd hate for my blasphemy to reach Kïer's ear. He's so sensitive."

Then the man stepped aside and waved Nikiatis through. The birdman slew the elves, entered the prison, and dove through the center of a winding stairwell. Exhausted elves cowered, and several arrows were fired, but there was room for Nikiatis to maneuver. He slew every elf he saw, demanding Devin-Brek's location. The elves of Vlörinclad resisted. Some of Räthinock's did not. If Giyavin was not present, then Nikiatis would set his other plan in motion, and it began with the General of Vlörinclad.

The rooms were large on this portion of the fourth floor, and that was the reason General-Dägin-Bok had it for his living quarters. He had many of the walls removed so that the fourth level became one large room, save for just outside by the stairwell, and furniture was brought in for his comfort. If nothing else, Dägin-Bok was obsessed with comfort. Mathew felt it made him lazy.

Devin-Brek had quickly usurped control of Dägin-Bok's belongings but was now preparing them for Sheligog with hopes of gaining the Kïen's favor. The physical work of preparing the lodgings, however, was given to another.

Mathew descended the stairwell and opened the door leading to the fourth floor. The General was shouting at someone, and Mathew could guess who that someone was.

"Is this the best an O'lor can do? Are you so weak that you can't even scrub a simple bloodstain from the floor? Why Kier puts up with your brethren is beyond me. You are all so very useless."

Mathew circled a pillar and found the General of Vlörinclad towering over an elderly man who scrubbed the floor vehemently with a cloth. Blood stained the carpet black, likely drawn from the chameleons that lay dead nearby. A closer study revealed that a gash split the General's shaved head and that there were piercings hanging from loose skin over his left eye.

"You were attacked I take it?" Mathew said as he approached.

His father looked up in surprise, but Mathew ignored him. Devin-Brek scowled at Mathew's approach.

"Have you not noticed?" Devin-Brek said. "The lizards have escaped."

"If you haven't noticed, they all have."

Devin-Brek eyed Mathew and then spat, just missing the elderly man. Mathew's father wiped up the spittle.

"Is this how you run an operation?" Devin-Brek shouted. "You place so many variables onto one ledge and hope to maintain some semblance of control? You set this prison up to fail, little O'lor, unless, of course, you intended for this to happen. Some might be fooled, but I see what you are, traitor. Sheligog will know of your incompetence!"

"Let us not forget that you usurped this operation days ago. I suppose an elf of your importance is immune to accepting your own failures."

"How dare you!"

Devin-Brek kicked Mathew's father in the head and then kicked him again until the man lay on his side whimpering. Then Devin-Brek drew his sword and approached Mathew.

"Such blasphemy will not be tolerated. I am your master race, and you will know respect! Kneel!"

Mathew simply smiled. He drew his sword, and Devin-Brek, for the first time, smiled with him.

They did not attack each other, however, for the sounds of battle caught their attention. Elves were screaming from the stairwell; there were clashes of metal, and then another cry sounded. The screech echoed. Recognizing the sound, Mathew fell to the floor seconds before Nikiatis flew over his head and collided with Devin-Brek.

The General of Vlörinclad was a lithe creature, however, and slipped from the birdman's grip. Their swords clashed, and Mathew considered joining them but thought better of it. He needed Devin-Brek to die, and this birdman was certainly up to the task.

He turned to go but then saw his father, Nathan O'lor, frozen where Devin-Brek had left him, his eyes glued to the vicious battle being fought. Would the birdman attack Mathew's father once Devin-Brek was dead? Would Devin-Brek kill Nathan and blame it on the birdman? Mathew cursed his soft-hearted concern. He refused to acknowledge one so weak, yet he feared for his father's safety. He cursed as he took Nathan's arm and dragged him from the room.

"Stay under there," he told the quivering old man as he shoved him beneath the stairwell. "If you whimper, it will be your own cowardice that kills you."

Then a scream filled the fourth floor and echoed throughout the stairwell. Mathew could only surmise from the scream that Devin-Brek was dead. He stood, held out his sword, and faced the inevitable attack. Instead of flying at Mathew, however, the birdman stepped calmly through the doorway with fire burning in his eyes. He held two swords: his own and Devin-Brek's.

Mathew cursed his own weakness. He should have left the old man to die. Instead, it was now Mathew who would face the birdman's wrath. He prepared for the death that would surely come, but the birdman did not attack. It stood erect, stretched its wings, and dropped Devin-Brek's sword to the tiled floor. It clanged and rattled with the General's hand still gripping its hilt.

"Give this sword to the Kïen that comes," the birdman ordered. "Tell him that General-Devin-Brek of Vlörinclad is the first of many and that others will share his fate. The spirits of Uuron Plauf will know peace only after every General and Kïen of Amon-Göl are dead, and then I will slay Kïer himself. So swears Nikiatis, the last king of Uuron Plauf. Do you understand?"

"I do," Mathew replied. He lowered his blade as to not challenge the beast.

The white birdman flapped his mighty wings and shot up through the open stairwell. Mathew waited until he was gone and then breathed a sigh of relief. *What an enemy Kier has made in that one.*

"You did not challenge him," Mathew's father stated from beneath the stairs.

"No, I did not. He had a message, and I would rather deliver it than become a part of it. There is something to be said of intelligence."

"I will give Sheligog the message."

"See that you do. You are his slave after all."

Nathan O'lor came out from hiding and placed a hand on Mathew's shoulder.

"Son," he said, but Mathew pulled away.

"I am not your son. I will not be associated with one so weak."

"You are my son whether you want to be or not."

"I should have left you to the birdman. Then your cowardice would have been removed from the lineage you so deeply taint."

"That's not fair, Mathew."

"You were strong once, but you cracked. You gave up. You volunteered to serve Sheligog out of fear, afraid of being slain by the elves you once served. I could never respect a man who willingly bows to the elves."

"We are O'lors, Mathew. It is our duty to serve them. That is our place in life and why we live as long as we do. It is for our best."

"Then you are a fool, and I have nothing more to say to you."

Mathew wiped the blood from his sword and slipped it into its sheath. For a brief moment, he considered running it through his father's neck but quickly discarded the idea. He could blame the birdman for Nathan's death, but that wasn't the point. He still loved his father no matter how much he pretended not to.

Moving forward, Mathew took Devin-Brek's blood-covered sword and removed the severed hand. Then he stepped through the doorway and surveyed the mess that Nikiatis had made of the General.

What an enemy indeed.

The white birdman had been seen diving into the forest, and it was reasoned that others were there waiting for him, humans most likely. A band of elves were making their way to the nearest exit. Their orders were to kill whoever they found and reclaim the escapees for the purpose of judgment. The transgressors would pay for challenging the master race.

They didn't question the dimness of the hallway or that the candles had been extinguished; it was a drafty building after all. It wasn't until strangers stepped from the shadows and cupped hands over their mouths that they realized their mistake. They had fallen into a trap.

Seven elves lay unconscious a moment later, tucked into corners and small, unbarred rooms. Four figures stepped out of the darkness and carefully advanced.

"Very good," Randall Whitaker whispered. "Quickly now."

"You're foolish to leave them alive," Ivan chastised.

"Murdering is not our way. They were simply following orders." He stopped when they reached a fork in the hall. "Which way?"

Ivan seemed to be struggling with his memory. Randall understood that the man, or elf rather, had been gravely injured upon his escape, but there was no time for this. Knowing that a battle was being fought on the prison's ledge terrified Randall. His daughter needed him.

"Quickly," he urged.

"I would guess left."

"Are you certain?" Trent asked. He was also eager, for Benjamin's sake.

"As I said, it would be a guess."

It was good enough. Randall jogged forward but then stopped and motioned for the others to follow suit. He listened. There were footsteps coming, not from ahead of them but from behind. They ran to the nearest candles, blew them out, and laid in wait on the edges of darkness.

"Randall?" a familiar voice said. "It's Gabe, and Kris is with me."

Randall let the two pass through the darkness until he could verify with his own eyes that they were who they said they were. His heart flooded over with joy at the sight of Kris Medair'yin, and he ran to him.

"You are a sight for this old man's eyes."

"What of the others?" Tramin asked.

"Where is Benjamin?" Trent queried, his voice wavering.

"Benjamin and Angela are still inside," Kris replied, "but Orlan's safe with Debra. I've memorized what I've seen of the building and have a good idea of where they'll be." He began drawing lines and circles on the dust-covered floor and talked them through it. They listened inquisitively as he laid out each level so that they understood what awaited them, and then, after describing the interrogation room where he thought Angela and Benjamin would be, he pointed at a separate circle. "There's another prisoner also, just off the stairwell on the fifteenth floor. I've not seen her, but I could hear her crying."

Ivan seemed to startle at this mention.

"Did you hear her with your ears or with your mind?"

It was an odd question, but Kris confirmed that her voice had been in his mind. Ivan paled a bit.

"Who is she?" Tramin asked.

"Someone I've wronged."

"Then I'm sure we can help you right those wrongs," Trent said. "Does his map sound familiar?"

"It does. We should follow it."

Trent nodded and stood impatiently.

"Come on, then. Kris, lead the way."

The six men backtracked slightly and then ran toward the stairwell that rose at the end of the hall. Randall glanced at Ivan, who was last in line, and noted how distracted he seemed. He fell back a few steps.

"The woman," Randall said, "we will help her."

"She deserves as much," he replied, "but you should do so without me. My presence would only make matters worse."

"Who is she, Ivan?"

The elf hesitated, and Randall noted that he was holding his wounded ribs.

"Call her my biggest regret and leave it at that."

"We should carry no secrets, Ivan."

"You will have to live with this one. The shame I feel for what I've done to that woman is far too great to speak aloud. It would surely kill me."

Ivan ran ahead, dodging further questions. Randall did not like secrets, but he found some comfort in Ivan's guilt. It showed compassion, and Randall clung to that. There was hope for Ivan Shaymolin. The disfigured elf could still be redeemed.

Angela screamed and fell to her knees. The vision was so sudden and the willow's scream so loud that it caught her completely by surprise. The image of Ivan was so vivid that it cut her mind like a knife.

"Is he here?" Benjamin asked, running up to the willow. He had obviously seen the vision as well. "Have they come for us?"

The willow screamed again, and Benjamin fell holding his ears. The images were back. Ivan was running through the halls. Angela recognized his location from when she had first arrived. Others were with him. She saw her father.

"They're here!" she shouted. "Willow, we have to find them."

The willow constricted violently and moved away from Angela, cowering at the suggestion.

"Returned," her voice echoed in Angela's mind. "Came for me."

"He's come to rescue us," Benjamin clarified.

"Listen to me, willow. If Ivan is here with my father, then he's here to help. My tribe, we believe that people can change. That includes Ivan. I remember what you showed me of your history, but if we want to live, we must find Ivan and my father."

Tears streamed down the willow's face, and her glow dimmed. She was kneeling, rocking, and her arms were wrapped tightly around her torso.

"Willow, please. I can't leave you here."

The willow did not respond.

"Have faith, willow," Angela tried. "Have faith in Ivan."

The willow looked at Angela with hollow eyes.

"No faith," her voice faintly echoed. "Not him."

The willow had made up its mind. She would go no further, and Angela knew it.

"Could you at least tell us how to find them?"

The willow locked eyes with Angela, and visions flooded her mind. Angela looked through Ivan's eyes, and she recognized where he was. Then willow pointed toward a stairwell down the hall.

"Down. Wait."

The image faded. Angela hesitated but then hugged the willow.

"Thank you. I'll come back for you if I can."

"No," the willow's voice echoed. "He will come."

"I can tell him not to."

"He comes. Alone."

"Then I wish you the best."

They could linger no more. Benjamin took Angela by the arm, and together they ran down the hall and descended the stairs. It was only one floor, and they paused on the bottom step.

"She said to wait, right?" Benjamin asked.

"She did."

They waited for what felt like an eternity. Then the footsteps came. Benjamin shouted and ran toward them but then skidded to a halt.

"What have we here?"

Elya-Ecshelï, one of seven heavily-armed guards, seemed just as shocked as Benjamin was.

Benjamin held out Mathew's knife, but Elya disarmed him easily enough. Angela rushed to Benjamin's side and pleaded with Elya for mercy. Heeding her pleas, the elves bound the humans and led them toward the stairwell.

Angela didn't understand. How could this happen? The willow's every prediction was accurate. Every vision. Every whisper. They hadn't run into a single elf due to the willow's foresight, and that accuracy told Angela that the willow intended for them to be captured. But why would she do that? Was this revenge for having left her behind?

"Have faith," she heard the willow's voice echo. "Have faith."

A rusted sign beside the door read *thirteen*, so Kris motioned for them to prepare. They had already fought through four bands of elves and were hurrying now. No elves had escaped thus far, and their presence was still a secret, but Randall worried. Things seldom went this well.

Tramin inched the door open and peered through it.

"Clear," he whispered.

"Clear?" Kris repeated. "The ledge was always guarded."

"Perhaps that was due to there being prisoners," Tramin suggested, "but it's a bit lacking in that department as well."

"The guards are still present," Gabe said. "They're dead."

"Nikiatis?" Randall suggested.

"Likely," Tramin confirmed.

They moved into the short hall, and Tramin rushed to the other stairwell and listened. There were footsteps.

"More are coming."

They blew out the lamps and hid in the shadows. Three elves appeared, followed by Angela and Benjamin, and four more elves marched behind them. They hesitated when they reached the thirteenth floor. They weren't expecting the bodies.

"The prisoners did this?" one questioned.

"They had help," the lead elf replied. "How is the prison?"

"Still operational."

"Are there any prisoners left?"

"Only the dead," a guard stated. "Four wildmen and fourteen chameleons are here."

"Fourteen?" the elf replied. "Peculiar. There were only seven in captivity."

"The largest wildman is still alive. It's wounded but living. Should I slit its throat?"

"No," the leader replied. "Take it to a separate room and nurse its wounds until we've been ordered to do otherwise. There might be a change in orders following today's events."

"Will the boy and girl be staying here?"

The leader surveyed the ledge, littered with bodies, and shook his head.

"Not until this is cleaned up. We'll take them to Dömin-Mathew O'lor."

They turned to go, but Randall could wait no longer. He leapt at the nearest elf and left a gash in his chest. Then he moved on to the next. He knew that it was wrong to kill, but he couldn't help himself. The next elf fell dead. The others joined him, and the last to fall was Elya-Ecshelï, leader of the guard. He stood his ground against the Bishop brothers, but Trent eventually disarmed him so that Tramin could render him unconscious with the hilt of his sword. All in all, three elves lay dead. Randall would pray for forgiveness later.

"Father!" Benjamin cried as he clung to Trent. Trent was sobbing uncontrollably, and Tramin stood over them both.

Angela ran to her father, and he held her for what felt like ages. It was not near long enough. He was reminded of how she used to cling to him after having a nightmare.

"It's okay, Angela," he said. "The nightmare's over."

"Not yet it isn't," Gabe reminded him. "Not until we've left this place."

"No!" Angela shouted. "We have to go back for the willow. She helped Benjamin and me escape. She knew our being captured again would lead us back to you, but she was too afraid to join us."

Randall couldn't fathom what Angela was talking about, having never met a willow, but Kris looked as if the last pieces of some unseen puzzle had finally fallen into place.

"Of course," he said. "The prisoner on the fifteenth floor was Ivan's willow."

The group looked at Ivan who, to their surprise, appeared dismayed. He lifted his hood to hide from the questions burning behind their eyes.

"She tore out my side when last we met. To upset her again would surely mean our deaths."

"She was afraid," Angela said. "We should help her."

"You will die," Ivan warned.

"That doesn't mean we shouldn't try," Benjamin stated in a manner that made him sound older than he was.

Angela noted the uncomfortable pause in Ivan's face. He tugged at his hood again.

Footsteps.

They hesitated as the sound drew closer, echoing from the same stairwell that Elya and his guards had come through. The noise told Randall that there were more elves coming than they felt comfortable facing, and so the people of Refuge retreated down the opposite stairwell and hid in various rooms and shadows. A large group of elves passed by them—two dozen at least—and they seemed to be in a hurry. The tribe slowly gathered once the commotion had passed.

"Do you think they're heading for the entrance?" Tramin asked.

"If they are, then we could have a problem on our hands," Trent replied. "Debra and Orlan are still out there."

Gabe beat his axe against the wall.

"I should have stayed with them," he said. That's what I was out there for. If something happens…"

"There isn't any time for that now," Randall interrupted. "Let's head their way. We can intervene if necessary, but only when necessary. We must remain unseen for as long as possible." He concealed a cough then motioned for Kris with a wave of his hand. "Can you lead us out?"

Kris nodded, favoring his side now. "Follow me."

They descended the stairwell as quietly as possible but the need to escape was great, and they were soon sprinting. Then they stopped. Sixty or more elves had gathered near the exit, preparing to attack whoever it was that aided the prisoners, and they were armed. Kris nearly stumbled down the stairs at the sight of them but was rescued by Gabe, who yanked him back by the shirt. The tribe attempted to hide, but they were too late. They had been spotted.

"Intruders!" the nearest elf shouted.

The cry of an angry mob arose, and arrows began to fly. The tribe scampered up the stairs and was sprinting through the second level hallway, searching for an unbarred room to hide in, when they heard a terrifying roar that sounded like metal grinding against metal. The commotion below intensified as the elves began to shout, yet none followed them up the stairs.

"What's going on down there?" Gabe asked.

"To the stairwell!" Randall commanded.

They descended the stairs and were startled by what they found. The stone giant was tearing through the elves, their arrows breaking as they bounced off its skin, and the rest of Arick Kasdan's men fought alongside it. Debra was with them, firing off arrows, and Nikiatis' screech caught Randall's ear, revealing his presence as he dove through the hoard with great thrusts of his blackened blade. The elves were being slaughtered.

Randall engaged an elf that attempted to flee, and they held the stairwell. None got by. It wasn't long before the elves, all sixty of them, were either dead or unconscious.

None spoke after the last elf fell. They fled into the woods, retrieved Orlan, and continued on until a large distance had been covered. Some fell into the mud while others bent over, gasping for air. It was only then that Angela began to sob. Randall held her.

"You are their leader?" one of the men asked.

"I am."

"My name is Arick Kasdan, and you have our gratitude."

Randall nodded, and the man left to gather his people. Randall watched him go and felt a small pain in his gut. He wanted to befriend the man who helped Refuge in their final escape, but he couldn't forget Ivan's words. This man was building an army and planned to wage war on the elves. Arick Kasdan had the potential to overthrow Kier himself.

He disregarded these thoughts, not wanting to remember Bethany's final words. No, he wanted to comfort his daughter, so he focused on that.

"I saved her, Bethany," he silently mouthed, "just like I promised."

"Randall?"

"Yes, Tramin."

"Ivan's missing."

Randall scanned every face and realized that Ivan was indeed unaccounted for. How could they have left him behind? How long had it been? He remembered seeing Ivan as they fought their way out of the prison. Had he been struck down without anyone noticing?

"He went back for the willow," Angela stated. "She said he would come for her."

"The willow?" Orlan asked, wide-eyed. "The prisoner in that room was Ivan's willow?"

"Why would he go alone?" Kris asked.

"I get the impression that he's been alone for a long time," Tramin replied. "He knows what he's doing."

"Then it's out of our hands," Randall said. "You're all safe. Let's just focus on that."

The prison felt like a tomb as Ivan Shaymolin crept through its deadened halls. The willow wasn't in her room on the fifteenth floor, but she was still present. He could feel her.

He had slain several elves during his hunt. Their numbers were fewer now, and he wondered how many could be left. Not many, he assumed. This prison was only a small holdout after all, not a tower like Räthinock or Vlörinclad.

Then he heard her. The willow's cry echoed in his mind, and he knew that he was near.

"Contrary to what you might think," he called out. "I've not come to hurt you."

The crying continued. It got louder as he approached a stairwell on the seventh floor. He spotted her crouching beneath the stairs. It was dark.

The willow began to hiss, so he stopped. She had torn four gashes into his side and nearly killed him when last he'd heard that sound. He stood at a distance, sheathed his sword, and waited.

"Why have you come?" her voice echoed in his mind. "Leave me."

"I've come to free you."

"Trickery."

"Guilt," he corrected.

The willow paused and sat up a bit. He could feel her in his mind, and so he allowed her to roam freely. She seemed surprised.

"Guilt," she repeated. "Compassion. Concern?"

He didn't reply as she slowly stood and approached him. Her fingers were still sharp, prepared to attack if need be, but he had no intention of defending himself.

"Softened heart." Then she paused. "Love?"

"I doubt there is love in me, but perhaps something like it."

"Refuge," her voice echoed. "Changed you."

"They haven't."

"Have."

He cursed them in his thoughts, and she flinched. He apologized without speaking. They *had* changed him. He tried his best to hide it, but he knew. He had come to their tribe hating the world, embittered by his role in its current corruption, but Refuge had changed him. They somehow created a crack in his black and bitter heart and instilled a grain of hope where there had previously been none.

A series of images flashed through Ivan's mind. He saw himself. He was young with beautiful white hair and flawless skin. Mankind's wars were concluded, and the world had been left black, covered in ash. The willows had come out of hiding, and he was drawn to the lake where they gathered. With their faith they could weave the lands. The lake was made crystal clear, and its shores became lush with vegetation. He befriended them, and they taught him their faith. The willows loved him unconditionally.

He led other elves to them, and they embraced the teachings. They embraced the willows' faith. They rebuilt the burnt and blackened world with what they had learned, but their hatred of mankind was too great. They refused to release that darkness and walked away from the willows. They built a kingdom to honor their king, Kïer, and as their darkness grew their faith diminished. Their ability to weave the world vanished with their lack of faith, and they grew angry.

Ivan's kin attacked the willows, demanding that the power be returned to them, but the willows could not offer what was not theirs to give. Many died. Unknown to most, the willows were the first victims of the elves. Ivan hid during these attacks and grieved for both his kin and the willows. He loved his people but hated what they had become. He blamed himself. He had introduced the elves to the willows, who lovingly equipped his kin with the means to heal the world, but with that power they also created an Elven Nation. Their pride grew, and their hair darkened. The willows had shared with them their faith and love, but it was not enough. They lusted for more and were never satisfied. Ivan blamed himself for the torment that was to follow.

Then, when the elves turned their hatred toward humanity, Ivan opted to defend mankind. He didn't particularly love the humans, but couldn't condone their being hunted. He abandoned them both before long, however, as his guilt and disappointment in both sides became too much to bear.

What was this new world? Was it so different from the last?

He found the willows again, in time, but they refused his presence. They blamed him. They believed that he had tricked them into empowering the elves, but they were wrong; his only desire was to heal the world. The elves were the ones who twisted his noble intentions into an empire of hate.

He pleaded with the willows, and then he cursed them. How dare they blame him! Had he not loved them? Had he not shared their faith? He lashed out. Many were killed, and he was very nearly killed himself. He was exiled. His faith faded, and his hair became charcoal black. He realized that he was no different than the rest of his kin, and so he grew bitter and isolated himself, no longer caring for the world or those who inhabited it. He was to be alone forever—no, not forever. Silus Rook found him, but that was not to last.

"Found again," willow's words echoed.

"Refuge is weak."

"Strong."

"You do not know them."

"God knows them."

"I do not care what God knows."

The willow hissed violently. She approached, and Ivan cowered. She held her menace for only a moment, but then she softened. He looked away.

"Teach them, Tröbin-Dur."

"I am not worthy," he said, his voice breaking.

"Find your worth."

"There is none left."

"Learn from them."

"I cannot..."

"Learn from them."

"But I..."

Then the willow cupped his face in her soft, gentile hands, the bark-covered talons gone, and stared deeply into his soul. In her eyes he saw the willows from long ago; the ones he trusted and loved; the ones who loved him in return.

"Have faith," her voice echoed in his mind, and he began to weep.

"I have none," he replied weakly.

"You will."

He clung to her, and she comforted him. The death-filled prison vanished as she sang a lullaby into his mind, seeping through centuries of hatred and confusion, and he felt safe. He curled into her arms and slept as she carried him from the prison into the forest. He dreamed of birdmen and humans who loved him. He recalled the words of Silus Rook and then the words again when they were spoken by Randall Whitaker. He remembered another elf among the humans, Shëlin-Vin, and then he recalled the children. They were asking him to play.

The willow laid Ivan in a shallow stream and left him to his dreams, memories of a happier time mixed with what could still be. She whispered a prayer for him before fading into the shadows of the Greysong Forest, and still he dreamed on. For the first time in two-hundred years, Ivan Shaymolin, who had once been called Tröbin-Dur, was content in his slumber.

Part VIII: Refuge United

Water cascaded from the rocky cliffs above as Joshua sat on the walkway between caves, patiently waiting for his tribe to return. Jillian and Pillar sat beside him, as was normal, but Jillian wasn't so patient.

"Do you see them?" she asked while fidgeting with the heart-shaped stone her father had engraved for her.

"No," he replied.

It had been more than a week since Gabe and the others left for the prison, and in that time, with Shëlin's guidance, Joshua assigned himself to Jillian's complete recovery. She clung to Joshua after Debra left, and they had been spending their days together ever since. He missed Phyllis and cried out for her often, but Jillian gave him something else to focus on.

"Do you think they'll all come back?" Jillian asked.

"I hope so."

"But what if my mom doesn't make it back?"

"She will."

"But what if…"

"Then you'll become a Harlow like me, and I'll keep taking care of you."

She leaned against him, and he put an arm around her. Jillian didn't ask the next question. What if Gabe didn't return? What would happen to Joshua and those like him if there weren't any more Harlows left to adopt the orphaned children? He cast the thought aside and not for the first time. There was no use in worrying about things that were beyond his control, but he prepared himself for the possibility that it could happen. Anything could happen.

Joshua had changed since his father's return from Uuron Plauf. He feared for his family now, and he no longer looked forward to hearing their stories. He had lost that innocence.

Then something caught his eye. He stood, and Jillian stood with him. Pillar began to bark.

"Quiet, boy," Tramin's called up, and Pillar dashed down the walkway, vanishing in the trees below.

Joshua and Jillian followed after the dog and saw their friends and loved ones racing toward them.

"We got them all," Gabe whispered into Joshua's ear after a long hug, "and then some."

Joshua clung to Orlan and Kris next and then to Benjamin. He cried and didn't care who saw. His family was back. They were not whole and would never be again, but Gabe and his brothers were alive, and for that at least, he was glad.

"Stretch your wings, my friend," Fagunol said.

Vetcalf, the blue birdman, stood and slowly did as he was told. He grimaced a bit but then spread his wings to their full extent.

"Very good."

Fagunol had been working alongside Shëlin-Vin while the tribe was away, aiding in Vetcalf's therapy. The blue birdman was recovering quicker than expected, as birdmen often did, but he wasn't quite ready to fly yet, though he was close. Another week or two perhaps, provided flight was restricted to short distances.

The greatest of Vetcalf's injuries, however, was his voice. His throat had been horribly slashed in Uuron Plauf, and his speech was permanently negated as a result. The birdman was mute.

Vetcalf was still wary of Shëlin, her being an elf, but she was earning his trust. She did this by teaching him a form of speech through hand motions. He had much to learn, but Shëlin calmly corrected him as he made mistakes, and he eventually grew to tolerate her methods. He was a fast learner, and Shëlin was a wonderful instructor. Fagunol was enamored by the elf's ability to care for other beings. He found it intoxicating.

"They're back," Shëlin said suddenly.

She ran from the cave. Fagunol told Vetcalf to rest and signed his instruction as well for learning purposes, and then he followed Shëlin out. She was already halfway down the walkway, and so he simply watched as members of the tribe appeared at the base of the waterfalls. There were four unfamiliar men among them and one giant. It had been quite some time since he'd seen one of those.

Then he spotted Nikiatis.

"How is Vetcalf?" the white birdman asked as he landed on the walkway and entered the cavern.

Fagunol was struck by the tint of red in Nikiatis' feathers. The blood from Uuron Plauf had washed out in time, but here it was again. The omen made Fagunol uncomfortable.

"He is recovering," Fagunol replied, "though he is mute."

"Can he fly?"

"Not yet."

Fagunol followed Nikiatis to where Vetcalf was resting but stood back as the white birdman approached the blue. Vetcalf saw him coming and knelt before his king. Nikiatis simply helped Vetcalf to his feet and hugged him.

"It is good to see you, Vetcalf," he said, "but our people are dead. I failed them. Though I am your king, I should no longer be revered until they are avenged." Nikiatis stepped back and turned toward Fagunol. "But their blood will be paid for. I have declared war on Kïer. I slew the General of Vlörinclad and have vowed to destroy every other General, Kïen, and even Kïer himself for what they have done to us."

"We cannot destroy all of Amon-Göl alone," Fagunol interjected.

"We need not destroy Amon-Göl, only its leaders. The rest of the body will crumble."

"Can we not simply move on?" Fagunol pled quietly.

Nikiatis grimaced.

"These people continue to eat away at your mind, these people and that elf. I will suffer no more of it," he said. "The debt we've owed them has been paid. Vetcalf is on the mend. We will leave this place when he is strong enough to fly, but you, Fagunol, must remember your proud heritage. You are a birdman of Uuron Plauf not a man or an elf. Reclaim your spine!"

Fagunol felt a fire in his belly but kept it from pouring forth. Instead he asked, "What of the traitorous Giyavin?"

"He was not at the prison, but we will hunt him as we destroy the leaders of Amon-Göl. The villain will receive his penance at the swords of his brethren."

Vetcalf pounded a fist against his chest, a sign that he and Nikiatis were of the same mind.

"Finally," Nikiatis said, "a birdman who has not relinquished the might of Uuron Plauf."

"Uuron Plauf is dead."

The words shocked Fagunol even as he spoke them. It was that shock which prevented Fagunol from defending himself as Nikiatis threw the golden birdman against the cavern wall and held him there by the throat. He could not breathe, but then Nikiatis, overcoming his rage, released Fagunol and spat at his elder's feet.

"There is no place for us in this tribe! Our place in this world is now one of vengeance, and you will aid in that endeavor. So orders your king."

Nikiatis turned and left the cave as Fagunol rubbed his fur-covered neck. He looked at Vetcalf, who was sitting wearily now, and wondered if there was any point in arguing with Nikiatis. He had hoped that they could simply exist with Shëlin and the people of Refuge, but that would never happen, not with so much unfinished business. He could refuse Nikiatis, but Fagunol still possessed that burdensome birdman pride. He could never stand by and watch as the last of his kin flew off to what would most likely be their deaths. He loved them far too much.

"Rest, Vetcalf," he said softly. "It seems that we will have even more blood on our hands before long."

Mathew O'lor stood at the door with his hands behind his back. He could hear the wildman screaming inside.

"Not fond of being chained," he stated plainly.

"No," Adviser-Mondel answered beside him.

Mathew could see that his Adviser was shaken by the creature's wrath, but Mathew did not scare so easily.

"Is there a reason you've asked me to join you, Mathew?" Mondel asked. "Do you need me to translate?"

"No. I know their language well enough. I want you to stand guard while I speak with it."

"Wouldn't an elf be better suited for that task? Captain-Ecsheli perhaps?"

"No, my friend. The meeting I am about to have with this wildman must remain secret; none can know that I was here. I cannot trust an elf to keep this secret, but I can trust you, Mondel. You are one of the few."

Mondel hesitated but then nodded.

"I will do as you ask."

"Very good."

Mathew placed a hand on Mondel's shoulder and nodded. The hall was clear, and so Mathew entered the room and closed the door behind him. Candles flickered, reflecting in the chains about Grot's neck and arms. The wildman was large and scarred; a truly frightening creature.

"Hello, Grot," Maximus said in the wildman tongue.

"What do you want?" it growled back in a similar dialect.

"I wanted to apologize for how you have been treated."

The beast lunged at Mathew, but the chains held. Mathew did not flinch.

"I am sorry to inform you that you are the last of your tribe. The others were killed in battle upon the prison's ledge, slain by both elf and cowardly men. You would have been slain as well if not for your own strength and the aid of an elf named Elya-Ecshelï who showed you mercy."

Grot howled in anguish. Mathew continued once the wildman had quieted.

"I wanted you to know that it was my predecessor, General-Dägin-Bok, who sacrificed your tribe to experimental testing. He infected your people with a virus that he hoped would spread to mankind, but the virus was ineffective. He planned to have your kind killed, blaming you for the virus' failure, but then he was murdered. I halted his kill order on you and attempted to give you a purpose, sending you to Refuge."

"I remember," Grot grumbled.

"Good. Then you know that it was not I who ordered that your people be killed?"

Grot growled, and Mathew smiled knowing that Grot was remembering that night.

"My Adviser overstepped his boundaries by ordering Maximus the hunter to slay your people. The full blame of that night rests on my Adviser's shoulders, Mondel O'lor."

"The hunter killed them all," Grot growled. "He slew Krom."

"The hunter was following Mondel's orders in the forest and was defending himself on the ledge. He is not to blame."

Grot barked but then backed away. He seemed confused, which was precisely how Mathew wanted him. He risked taking a few steps toward the wildman.

"A hunter is one who has sworn away all loyalties and works for his own selfish gain. He does not side with the elves, mankind, or anyone else. He has no place in this world save for the one he creates for himself. I have a lot of respect for hunters in that way."

"What of it?"

"I have a proposition for you," Mathew said. Grot listened closely. "You are unaccustomed to being alone, and so I propose that you take up the mantle of hunter and work for me. I will pay you in food, shelter, and whatever else you desire, and you will fulfill the contracts that I prepare for you."

"Why should I do this?"

"First off, a hunter is immune to punishment, provided they do not challenge the elves. Secondly, you serve none but yourself. You would work for me, but not serve me. You would accept only the contracts that serve you best and are free to come and go as you please. And finally, if you fulfill my contracts, then I will keep you protected above and beyond that of a normal hunter, such as I do for Maximus."

Grot growled.

"And what do you get out of this," he asked.

"I gain a clever killing machine. You are not as stupid as the elves think you are. I know this."

"What sort of contract would I fulfill?"

Mathew smiled and nodded toward the door.

"The sort you'll enjoy," he said. "In fact, your first contract is standing just beyond that door: Adviser-Mondel, the man who had your people killed. I need him eliminated, and I want you to do it. If you kill him, then I will pay you your first wage—your freedom."

Grot began to salivate and tugged at his chains.

"I can unlock those, provided you do not attack me. I am offering you a job and a place in this world. You will kill, you will feast, and you will live a greater life than any wildman before you. I have great plans for you, my friend, if you will only trust me."

"Unlock me," Grot demanded.

"Then we have a deal?"

"I will hunt for you."

"Good." Mathew drew a key from a pocket and approached the wildman. He would be lying if he said he wasn't nervous, but his nerves did not show. He made sure of it. "I will unlock your shackles, but for the moment I want you to hold them as if you were still chained. I will send Mondel in. Once the door closes, he will be yours to do with as you please. Wait one hour before leaving this room so that I may prepare your new status, and then you may leave. Be wary of elves, but do not threaten them. Give them no reason to fear you, and you will know freedom."

"Deal."

Mathew unlocked the shackles and backed away.

"Here's to a long, bloody future together, my friend."

He opened the door and found Mondel several paces away, seemingly afraid.

"Have you finished?" the Adviser asked. "Can we go now?"

"Not yet, my friend," Mathew said. "I cannot convince the wildman to trust me. He will not speak… coherently anyway. Perhaps you would be better suited to the task. You are more fluent in their barbaric tongue than I."

Mondel seemed stricken.

"I don't know if that's…"

"Have a look, Mondel." He motioned into the room where the candlelight reflected in Grot's chains. "He is restrained. If he does not speak, then I will slay him myself."

"What would you like me to ask him?"

"Whether or not there are other wildmen in the area. Useful things of that nature."

Mondel shook slightly but nodded.

"Very well," he said. "I will return momentarily."

He stepped into the room, and Mathew shut and locked the door. Then Mondel shrieked in terror as Grot howled, and a sudden impact nearly broke the door from its hinges. His screams did not last long. Mathew waited until he could hear nothing but the sound of Grot feasting, then he unlocked the door and walked away. The creature would be busy for the next hour.

He needed to inform Maximus of the wildman's acceptance. The hunter had originally been against training the beast, but he came around to the idea once Mathew offered him a more lucrative fee than normal. Truth was, Mathew needed Grot. A wildman could remember a scent for years, and if Mathew was going to find the people of Refuge, then he needed the wildman's nose.

Mondel had been a good Adviser once but grew cowardly and lazy, and he knew too much. Mondel knew that Mathew had been bested by a mere boy, and that could have been devastating if the Adviser chose to exploit it. Mathew's impeccable reputation was at stake.

Offering Mondel to Grot served to gain the wildman's trust while ridding Mathew of a potential threat. The sacrifice was necessary. There were other Advisers after all.

Mathew had to consider his place in Räthinock as well. After the fall of so many, Mathew was now its highest ranked official. If he was to become General, then he needed to distance himself from humans and begin associating with elves. Besides Mathew, Adviser-Mondel was only one of two other eligible replacements for the role of General, the other being Elya-Ecsheli. Mathew had spoken with Elya, however, and learned that the elf did not feel prepared to claim such a prominent position. However, he found the Dömin of Forces position entirely reasonable. Mathew did not trust Elya of course—he was an elf—but that was a concern for another day.

He had other things to worry about. Sheligog had finally arrived, and the Kïen was not pleased. If Mathew was to become General, then he needed to appease Sheligog by removing himself from this fiasco and making himself respectable again. Much had already happened to allow for this, Mathew just needed to twist the scenario to his advantage.

"You may enter," the hollow voice echoed.

Mathew opened the door and found Nathan kneeling, cleaning the stained remains of General-Devin-Brek from the floor. Mathew passed his father without a glance and found a rather large elf sitting in a chair near an oak table.

"You have much to explain, Dömin."

"I do, your excellency."

Sheligog of the Kïen was a towering presence. He wore armor that was the color of smoke with the symbol of the Kïen on his chest, that of a golden crown. None had ever seen his face, for Sheligog, like all Kïen, wore a mask. It resembled an elf's face, though every aspect of the mask was horribly exaggerated from its pointed ears rising like horns to its teeth appearing as fangs. There were indentations where eyes should be but no visible windows for Sheligog to peek through. Mathew wondered if Sheligog could see through the mask or if there was some dark magic involved.

Much of the mask, however, was hidden by a green hood that fell to a point between the two horn-like ears, covering much of Sheligog's face. The hood was connected to a ragged, green cape that was now draped over the back of the chair and floor. In Sheligog's hand was a massive sword. Its blade scratched the tile floor as he rotated its handle slowly with his metal, talon-like fingers.

"Nearly three hundred elves dead," Sheligog spoke. His voice was deep, potentially amplified by the mask or magic. "How did this happen, Dömin-Mathew O'lor?"

"I offer no excuses, but rather, explanations."

"Begin."

"We were invaded by unseen forces. The people of Refuge had found the prison, we assume, by following trails left behind by Adviser-Mondel O'lor and the wildmen. They attacked in unison with a large tribe of chameleons that were attempting to rescue their kin."

"Explain the chameleons."

"Before his death, General-Dägin-Bok found a group of chameleons stealing from our stores, and so he captured them and began serving them for meals. There were seven chameleons left on the ledge at the time of the attack, yet we've uncovered nearly thirty bodies scattered throughout the prison. We believe that the chameleons' kin had been making their way through the prison when the people of Refuge attacked. Their ability to mimic their surroundings made this infiltration difficult to detect. I believe that Sölva, Master of the Guard, was so intent on keeping the prisoners on the ledge that he turned a blind eye to the rest of the building."

"And what has become of Master-Sölva?"

"He fell from the ledge during the battle. His body has been recovered."

"Dismember it and cast his limbs to the wind," Sheligog demanded. "Continue your explanation."

"By the word of Captain-Elya-Ecshelï of Räthinock, Master-Sölva had ordered an attack on the prisoners without General-Devin-Brek's approval. He opened the gates, and a battle began that would ultimately lead to the prison break. Therefore, the initial riot was also due to Master-Sölva's incompetence."

"Is the word of Captain-Ecshelï trustworthy?"

Mathew thought this over for a moment. Now would be the time to cast doubt on the elf, but he opted to stay honest. He feared that Sheligog would see through his lies.

"Yes, to the best of my knowledge. He is a loyal elf of Räthinock and came to me once Sölva chose to follow his own path. He should be commended for his wisdom and his readiness to act. He was the only elf who spoke against Sölva's folly."

"He came to you and not General-Devin-Brek, who ranked your superior?"

"He attempted to inform General-Devin-Brek first, as he should have, but could not find him. The General, I am sorry to report, was more concerned with your coming than the workings of the prison. I feel things might have gone differently if he had been more focused. Your O'lor servant will attest to this."

"Do you feel General-Devin-Brek was wrong to prepare for my coming?"

Mathew took a deep breath.

"I do, your excellency. Your servant is my father. He needed no help preparing your quarters, yet General-Devin-Brek chastised his every move as a means of belittling me. The General told me himself that he assumed command of this prison with the intent of undermining my newfound authority. He was not fond of an O'lor leading an operation of this size and made it well known. Knowing his superiority, I willingly stepped aside and allowed him to take control of the prison. General-

Devin-Brek, however, was so focused on undermining my role here that he seldom considered the building's operations. It is my opinion that this is what failed both you and this prison, my lord. If he had given half a mind to the task at hand, then we might have been able to defend ourselves to more satisfactory results."

"And what of you, Mathew O'lor? Have you failed me?"

"I have, to the extent that I did not alert you of General-Devin-Brek's distractions. I stepped aside when the General arrived and merely performed my duties as Dömin of Intelligence. Before the General's arrival, I saw to it that Refuge was found. The wildmen under Adviser-Mondel O'lor's leadership failed to perform as I had hoped, but they did manage to return with hostages who I put to good use by means of interrogation. We learned a great deal from them."

"Tell me of Adviser-Mondel O'lor."

"Adviser-Mondel served me loyally for three years, a promotional transfer from the tower of Olergöl. Sadly, this was his first experience with battle, and his performance was less than desirable. Captain-Ecsheli found him cowering in a room while others fought off the invaders. This was after I had ordered him to retrieve two prisoners who had escaped his grasp. Adviser-Mondel was later mauled to death by the last surviving wildman."

"Good. Such cowardice is not to be tolerated in Kïer's kingdom. What has become of the wildman?"

"Being the last of its tribe, the wildman has declared its intent to become a hunter in Kïer's service. Maximus, my top hunter, has agreed to train him."

"Is there benefit to the wildman working with us?"

"Yes, your excellency. He has the prisoners' scent."

Sheligog pondered this a moment and stood. There was something about the Kïen that seemed askew, as if Mathew were looking at him through a haze. His green cape flowed softly as he paced.

"Tell me about the prisoners."

"I've told you what I know of the chameleons. There were four wildmen, three of which died on the prison's ledge, one of whom I slew myself. There was a stone giant, which General-Dägin-Bok had imprisoned with hopes of converting to our side. There were four humans charged with General-Dägin-Bok's murder, and of course, the four young prisoners from Refuge."

"Why were they imprisoned in one place?"

"General-Dägin-Bok had constructed the prison for the giant and then threw the chameleons in with it. I added General-Dägin-Bok's slayers to the ledge and ordered that a second prison be prepared, but General-Devin-Brek halted all of my orders upon his arrival. He then ordered that the young prisoners from Refuge be thrown in with them as well. I voiced my concern, but as you can imagine the General would heed none of my advice."

"And General-Devin-Brek is dead."

"He was slain by the white birdman who was once king of Uuron Plauf."

"My servant has informed me of the birdman's declaration."

"I heard it myself, my lord."

"Was the birdman with the people of Refuge?"

"I believe so. In fact, it is my belief that they were all functioning as a single unit. The chameleons would be the lone exception."

This seemed to capture Sheligog's attention.

"Explain," he ordered.

"When the elves captured the original four men, there was a fifth with them. The fifth prisoner, a disfigured man in a black hood, had escaped the prison."

"Why was this not reported?"

"I only just learned of it myself. Master-Sölva had lied about the man's escape, claiming that he had died. The youngest prisoner brought the lie to light just prior to the chameleon and Refuge attacks."

Sheligog considered this and then laughed. It was an eerie sound.

"Dismemberment is not punishment enough for the Master of the Guard. Feed him to the wildman."

"I'm sure the wildman will appreciate the gesture."

"So this fifth prisoner?"

"According to the boy, he had wandered into their camp and informed them of the extermination order on Uuron Plauf. That was how their people learned of the raid, leading to their interference."

"And what do you think, Dömin?"

"I think that the man was a member of Refuge all along. In fact, it is my belief that all nine of the human prisoners were from the same tribe. I learned from my interrogations that one or more elves might reside with them as well, and reports state that General-Dägin-Bok's slayers were attempting to recruit a willow to their cause before being captured. They also convinced the giant and the wildmen to fight alongside them during the prison break. Maximus the hunter claims that the giant had rescued three humans during their escape and the white birdman three more."

Sheligog watched Mathew curiously, though whether this was a good thing or not was uncertain. Mathew let his claims float in the air a moment before finishing up his theory.

"It is my belief that the remnants of Refuge are raising a diverse army to challenge Amon-Göl. Men, birdmen, willows, giants, elves—they are recruiting any who would side with them. I believe there is a war coming if we do not stop it and that the people of Refuge are directly responsible."

"That is a powerful accusation, Dömin."

"But there is merit to the accusation, is there not? I request permission to validate my assumptions by searching out this army's existence."

"And how would you do this, Dömin-Mathew O'lor?"

"With the permission of Kïer, I would like to lead Räthinock in a search for Refuge."

Sheligog straightened, and Mathew felt that the elf was sneering at him.

"A General alone leads the tower of Räthinock, and a General you are not."

"No," Mathew said with a bow, "but as Dömin of Intelligence, I am Räthinock's highest ranked official. I request the honor of replacing Dägin-Bok as General."

Sheligog seemed to consider this.

"What of the Captain of the Guard? Elya-Ecsheli seems worthy of the position."

"In that we agree, but he has confided in me that he has no interest in filling the role. I see potential in him though, and I request that he be promoted to Dömin, replacing the departed Vlö-bek as Dömin of Forces. If I am not made General, then I would like to work beside him as an equal."

"Interesting," Sheligog said.

He began to pace, considering all that Mathew had shared, and then the room grew cold. Mathew began to shiver as a chill ran through his body. He considered asking Sheligog what the cold meant, but the Kïen was silent, his head lowered, ice forming over his smoked armor.

"It is done," the Kïen said a moment later.

The room warmed immediately. He approached Mathew and asked that he kneel. Mathew did as he was told and lowered his eyes. Sheligog rested his sword on the top of Mathew's head, and Mathew gritted his teeth in anticipation.

"By the declaration of Kïer you have been deemed worthy," Sheligog stated. "I now declare that you are Mathew O'lor, General of Räthinock."

The edge of Sheligog blade dragged smoothly across Mathew's scalp, leaving a slight trail of blood. Mathew resisted the urge to flinch.

"Stand."

Mathew obeyed. "Thank you, lord."

"Thank Kïer, human. It was he who accepted your request. I am only his voice, and his voice would not have been so rewarding." Sheligog sheathed his blade and faced a window. "Never has an O'lor reached the rank of General. Are you up to the task?"

"I would not have requested the position if I felt otherwise. I serve Kïer readily."

"Good. Now go and compose a list of elves who might fill other vacancies. Räthinock must be put in order before I travel to Vlörinclad."

"And what of Refuge?"

"We will discuss the threat that Refuge presents in the weeks ahead. We must first put our towers to order."

"As you wish, my lord."

Mathew bowed and marched for the door.

Nathan O'lor mumbled something about being proud, but Mathew ignored him. Something inside leapt at the idea of his father's approval, but he cursed that part of himself and shut it out. The last thing he needed was to show such weakness in Sheligog's presence. His father was a slave and not worthy of his attention or affection. He had bigger things to worry about now, such as finding a new Dömin of Intelligence and other such positions of hierarchy. He sent the nearest guard to retrieve Elya-Ecshelï, soon to be his Dömin of Forces. There was much to be done.

An elf knelt on the edge of a cliff that overlooked the various waterfalls, the same falls that had been serving as a house of healing for the people of Refuge. He watched as they and their guests gathered along the river's shore and shared comforting words with one another. It was finally time to say goodbye to their loved ones: Payson Gibson and Phyllis Shepherd. He could hear every word. He hadn't heard this clearly in nearly fifty years, not since the fall of Refuge.

Ivan Shaymolin arrived at the top of the falls hours ago but was uncertain of how to proceed. The words of the willow still echoed in his mind, but who was he to teach these people? What would he teach them? Their faith, which he had followed in his youth while in the company of the willows, now perplexed him. He couldn't understand how they believed in a God after everything they'd been through, after everything the world had been through. Perhaps it was a sign of how truly astounding they were.

"You've returned."

Ivan cursed his wandering thoughts. What good were ears if you were too distracted to use them? He tugged at his hood, further hiding his features.

"How did you know?" he asked.

Shëlin-Vin pushed through an overgrown path and sat beside him.

"I spotted you a few hours ago, but I thought it appropriate to give you time."

"Did you tell the others?"

"Yes. Randall recommended I come alone."

"Wonderful." There was no enthusiasm in his voice.

"Why did you go back to the prison?"

"To repay an old debt."

"The willow?"

"Yes."

"And did you rescue her?"

"She is safe, though I do not know where she is."

"I'm glad to hear that. I've not met a willow, but I hear they are wonderful creatures."

"Elves don't typically have good opinions of willows."

"My opinion comes from Angela's description of her."

Ivan sighed.

"Angela is correct," he said.

He stood and turned away from Shëlin. There was an uncomfortable silence between the two elves, and Ivan wasn't sure how to break it. He didn't need to.

"Will you be staying?"

"I haven't decided."

"It would mean a lot to me if you did. I love these people, but I miss my kin. To have another elf around…"

"I'm not sure I'd fit the description of the elves you once knew."

"I don't believe either of us would," Shëlin replied with a laugh. "I think we're examples of what elves could become."

"You think too highly of me."

"I don't think so. You obviously carry a heavy burden, but I see potential in you. Randall and the others agree. We would love to have you. I would love to have you."

She extended a hand.

He wrestled with his own thoughts. His every instinct was to turn away and continue being the enigmatic hermit he had grown accustomed to being, yet something inside him longed to take Shëlin's hand. As Tröbin-Dur he fought for equality between elf and mankind—that dream was being fulfilled in Refuge—but time had changed him. The amazing stories that branched from his early adventures were exaggerated. He wasn't the legend that some proclaimed him to be. He wasn't the hero that these people needed.

"Please, Ivan. Stay with us."

Ivan's feet began to move, feeling as if bags of sand were weighing them down. He reached out a shaking hand, accepting Shëlin's offer, but then Shëlin recoiled, pulling her hand away. She was shocked at first but then studied him more closely. Then, cautiously, she took his hand and rolled up his sleeve. His forearm was without blemish. He stood perfectly still as she pulled back his hood, revealing the beauty of his perfected features and white hair. He looked exactly as he had when he first discovered the willows, young and vibrant. Imagine his reaction upon catching a glimpse of himself in the stream that he had awakened in.

"Ivan?"

"The willow healed my wounds with a lullaby. It seems that I am noticeably an elf once more."

"An elf of the old world," she whispered.

She studied him with tears in her eyes, and then she wrapped her arms around his neck and squeezed. He held her, and the bags of sand that weighed him down fell away. To be loved as the people in this tribe loved one another was so strange, yet so wonderful. He could find no reason not to stay.

"We should probably join the others," he said hesitantly.

She pulled away and studied him again. She was pondering something, and so he prompted her to ask.

"What was your name before you became Ivan Shaymolin? Will you go back to it?"

He opened his mouth, but *Tröbin-Dur* did not come out. He could never live up to that legacy, so he opted not to try. Let the myth continue. The stories gave people more hope than he ever could; why extinguish that with the disappointing truth of his actual life? He was not Tröbin-Dur the myth. He was a different person now, an imagined character that he ultimately embraced.

"Who I was no longer matters. I will go on being Ivan Shaymolin if that is alright with you. I have grown comfortable with the name."

"I don't mind at all."

"And one other thing."

"Yes?"

Ivan wrestled with what he was about to ask. The willow had planted the thought in his mind, but he had no desire to give in to that side of Refuge. He bit down his resentment and asked anyway, if for no other reason than to show Shëlin's people that he was willing to learn.

"Could you teach me your faith? I doubt I will ever believe as you do, but I would like to have an understanding of it."

Shëlin smiled and took his hand. "We can teach you a great many things, Ivan Shaymolin, but yes, I will instruct you in the ways of our belief. We all will. Welcome to our family."

Ivan flinched. She did not call them her tribe, but rather, her family. Ivan had stopped believing in the concept of family long ago, but something about that term jostled him. He felt his private barriers beginning to crumble. These people were far greater than any he had ever met, and now he was considered one of them. It felt wrong.

They descended the winding path to the base of the cliff where the river ran. There Ivan found the others dispersing. Some were left crying over empty graves, the birdmen took to the skies, but the rest came to him.

They made him feel uncomfortable with talks of his miraculous healing, but he did not rebuke them. They were merely surprised, much as he had been upon the realization that he was no longer disfigured.

"He has accepted our invitation to stay," Shëlin announced to the crowd. They were pleased.

Randall extended a hand, and Ivan took it.

"I admit that I had reservations at first," Randall said, "but you helped save our children, and for that I am thankful. You've earned your place here."

Others shook his hand. They embraced and welcomed him, but it all felt wrong. He hadn't known love since before he betrayed the willows, and he knew not how to react to it. He pulled away.

"I accept your offer, but I am not accustomed to your ways. Bear with me."

Then Debra, who had stayed behind to mourn, stepped forward. She did not seem quite as happy as the others, but she studied him and finally extended a hand.

"I do not deserve your acceptance," he said. "My selfishness cost you your husband."

"I refuse to hate you for that, Ivan. I forgive you."

Slowly, Ivan reached out and took her hand. The last barrier began to crumble as he fought a tear from falling. Then she hugged him, and he heard the heaviness in her voice.

"I was once a wild vagabond living in the forest," she whispered into his ear. "These people changed me for the better. They can change you."

"I do not deserve this," he whispered back.

"We've decided differently. Welcome to Refuge."

Randall watched as Ivan broke upon Debra's shoulder. It was unlike the man, or elf rather, to sob, but Randall had seen stranger things. Ivan was simply discovering that he was no longer alone. He remembered a similar reaction years ago when Debra had cried upon his own shoulder. It warmed Randall to see Debra embracing forgiveness, which could, in turn, help Ivan forgive himself.

"Randall Whitaker," Arick Kasdan said. "Might I have a word with you?"

Randall's smile vanished. There was no reason for him to dislike this man other than for a vague prophecy that escaped his wife's dying lips. He tried to forget those words, to pretend they were simply the hysterical illusions of a dying woman, but he knew better. They predicted a war. They predicted that the person who surpassed Kier could become an even greater threat than Kier himself. Arick Kasdan had the potential to fulfill that prophecy.

"Of course," he replied. He attempted a smile but wasn't convinced of its authenticity.

The two men walked along the river, passed the giant and Arick's men, and entered the forest.

"I must confess," Arick said, "I find your tribe a bit odd. I've never seen people act as you do. While on the ledge, your people shared what they could of your faith. To be honest, I thought it a misdirection to confuse eavesdropping elves, yet here we are, and you still believe. I am genuinely happy that your people find this way of living acceptable, but I am not so naive."

"You might believe still—given time."

Arick laughed.

"Thank you," he said, "but religion is not a crutch I can afford. You see, my people put their faith in *me*, in the fullness of my vision. Your faith would simply distract from that. There is a tribe forming..."

"I know about your tribe, Arick Kasdan. You are raising an army to confront the elves. Ivan shared a little with us before we left to rescue you."

"Then you understand the importance of this uprising for humanity's sake. If you would accept, I would like to offer you..."

"We in Refuge are not a people of war. I am sorry, Arick Kasdan, but I am going to have to decline your offer."

"I understand your caution, but do you not care about the longevity of our race?"

"I care very much about the human race. However, I suspect that your method of solving things will only hasten our demise."

"I would rather die fighting than wait for the Elven Nation to kill us while we dream."

"Our dream is to teach the elves what it means to love."

"That dream nearly cost you your children."

"It is not an easy path, I admit, but it is certainly worth the effort. What happened in Refuge will never happen again."

"It nearly did."

"Then we will continue to move beneath the elves' attention."

"You will run, you mean. There is no hiding from the elves now. They know you exist. A small intervention in Uuron Plauf nearly cost you everything, and now you've broken into their prison and killed who knows how many elves to retrieve your people."

"We did not kill..."

"The elves will not see it that way. They will not differentiate you from us, or the birdmen, or the wildmen or chameleons. They will lump us all together as one threat. They will pursue your tribe as soon as they recover from what they've lost, but I am offering you protection."

"We will not march to war!"

"You will not have to!" Arick said, frustrated now. "I am merely offering you a safe place to rest. But should any of your people decide to march with us when the time comes, it would only benefit the race of man."

Randall wanted to argue, but Arick stopped him and motioned to where the others were still gathered.

"It should be their decision, Randall, not yours alone."

"I lead this tribe, and what I say is final."

Arick took a deep breath and finally nodded.

"I am sorry to hear that. I am also sorry to inform you that my men are offering this same deal to the rest of your tribe as we speak."

Randall grabbed Arick Kasdan and nearly beat the man. He was interrupted, however, by a sudden fit of coughing, betrayed by his own tired throat. Arick backed away from Randall and waited for the fit to pass.

"You are not well."

"I've been sick of late with no time to heal."

"How long have you been sick, Randall?" Arick asked, suddenly concerned.

Randall didn't bother to answer. He rushed from the forest and found the people of Refuge intermingled with Arick's men. Only the giant stood aside.

"Do not speak with them!" he shouted, but it was too late.

"Do you think the elves will come for us again?" Debra asked.

Randall didn't know how to answer. Well, he did know the answer, but it wasn't one anybody wanted to hear. Yes, the elves would come. They would hunt them, just as Arick had predicted, but did they really need Arick's tribe to escape?

"They will come," Arick called out from behind him. "We can protect you, but we must leave now. The longer we wait the fresher our trail will be."

"We will not fight for you!" Randall shouted, and he began to cough again.

"Then don't," Palin said calmly. "Your people have done us a great service already. Let us repay you. Come with us. We will not force you to fight."

"And if war comes to you?" Trent asked.

"Then we will protect each other as we did on the ledge," Palin replied.

"We will not force you to come," Arick said, "but the offer is open. I feel we would benefit from your presence. Your tribe would be refreshing if I might speak so bluntly—our people are not always so kind—but you must decide now."

"And if we do not agree?" Gabe asked.

"Then we will leave you with our best wishes. Come, men," Arick said to his people, "give them space."

Palin, William, and Jon joined Arick, and they walked along the river. Randall watched them go and felt such wrath at their even being there that he could scream. They should have parted ways before now. The falls might have served as a new home for the tribe if not for Arick's men knowing its location.

"You think we shouldn't go?" Trent asked.

Randall turned to find his tribe looking at him.

"They are a people of war," he replied. "We do not believe in murder."

"No," Trent replied, "but murder and war are not necessarily the same thing. God's people fought in many wars when He requested it of them."

"And they aren't forcing us to fight," Debra said. "What happens when the elves find us alone?"

"We will run," Randall said quickly.

"But how long would we last?" Kris jumped in. "Now that they know we exist, how long before they find us? A month? A year at the most? I highly doubt that they would forget about us and move on."

"They won't forget," Ivan replied. "It's been over two hundred years since mankind nearly broke the world and still they remember. They will not forget when a small group of men bested the elves of Räthinock and Vlörinclad."

"The elves will not rest until we are found," Shëlin added. "They saw Nikiatis and the giant escaping with our tribe. They will hunt us for fear of racial unity if nothing else."

"Shëlin's right," Orlan said. "We could always leave if there's a problem, but for now I think it's best if we go with them."

"I agree," Angela said. She sounded slightly ashamed and wouldn't look Randall in the eye.

"We cannot..." Randall tried but his voice failed him. He didn't know how to convince them to stay. What they were saying made sense. For the safety of the tribe they should probably accept Arick Kasdan's offer, but what about Bethany's prophecy? Would he have to reveal that horrible event to everyone?

"Bethany," Trent said.

Everyone faced Trent Bishop, and Randall cursed himself for sharing her prophetic vision with him.

"What about my mother?" Angela asked.

"Trent, you promised…"

"Tell them, Randall," Trent said sternly. "If you are going to make decisions based on that moment, then the rest of the tribe should know."

"She was dying, Trent," Randall said softly. "She was speaking nonsense."

"Then what other reason is there to turn away that man's offer?"

Randall and Trent simply stared at each other. He was becoming frustrated with his second-in-command, but then he sighed. Trent was right. What he was attempting to do, make decisions based on a secret, was wrong. It was the wrong call.

Then Angela took Randall's arm, and gently touching his chin, she turned his face so that their eyes met.

"What does this have to do with my mother?"

Randall groaned and sat on the ground. He took a deep breath and revealed Bethany's final moments; the true moments. They had once been told that she suffered a stroke in the night and that she had died while they slept. He cleaned her up and requested to prepare her for burial alone. He couldn't stand to let others see her like that, but now they knew. Randall had another coughing fit as Angela wept. They waited for him to recover.

"Do you remember the words exactly?" Shëlin asked.

With a heavy heart Randall repeated the words etched into his memory: "Upon broken ledge Refuge begins their descent, and war is soon to follow. The one who takes the throne shall strive to surpass the last. With a forked tongue evil is halted, but only for a while. It comes again. So speak the gri'ori."

"What does that mean?" Benjamin asked.

"*Broken ledge* likely refers to the prison," Trent deciphered, "and *war is soon to follow* is the part that Arick seems to be promising."

"And the rest?" Joshua asked.

"The rest," Randall interrupted, "is why I do not trust Arick Kasdan. It's saying that whoever replaces Kïer will become a worse tyrant than Kïer ever was."

"Or they'll attempt to be," Trent corrected.

"Who's to say it's talking about Arick at all?" Angela asked. "I don't know him as well as I do William and Palin, but he doesn't come across as one who would become a tyrant."

"'With a forked tongue...'" Randall began.

"This needs to stop," Kris interrupted. "We are deciding the fate of our tribe based on what may or may not have been a prophecy given by the gri'ori, which may or may not even exist. I'm not saying her vision meant nothing, but we cannot base this decision, or any decision, on something we do not understand. We need to do what's best for Refuge. For what it's worth, I think we should go with Arick. Our tribe will be safer alongside his, and that's what we should be focusing on right now."

"And what if the danger comes from within their tribe?" Randall asked.

"What have they done to earn our distrust?" Kris replied. "They protected us on that ledge, and they returned for us after we found Angela and Benjamin. We would be dead if not for them. Let Bethany's final words go, Randall. Think of what's best for the tribe."

"He's right, Randall," Gabe said. "I'm sorry for how Bethany died, but we can't run from our only chance at survival. If something comes of that prophecy, then we should see it coming. We'll know how to react. But for now, I think we should go with Arick."

"Do you all feel this way?" Randall asked.

None spoke, but he understood. He was alone in his decision. No, not entirely. There was still fear in Jillian's eyes. That fear, however, began when he mentioned the gri'ori. So why was it that only he and a child feared the prophecy? Was it because he had somehow been made to believe a fairy tale—a child's fairy tale? He finally sighed and covered his face.

"I am sorry, everyone. I am old, I am sick, and I am no longer capable of deciding what is best for our tribe."

He felt the sob in his throat and tried to fight it, but it came anyway. Angela was the first to hold him, then Shëlin, and others followed.

"You've led us well, Randall," Trent said. "There is no shame in recognizing when your time has come."

"It has come," Randall said with a heavy heart. He coughed again and noted the specks of blood on his fist. "I am sorry."

"Rest, Randall," Trent said as he hugged the man who taught him everything he knew. "I'll relieve you of your duties."

"So will I," Kris stated.

Randall looked at the young man standing before him and nodded. Kris was not quite ready yet, but he would make a splendid second-in-command. He and Trent would do well together.

"Tell Arick that we will be accompanying his tribe," Randall finally said, "and that is my final command."

Trent nodded and went to where Arick and his men were gathered. They returned a moment later. William and Palin seemed pleased. Jon was indifferent. Arick, however, appeared concerned.

"I promise to look after you," he told those who had gathered, "but a greater concern has unfolded, I fear."

"What do you mean?" Trent asked.

Arick knelt and studied Randall closely. "When did you begin feeling symptoms?"

"Upon our return from Uuron Plauf."

"And no one else feels as you do?"

No one spoke. It was obvious that Randall was the only one sick.

"Randall," Arick said, "We learned of an illness created by General-Dägin-Bok, carried by wildmen. It was thought ineffective, but I fear you might have contracted it."

"No," Orlan whispered.

The faces surrounding Randall sank. Angela clung to him as Palin, Ivan, and Shëlin began studying every inch of his face and hands.

"Is it contagious?" Gabe asked.

"The virus did not seem to take, and so the project was abandoned," Palin replied as he studied Randall's left eye, "but perhaps it did. Perhaps the illness only infects humans with a unique trait, a blood type perhaps. If he alone possesses this trait, then no one else would become infected. But let's not jump to conclusions. This could still be a common cold or flu."

"This is neither of those things," Ivan said. "I recognize these symptoms. There was an illness that spread through the elves about a century ago. I remember it was devastating and likely prolonged humanity's survival by a hundred years."

"What symptoms are you seeing?" Palin asked.

"His skin is slightly yellow," Shëlin answered. "It's so faint that I hadn't noticed before, but now…"

"The blood on his hand," Ivan continued, "it has an orange tint to it. When was the last time you felt rested?"

"I cannot remember," Randall replied. "I've not had time to sleep."

"And when you do sleep?"

"I wake up feeling just as tired."

No one spoke. Randall had been feeling tired and sick since returning from Uuron Plauf, but he never suspected it to be anything more than his age. He wasn't sure what to make of this new possibility.

"I am sorry to worry you," Arick said. "We have various forms of medication in our tribe. They might help. The sooner we get him there the sooner we can treat him. It's a twelve day walk. Ten if we rush."

"We have only basic medicine here," Shëlin reported. "Nearly all of our supply was destroyed in the wildman raid."

"How did the elves overcome the virus?" Trent asked.

"With plants grown in Amon-Göl," Ivan answered.

"Grëoform?" Palin asked. "We have people who grow Grëoform."

"No, though Grëoform could have an effect."

"Then find the birdmen," Trent ordered, his first as the new leader of Refuge. "Inform them of our decision and gather what little we possess. We're leaving right now."

The days passed, and Orlan, like everyone else in the tribe, hoped that the illness would fade. He had lost his mother Danielle, his father Fredrick, and Phyllis, who had adopted him after their deaths. Now he was losing the man who was like a father to them all.

No! He had to think positively. There was still hope. Arick's tribe possessed medicine that could potentially save Randall's life. He could survive. There wasn't even a certainty that this illness was fatal.

Then Randall erupted into another fit of coughing, and Orlan turned his head. Spit splattered Orlan's shoulder, specks of blood filling in the gaps where the previous specks had landed. Randall's skin was like fire against Orlan's neck. His condition was worsening without question.

"Do you need a spell?" Kris asked, but Orlan shook his head.

Randall had walked the first few days but grew tired, and they began to lose daylight due to their slow pace. Gabe took Randall upon his back, despite Randall's protests, and they had been carrying him ever since. He no longer had the strength to carry his own weight.

"I am sorry, Orlan," Randall whispered into his ear.

"Don't be sorry, Randall," Orlan replied with forced enthusiasm. "I've had enough blood on me of late. A little more won't hurt."

He carried Randall for an hour more before finally allowing Kris his rotation. It wasn't out of pride or his love for Angela. It was for the respect of a man who had taught him—taught them all—so much. He gave them hope. He gave them faith.

With Randall passed on to Kris, Orlan made his way to Angela and walked silently beside her. She was reasonably upset. Her eyes were swollen red, and she hadn't slept but a few hours since leaving the falls. She was crying again. There were no more words to say, so he took her hand and kissed it. He continued to hold it as they marched.

He knew what it was like to lose both parents, how lonely it felt, so he was going to stand beside her every step of the way. He would encourage her and love her, despite the fact that she didn't return his love. They were friends, and that was all that mattered.

He would be there for her when her world fell apart and it would. Somehow, he just knew. No one talked about it, but he was fairly certain everyone knew. Randall was fading too quickly. Orlan hated the idea, but he was preparing himself for the loss—for him and for Angela. Randall Whitaker was going to die, and there was nothing anyone could do about it.

"Give it another try, Vetcalf?" Fagunol asked.

The blue birdman nodded and stretched his wings.

Trent granted permission to scout ahead, and so Fagunol, Vetcalf, and Nikiatis flew. They had been flying in short spurts since yesterday, giving Vetcalf time to recover between flights. The practice was for his benefit more so than the tribe's. They glanced ahead, saw no reason for concern, and flew higher.

Arick's tribe and the people of Refuge had stepped from Greysong's eastern border early that morning and were now approaching the tip of a southern extension of the forest that curved out and up. They had originally planned to traverse all the way south until Greysong connected with Rïnwood, the southern forest which ran west to east. They would have followed that under tree cover until they reached the Southern Caves where Arick's tribe resided. Time, however, grew short for Randall Whitaker. Against Arick's better judgment, they were forced to alter their course and make a straight line for the caves, exposing themselves on open plains.

It was a dangerous path, but they weren't all that worried. The forces of Räthinock and Vlörinclad were depleted and needed rebuilding, and they were too far south for other towers to be a concern. There were other things in the world to be afraid of, however, and these were the creatures that the birdmen searched for.

Vetcalf pointed south to where a curved portion of Greysong turned northward. Fagunol noted the wildmen darting into the forest, but these were yellow backs, meaning the hair that grew from their heads and backs was blonde. They were a skittish race of wildmen who ate only rabbit and occasionally deer. They did not enjoy conflict and evaded other tribes. They were not a threat.

A beastly troll was spotted moments later. It was sitting out in the open, roasting what looked like a chameleon over a fire. This oversized, humanlike creature was certainly a threat. Fortunately, it seemed content with its meal. They would give it a wide berth to be safe.

The birdmen circled back and relayed what they had seen to Trent and Arick. The tribe adjusted accordingly.

How long had it been since Fagunol last took to the skies beyond Uuron Plauf's borders? Despite his concern for Randall Whitaker, the golden birdman felt a great amount of joy flying beside Nikiatis and Vetcalf. In a way, it reminded him of his youth. If only he hadn't squandered that youth in pride and politics. Perhaps he'd have been a happier birdman, less judgmental. He stole glimpses of Shëlin-Vin, who walked between Joshua and Ivan Shaymolin. Perhaps, in his youth, he might have discovered love.

The sun fell and rose and fell again. The night was cooler this far south but not intolerable. Still, Angela shivered. There was no warmth left in her body, so she was gracious when Orlan offered her a blanket.

"Thank you," she said as he sat beside her.

She watched as Shëlin attempted to make Randall comfortable, and she sighed. She thought she'd shed her last available tear, but still another managed to seep through. She wiped it away as Orlan put an arm around her. It was nice. Though her father dominated her thoughts, she did have time to consider other things.

Orlan's love, the willow had called her. She hadn't time to consider what that meant while imprisoned, but that was days ago. There was no question that Orlan was in love with her, though she wasn't sure how long that had been true. She always knew in some small way—the signs were there—but she was blinded. For her, there was only Kris.

Yes, there was only Kris, but she could see now that for Kris there was only the tribe. He was constantly focused on how to best prepare himself for the task of leading them. Even now, he sat with Trent and Arick Kasdan, discussing their next course of action. And here was Orlan with his arm around her, comforting her. It was where he'd been for as long as she could remember.

Kris would fall back to check on her at times, but those times were few and far between. They were friends, of that there was no question, but her views of him were changing. She still loved him and respected him as a leader, but the intensity of what she had previously felt was fading. She knew that Kris loved her—he loved everyone—but he didn't love her like Orlan did.

How could she have been so blind?

Angela leaned her head against Orlan's shoulder. She had always loved him in the way that Kris loved her, as a friend, but that was changing. His love was pure, and his determination to take care of her did not go unnoticed. This was not a happy time. But in the midst of these dark days, she was finding a light—as faint as it was—in Orlan.

"I am dying, Tramin."

The time had come.

The yellow tint in Randall's skin had grown deathly pale, and his breathing was heavily labored. To touch him was like touching ice. They were somewhere north of the Rinwood Forest when Tramin called for everyone to stop. He lay Randall on a bed of leaves and covered him with a blanket. It provided no warmth.

Randall saw his family as they crowded around him. His eyes weren't functioning as well as they should have been, so he had to squint. Someone took his hand, and it took him a moment to realize it was Angela. He squeezed her hand, but there was no strength in his grip.

"What medicine do we have left?" Debra asked Shëlin, but Randall waved her off with his free hand. It wouldn't help. It never helped.

"I miss Bethany," he said, and he heard Angela's voice break.

Orlan put his arm around her, and Randall attempted a smile. He wondered if Angela realized how much the boy loved her. He had known for quite some time but respected Orlan's choice to remain silent on the matter. He had always approved of Silus' grandson. He wished he could offer Orlan her hand in marriage if that time ever came. The thought made him sad.

"How do you feel, Randall?"

The voice belonged to Kris, who was destined to lead their people. He was the last of his family, the last of the

Medair'yins, and he bore such a burden. Randall questioned whether he had pushed the boy too hard or not hard enough. No, he decided. The boy had his own drive. Kris would be a great leader in time. His parents would be proud.

"I am cold," Randall answered.

"Gather blankets," Kris ordered.

They piled every blanket they had on Randall, but it did little to warm him. His breath came in haggard waves now. He was losing himself at times, forgetting where he was, but then he'd come back again and they were still there—his family.

"Never forget who we are," he said faintly. "Never lose faith."

"We won't," Trent, his wisest pupil, replied.

"I love you all," Randall said, though he was certain his voice had failed him.

"I love you too."

The voice did not belong to any of those surrounding him. His heart skipped, and for just a moment, he felt a warmth flood over him. He hadn't heard that voice in years, often struggling to remember it. Her voice had long since been replaced with the disturbing sound of prophecy.

"Bethany?" he whispered.

He could faintly hear crying. It sounded like Angela. He wanted to comfort her but couldn't move. Then he heard Bethany's voice again.

"He will care for her."

"Orlan?" Randall mouthed.

Those around him leaned in but showed no sign of understanding his mutterings. The sun above them shined brighter now.

"Yes, Orlan," Bethany's voice said, "but God even greater than he."

"Thank you," he said, and the light overtook the faces of his loved ones.

The pain faded, and he felt as if he were floating. The world he had known since birth was gone, lost somewhere in a distant memory, and he felt Bethany's hand in his. They embraced.

"I've missed you so much." He wasn't sure which of them had said it.

The light surrounded them now, and there was an overwhelming sense of goodness dwelling within it. Then he heard a voice that did not belong to Bethany. He recognized it, despite having never heard it before, and it brought him more joy that he had never known.

"Well done, my good and faithful servant," it said as he wept. "Welcome home."

Randall Whitaker was buried beneath a tree on Rinwood's northern border. The words spoken were kind and unlike any that Fagunol had ever heard. Birdmen respected their kin, but they did not mourn as these people mourned. The love harbored by the people of Refuge was overwhelming, and for the first time since the days following Uuron Plauf's demise, the golden birdman wept.

Flowers were laid around the grave, which was marked by a stone, and they said a prayer for his soul. Fagunol found this notion touching and wondered if such a thing could possibly exist.

Angela had asked them to carry her father's body to the Southern Caves, but Arick refused the request. They knew so little about the illness that took Randall's life, and Arick feared that it could still spread to those under his watch. The tribe was saddened by his decision, but Fagunol understood Arick's concern. They all did.

They did not travel for a full day, allowing Angela and those like her time to mourn, but they did eventually move on. It was particularly difficult for Angela, and Fagunol mourned for her, but the young man named Orlan Rook held her as they went. Kris Medair'yin was also with her for the majority of that first day, though he eventually made his way back to Trent Bishop and Arick Kasdan. Fagunol wondered if he had ever had friends such as these. He had associates and acquaintances but never friends. How misspent his life had been. If only he could have met these people sooner.

"Nikiatis," he said during one of their flights. "I would like a word with you."

"Speak," Nikiatis replied.

"I have come to a conclusion."

"Regarding what?"

"I will help you find Giyavin, but that is where our journey together must end."

"Excuse me?"

Anger ruffled the white birdman's feathers, but Fagunol no longer cared.

"I will not be accompanying you when you exact your revenge upon Amon-Göl. I have chosen to wash my hands of that matter. These people of Refuge are my tribe now, and I pray that, in time, they become yours as well."

"You pray?"

Fagunol couldn't hold back the smile.

"I suppose I do."

The anger on Nikiatis' face was clear, but his wrath did not extend beyond that.

"So be it," was all he said, and then he flew in Vetcalf's direction, likely to inform their kin of Fagunol's decision.

Fagunol worried for his brethren but was at peace with the decision he had made. He loved his king, but he could not live the rest of his years bitter and grieving. Unlike Nikiatis, he had learned to forgive.

Fagunol smiled as a weight fell from his wings, and he soared higher than he had in years.

He was free.

They came to the place where Rïnwood met the Sïren River, and there the men and women separated and bathed. Angela had grown so accustomed to having Orlan by her side that it felt strange being separated from him. She lay in the sun to dry and then clothed herself, thinking of her father as the others finished up their baths.

Randall had struggled to recover from Bethany's passing but could never adequately close that chapter of his life; he loved her too much. The idea of their being together again made Angela cry. Not because it pained her, though it did, but because she knew how happy they must be. She longed for the day when her family would be together again. She missed them so much.

"We love you, Angela," Debra said as she sat beside her, taking her hand.

The men had already caught several squirrels and were preparing for supper when the women returned. Angela spotted Orlan and sat beside him. He put his arm around her as usual. It felt nice.

"How are you holding up?" he asked.

She had been asked a variant of that question a hundred times since her father's passing, but she didn't mind. The tribe's concern reminded her that she wasn't as alone as she felt.

"I miss him," she replied.

"We all do."

He pressed his scarred cheek against the top of her head, and she snuggled into his neck. Then, with a little hesitation, she tilted her head back and kissed his lips. It was gentle but quick. If she were in a jovial mood, she would have laughed at the silly expression he wore as she pulled away.

"Thank you, Orlan."

He smiled as she took his hand and curled up against his chest. He wrapped his arms around her, more snuggly this time, and rested his chin on top of her head. She felt safe.

"I love you," he whispered. It was obvious by the way he spoke that he had been holding those words in for quite some time.

"I know," she replied. "Thank you."

It wasn't the reply that Orlan most likely hoped for, but he gave no sign of disappointment. She was in no mood to swear her love to anyone, and he knew that. She was in too much pain. But yes, she was beginning to love him. Fortunately, he was patient.

They had time.

The Southern Caves came into view the following day, and strangers rushed out to meet them. They clung to Arick Kasdan and his men but did not greet those who followed. If anything, the strangers were cautious of them. They were not like the people of Refuge, but that was to be expected. Few were.

Arick led everyone into the caves, and William told their story to all who would listen. He told of their imprisonment and of these people who had helped them escape. Only then did the strangers extend their hands.

The people of Refuge clung to one another in this foreign place. They had lost mothers and fathers, but they were not alone. They took comfort in knowing that they were together. They vowed to never lose sight of the love they shared for one another and refused to let the harshness of their new world sway them.

They were family and would remain so for the remainder of their natural lives and into the eternity that follows.

Acknowledgments

When I first decided to write a book on my own it was this novel that I attempted to write. I wrote the first two chapters but quit after receiving some harsh criticisms regarding my lack of writing ability. If not for Kyle Deckard encouraging me to continue, I might never have typed another paragraph again. So I would like to thank the Iceman himself for encouraging me to realize my dream. I owe you big.

Following my decision to continue with the book, I received a lot of feedback and encouragement from my three biggest fans: Sandy Sexton, Joanne Whitaker, and Debra Harlow (sound familiar?). Even after I made the difficult decision to abandon the book for other projects, you still encouraged me and asked when I would finish the story. Now that I've returned to the Refuge series as a matured writer, I'm reminded of all those hours you spent reading and correcting my horrible first draft, helping me grow into the writer I would eventually become. I'm glad to finally finish *From the Ruin of Extinction*, and I hope that you get as much enjoyment out of reading the final product as I did in writing it.

And lastly, I'd like to give a HUGE thank you to Ryan Campbell. Ryan's been an indispensable friend of mine for the past seventeen years. He's such a good friend in fact that he's labored over the covers to every book I've written, as tedious as they might have been, for the low low cost of zero dollars and zero cents. That's a pretty good price for the quality I get, especially for someone as—how should I put this—financially challenged as myself. If not for Ryan's help, my books wouldn't be nearly as attractive as they are. So thanks, Ryan. Your help and friendship is and always has been appreciated.

About the Author

Bradford Combs is a self-taught writer who nearly gave up his dream before it began. Having never taken a writing course, he began writing as a hobby only to be told he lacked the talent. He gave up for two years until an online friend read his work and encouraged him to continue. Bradford decided at that point to utilize every outlet available to make himself a better writer and continues to do so to this day. "Mr. Brad" is a school janitor by day and an author by night. He lives in Hamilton, Ohio, with his wife and two daughters.

— bradfordcombs.tk —

Made in the USA
Middletown, DE
17 February 2019